To Joe Hone
with affection
gratitude for
& creative flle
Tom Crowe
7.03.08.

THE DARK TOY

THE DARK TOY

Tom Crowe

ATHENA PRESS
LONDON

The Dark Toy
Copyright © Tom Crowe 2007

All Rights Reserved

No part of this book may be reproduced in any form
by photocopying or by any electronic or mechanical means,
including information storage or retrieval systems,
without permission in writing from both the copyright
owner and the publisher of this book.

ISBN 10-digit: 1 84748 178 7
ISBN 13-digit: 978 1 84748 178 8

First Published 2007 by
ATHENA PRESS
Queen's House, 2 Holly Road
Twickenham TW1 4EG
United Kingdom

Printed for Athena Press

For Lis

Acknowledgements

'The Island' was published in *The Dublin Magazine* and broadcast on BBC Radio 3.

'Madame Lussac's Madness' was published in *The Dublin Magazine*, and broadcast on the English Service of the SABC.

'Tristesse de Voyage' was broadcast on the English Service of the SABC.

A variant of 'The Dark Toy' was published by Hamish Hamilton in *Irish Ghost Stories* (ed. Joseph Hone).

These things either matter or they do not matter. It depends upon the universe, what it is.

Saul Bellow, *Herzog*

Contents

The Island	11
Madame Lussac's Madness	28
Tristesse de Voyage	56
The Quick and the Dead	63
Van Tonder's Mistake	77
Lonely Hearts	90
The Omega Point Theory	113
The Red Dress	130
The Tale of the Yellow Wolves	147
Field Work	169
Heading for the Rocks	190
Ice Thoughts	212
The Dark Toy	224

THE ISLAND

From where they were resting at the top of a steep hill they could see Lough Derg shining below them, a placid brilliance thirty miles long. Dermot McEnchroe, the younger of the two boys, felt his excitement grow as his eyes searched for a small island on the big lake. Glimpses of it from the opposite shore in Clare had haunted him throughout his childhood, and the faintness of this far off place had given it a mystery which obsessed him still.

The sweat prickled like ants crawling over their skin as they leaned on their bicycles in silence. After a few minutes the older boy stood up. This was Delmege, thick-set and assured, untroubled by the inner life. He pointed to a clump of trees near the lake's edge which seemed to strangle a flesh-coloured chimney, rising like a throat from the dark foliage.

'That's where they live,' he said, 'Captain and Mrs Slade. Captain of *what* I don't know. And allow me to impart to you this item of information: Mrs Slade's daughters are the most gorgeous pair of grinds in Tipperary.' He grinned. 'They'll lend us a boat.'

Dermot, who had just turned sixteen, saw no reason for grinning about the boat; he understood it to be the essential purpose of their journey. He was two years younger than Delmege. Their fathers' acquaintance had steered them into an ill-matched friendship at their Protestant school near Dublin, and Dermot was now spending part of the summer holiday at Delmege's home in Nenagh. They had brought beer and sandwiches for the long ride to Lough Derg.

It was nearly four o'clock when they reached the entrance to the Slades' property.

'The avenue's pretty steep,' Delmege said, 'and I've no brakes. We may as well walk from here. We can leave the bikes at the gate.'

The avenue plunged down through laurel and rhododendron bushes which almost joined over the boys' heads. Dermot ran two fingers across the soft hair on his upper lip.

It's a give-away, he thought, I ought to have shaved it off this morning.

The sound of a saxophone rose like a warm vapour, as though exhaled from the vegetation that smothered the back wall of the house.

'That'll be Janet,' Delmege said, 'she plays records all day long lying on the drawing room floor. She's a hell of a girl!' He gave a long, indrawn whistle and shook his head slowly.

They followed the avenue round to the front of the house. Not far from the door there was an abrupt slope of fifty yards down to the water, but the lake was hidden by a hedge enclosing a gravel sweep. Mrs Slade was standing at the door calling the dogs when the boys arrived. Her presence was somehow theatrical, excessive and when Dermot saw her he felt the simultaneous impacts of heat and colour. She was in her middle forties and had once been very attractive, though now she had ballooned into the pink convexities of those women on lewd postcards. Last year, she had married for the second time. The two girls were her daughters from her first marriage, and the house belonged to her. She had money and had been quite a girl with the Limerick hunt. For three years after her first husband's death, seedy Protestant bachelors in Limerick and Tipperary – and one in Clare – had thought of her carefully over their lonely dinners; until last summer when Captain Slade, arriving softly from somewhere in the East, had crept in among them and stolen her.

Dermot was introduced and her soft damp hand held his as she looked at him and said, 'How nice!'

Delmege said, 'Dermot's from West Clare. He's staying with us for a week or so.'

Mrs Slade looked Dermot up and down and said again, 'How nice!'

Captain Slade came round the corner of the house with a prepared smile. He was a man of nearly sixty with a very sharp face. He wore khaki trousers and a sleeveless dark blue shirt. His muddy-grey hair was brushed back from his forehead without a parting and was slicked to his scalp with pungent oil. Defying the afternoon's heat he wore a drab army-issue tie and under the knot of this a gold tie-pin across the wings of his collar. He had done some tea-planting in Ceylon.

'Salaam!' he said, 'How-do, how-do? So young men hunt in pairs now?'

'Be quiet!' said Mrs Slade. The reproof was tolerant, as though made to a bounding Labrador. Captain Slade winked at Dermot to convey his irrepressibly high spirits.

The saxophone, which had eerily accompanied the introductions, stopped, and a few moments later Janet came drowsily to the door. She was dressed in jeans. She wore a silk scarf knotted at the back that covered her breasts. She had absolute self-possession as she casually joined the group with no more than a smile at Delmege.

'We were wondering when you'd bring another friend along to see us,' said Mrs Slade.

'Oh well – mustn't come too often, Mrs S!' Delmege said, grinning.

'Can never overdo a good thing though, can you?' said Captain Slade, hitching up his khaki trousers and winking again at Dermot who wondered whether he should wink back. He wanted to be a credit to Delmege but decided it was impossible to wink at this man.

'You men!' said Mrs Slade.

'Eh?' said her husband, nudging Dermot. The nudge wasn't quite friendly, as though his earlier jollity had meant almost nothing.

While Delmege and Mrs Slade were talking, Janet moved over to her stepfather and they began stealthy horseplay. He gripped her arm and twisted it behind her back and when she had broken free of his grip he slapped her buttock. Then they put their arms around each other's waist – Captain Slade was much practised at this – but while they appeared to be listening to Delmege, Dermot noticed that Janet's hand had covered Captain Slade's and was moving it higher up. Then he saw their fingers move with a firm pressure.

Mrs Slade had seen this too.

'Janet,' she said sharply, 'go in and fetch Doreen.'

When Doreen appeared she looked bored. She raised her eyes only for a glance at her stepfather who quickly looked down at his feet.

'Somebody for you to meet, Doreen!' said Mrs Slade.

'New pupil,' Delmege said, sniggering. Dermot realised that they were introducing him to the girl. He jerked his hand out awkwardly and said, 'How do you do?'

'His name's Dermot McEnchroe,' said Delmege, 'and he wants to go to the island.'

'Oh yes?'

Doreen was blonde and wore a red sun-frock which showed a very full figure. There was a sudden intensity in the heat and Dermot became aware of how enclosed this place was, with the hedge obscuring the lake, the steeply rising ground at the back of the house and the dense trees and bushes all around. The wide country through which they had ridden from Nenagh could have been a different continent. He noticed that Captain Slade was the only person who wasn't sweating. He was dry, rather as you might expect a lizard's body to be dry in the sun.

'Your move,' Doreen's eyes seemed to say. It troubled Dermot not to know whether she was being hostile or friendly.

'We were hoping to go to the island,' he said. 'Delmege thought you might lend us your boat.'

'Del said that, did he?'

'Yes. Where do you keep the boat?'

'In the boathouse.'

Captain Slade looked at the sky. 'Might change your minds about the island before long. It's all right now, but there are clouds coming up from the Limerick direction. Can't trust our Irish weather, you know.'

Thank you, thought Dermot, I've been here for thousands of years and you have to fill me in about 'our Irish weather'. For a moment he felt the foreignness of these people, including Delmege, whose family had been in Ireland for three generations. They seemed shifty, they dropped their personal pronouns and they sniggered.

'Can't hold Dermot back, I'm afraid,' Delmege said, 'he's too eager!'

They all smiled, so Dermot smiled too. Captain Slade left them and strode into the house.

'Off you go, then,' said Mrs Slade.

As they turned to go, Dermot saw the gleam of the lake behind the hedge. Then, through a small chink in the leaves, he caught a sight of the island.

They walked steeply down through thick bushes. Again there was dense foliage overhead that seemed even darker after the glaring light. No one spoke as they moved in single file, like tourists entering a tomb. They stopped at the boathouse. From here a path led into a tall wood and through the trees Dermot could see a crude hut built of logs. Their breathing was heavy in the silence and he was conscious again of the still heat and their faintly animal smell. Delmege's face had the grin of a dog. Dermot wouldn't have been surprised if a long pink tongue had poured itself from Delmege's mouth and he had started to pant. The face that was so familiar at school had lost human personality. He felt isolated.

'Doreen will show you the boathouse,' Delmege said to him.

'Show me the boathouse?'

'Yes, you're a lucky man.'

'Oh get lost,' Doreen said. Everything seemed to bore her.

'But aren't you coming too, Delmege?'

'I shouldn't have thought you'd have wanted me in there as well…'

'To the island, I mean, I thought we—'

'Oh God! Yes, of course, the island. All right, we're all going to the island. Only first, Janet and I are going to the summer house. We've got things to talk about.'

'I can read you like a dirty book,' Janet said glumly.

'So you start getting the boat out with Doreen,' Delmege said, patting Dermot on the back. He went off with Janet in the direction of the log hut among the trees.

Dermot and Doreen were a few yards from the lake. He looked across the calm surface and almost cried out at the appearance of the island.

The island was a freak: a thin sliver of land nearly half a mile long, traced faintly where the water met the sky. A row of slender trees grew along its entire length. The land was quite flat and from this part of the shore it was a hair's breadth over the horizon, so that the trees seemed to stand miraculously on the water. They were serenely beautiful, set wide apart. Dermot gazed at them. They were so distant and so free. And so balletic. Springing from the still water on their dainty stems you felt that music would have made them dance.

'Shall we go in?' Doreen had pushed open the door of the

boathouse. When they were inside with the door shut he felt the thumping of his heart. She would tell Delmege if he made a false move. It would be remembered for ever. What if all his brilliantly inventive boasting at school was revealed as a sham? He would lose the flattering attention of older boys and the sweet respect of his contemporaries. They would no longer accept his addiction to Shelley on Sunday afternoons, the scribbled verses in exercise books and the records of Debussy.

The far end of the boathouse was open to the lake. Along one side of it there was a wide bench covered with cushions, and on the floor a large ashtray full of stubs. A gin bottle and two glasses stood on a shelf.

'Do you come here often?' He cursed himself for asking the question almost as soon as it left his lips.

'Fairly often.'

'You've certainly made it very comfortable. You could almost sleep here.'

'I suppose you could if you wanted to.'

She sat down on the bench and smiled at him. There was no warmth in her eyes.

'Ah, the boat,' he said.

It lay in a narrow inlet of murky water in the centre of the floor. He saw that it had an outboard engine and that it was secured by a chain and padlock to an iron post.

'The next thing we seem to require is a key,' he said, astonished at his pedantry. Why, because he was with this girl, did he have to speak like a man of eighty?

'I'm afraid the key's lost. It dropped down into the water there.'

'Oh dear, that's not very good, is it?'

'Are you any good with a wire?' she asked.

'With a wire?'

'I mean, could you open the lock with a piece of wire?'

'Ah, that's a good idea. I'm sure that with all my experience of housebreaking I'll be able to manage that.'

She took a short piece of thin wire from a tin and handed it to him. He knew he could do nothing with it but he took it from her and, standing over the lock with his back to her, his frantic hands began to fiddle. If only it would open and he could give her a smile of triumph, and shout for Delmege – but the wire bent like string, then it folded up and disappeared into the lock.

Doreen sat quite still behind him. Irritation had tightened her lips; an afternoon was going to be wasted. What on earth was this boy doing? She considered the young and almost incredibly thin shoulders, the soft, encouraged down on the cheeks, the body bent awkwardly over the lock as he fumbled with the wire.

'How old are you?' she asked.

'Seventeen.'

'Brothers and sisters?'

'No.'

'Father and mother?'

'Father yes, mother no. She died when I was eleven.' He wondered if she was filling in a form behind him.

'What's your father like?'

'I don't see much of him. He's away a lot.'

'Away where?'

'I don't know.'

This brought to his mind the extraordinary isolation of his life since his mother's death. Few friends now came to the big house with its threadbare carpets. His father was at best little more than an uncongenial stranger to him, at worst a brutish source of fear. The trouble arose from Dermot's growing addiction to writing down bits of stories and poems. His father was a man of robust skills, an intrepid horseman and a brilliant shot. To him, reading was an unhealthy occupation and writing was unmentionable. He was no ordinary philistine but a dedicated and resourceful opponent of the arts. He had once snatched a book from

Dermot's hands, torn it in two and flung it into the fire. In his early years Dermot had a nanny called Miss Williams, an incarnation of loyalty who was fiercely protective of her charge. She had stayed on as housekeeper. She was now old, myopic and frail but her courage bordered on the reckless. This courage went right through the rock and she would have gone to her death for Dermot. His reading was now done secretly, by day in Miss Williams' bedroom and by night under his bedclothes with a torch. His gramophone records were moved in stealth from one outbuilding to another and his books and scribblings were stowed under Miss Williams' bed. One day this would be discovered and she would take the blame, exulting. 'I wouldn't mind a fight,' she had told him. Meanwhile, these two allies advanced together and Dermot indulged his covert appetites with stubbornness and guile.

'Come and sit down,' Doreen said.

'I suppose I could do with a rest after my strenuous exertions with that lock.' His words made him wince. Nervously facetious again! If Delmege tells them my real age I'll die, he thought, I'll just die.

He sat down beside her but remained primly upright. She was leaning back on the cushions, her head lolling against the wall.

'You twit!' she said, managing a smile.

'You mean because of my not very expert performance with that lock? I'm afraid it wasn't very good. I don't know what we can do now – about getting to the island.'

'Why do you want to go there so much?'

'Because – I don't know. I've always wanted to, it looks wonderful.'

'Wonderful?'

'Well, yes, the way those trees seem to balance on the water. They're so perfect. They're like the thought right at the end of your mind that you can never quite think.'

'Are you totally, completely and utterly beyond help?'
'What do you mean?'
'Crazy, off your head?'
'No.'
'Feverish or anything?'
'No, thank you, I feel very well.'

'There's just miles of water on the other side and then the other shore which is County Clare. And the trees grow out of the earth. It's quite ordinary when you get there.' With a frown of curiosity, half mocking, half genuinely puzzled, she looked at his miserably embarrassed face. Surreptitiously, Dermot dried his damp palms on his trousers. He saw the swelling whiteness below the top of her frock.

'Nuisance about the key,' he said.
'You could always take off your trousers and wade for it.'
'Oh, I don't think I'd better do that.'
'Why not?'
'Oh well – you know!'

She leaned back and nearer to him, and when she moved her hair brushed his cheek. He knew that if he turned his head his lips would meet the skin of her shoulder. He looked at the soft flesh of her upper arm and saw what might have been a pimple, or the remains of a sting. The bare arm was so close to him; but it belonged to her, not him. The shoulders, the soft blonde hair and the cool eyes were someone else's, and someone else was like tomorrow: you weren't *there*, you were *here*.

'Have you ever been stung by a wasp?' he asked.
'What put that into your head?'
'I just thought perhaps that was a sting you have on your arm.'
'Where? Oh no, that's only a spot. But actually I was stung about a week ago.'
'I'm awfully sorry. Where?'

'Here,' she said, pulling the top of her frock away from her chest, 'down there.'

'Goodness,' he said, staring across the lake.

'You can look if you want to.'

'That's very kind of you,' he said formally.

'Well, look then, you silly twit.'

He looked quickly and politely, as though she had offered him a bag of sweets. He sat up straight again, but felt her arm touching his own from the shoulder down to the wrist. This was what Delmege would have called having it offered to you on a plate. The stiffening in his trousers scared him. If only he could say something. For Christ's sake, was there nothing in the whole wide world that he could think of to say to this girl?

After nearly a minute he said, 'Have you ever read Dunne's *Experiment With Time*?'

'No.'

'It's awfully interesting.'

'Oh?'

'About time, you know.'

'I see.' He really is mad, she thought. Trust Del to bring a nutter.

There was a whisper of cool wind. It disturbed the bright water of the lake. The girl stood up.

'It's about time we stopped wasting the afternoon. We'd better go in to tea.'

'Wait!' he said. But they heard Delmege's shout. 'Time's up, you two, and it's going to rain.'

They left the boathouse and found Janet and Delmege waiting for them with arms linked. The sisters exchanged quick glances. Then they all started to walk back through the bushes, in silence.

The sky was boiling over Killaloe and a swelling lump of dark clouds was drifting towards the Slades' house. In the wood the leaves hissed, turning their pale bellies to the wind.

'I hope everyone had a nice time!' said Mrs Slade, smiling at Delmege. She didn't seem to expect an answer and no one spoke of the island. Captain Slade appeared, carrying rugs and cushions.

'This is a very nice place you have here, sir,' Dermot said with his best manners.

'Very-pretty-come-in-and-have-some-tea.'

Captain Slade's movements were short and quick. Dermot noticed that when he smiled his eye teeth had no cutting edge but were tapered to sharp points.

At tea Dermot sat beside Mrs Slade. Delmege and the girls squatted on the floor amidst a welter of fashion magazines and gramophone records.

'I see you have a lot of records, Mrs Slade,' Dermot said.

'Oh those, they belong to Janet.'

'Do you like Shostakovich, Mrs Slade?'

'I beg your pardon?'

Her husband answered for her. 'Don't quite rise to that level, I'm afraid. Don't mind a spot of Elgar, though.'

'He seems to have plenty of juice, if you know what I mean,' said Mrs Slade.

'Juice?'

'Yes, juice,' said Captain Slade. He handed over his cup to be refilled. He smiled at Mrs Slade over the cup. It was the smile they had for each other. It kept you out.

Mrs Slade offered Dermot a cigarette and took one for herself. Dermot's match was politely struck and burning when Captain Slade said, 'I'll do that, old chap.' He took his wife's cigarette and put it in his mouth with another for himself, lit them both and handed one back to her. She glanced at him with a meekness which seemed out of character. Captain Slade's eyes were seldom far from his wife. Dermot thought of the overripe pear he had picked up that morning in the Delmeges' garden. He had looked into the hole and seen the palpitating rump of the wasp as it gorged in the soft darkness.

The rain started.

'See what I meant about the weather?' Captain Slade said.

Mrs Slade said it would only be a shower.

After tea, Dermot went to the window. The lake was grey, dimpled by heavy rain, and the island could no longer be seen. He didn't understand these people who, with their covert smiles and glances, made all friendliness seem stupid. Some monstrous private joke seemed to have drained their innocence away. He looked out over the lake towards his home. Fifty miles beyond that wall of rain there was the bare strength of the Burren where his roots had sprung. Those mountains of grey stone were always there, the bedrock of his life.

Behind him, a grandfather clock hiccoughed, retched and chimed. Six o'clock.

'Pinkers!' squeaked the girls.

Mrs Slade smiled slowly.

'Pinkers!" said Captain Slade. 'Pinkers all round? Pinkers, Del?'

'You bet!' said Delmege.

Captain Slade seemed to grow taller. The eyes of his wife and stepdaughters followed him as he expertly moved with bottles and glasses. He began to officiate at the drinks table like a priest. Lovingly, the angostura was applied, then the gin and water deftly poured. He served the girls and Delmege. Then he took out a large cut glass for Mrs Slade. He mixed her drink devotedly, tasting it several times as he carefully poured. He brought it to her, holding it as though offering a chalice. Dermot noticed that her hands enclosed his for a moment before taking the glass.

Finally he mixed his own drink, put it to his lips, then added more gin. An astonishing change came over him. The moment he raised his drink, the years fell from him; he was reborn. Mrs Slade and her daughters, who had watched his resurrection every evening, were not surprised. But to Dermot, its suddenness seemed unnatural. The pouched and pitted wilderness of his face had bloomed; he burgeoned like a flower. Turning sharply as if he had just remembered Dermot standing at the window, he said, 'Pinkers, Dermot?' He winked at the others. He didn't like the sons of native gentry and this one seemed like a wet into the bargain. 'Pink gin, y'know,' he added.

'Oh, thank you, sir, but—'

'But what?'

'Only a little gin. More pink than gin, sir, please.'

'More pink than gin? Good God. The chap's a terror! We'll have to lock up the bottles when he comes!'

He made the most of the joke. He guffawed and chortled and flashed brilliant glances at his women. He punched Dermot in the belly and slapped him on the back. Then he gave him an orange squash. Cruellest of all, he put his arm around his shoulders.

'Never mind, old chap. I don't know what they teach you in Clare but we'll certainly teach you to drink in Tipperary. You'll have to grow another skin or two before you're ready for the world.'

Dermot felt the scraggy brown claw discovering his youth and thinness as it moved up his shoulder blades in mock protection from the titters in the room; titters to which, he noticed, Delmege added. To be protected by this man, even *comically*, was nightmarish. Dermot stood still trying not to breathe the musty aura of Captain Slade's despair.

At last the paralysing arm was lifted, glasses were filled again and the atmosphere became tropical behind the closed windows blurred with rain. The girls and Delmege chattered like monkeys and Mrs Slade expanded secretly like a jungle plant.

Later the rain stopped and in a few minutes the exhausted sky was a tangle of cloud and light. The evening sun fell extravagantly on Mrs Slade's bosom and caught the hair on her husband's thin forearms. He had finished his third pink gin. He became bouncing and boyish and made fantastic proposals; they would all go for a swim starko; paint Nenagh red; ride the ponies bareback. He offered to row them to the island and swim back behind the boat.

'Once more unto the beach, dear friends, once more!' he said, with arm outflung. He noticed that Dermot hadn't laughed.

'Once more unto the *breach*, dear friend,' he said, 'Longfellah, y'know.'

'It isn't, it's Shakespeare.' The words came in a hiss through Dermot's teeth, all politeness gone, 'And it's "*into* the breach".'

'Oh, Shakespeare, eh?'

'*Henry the Fifth*, Act Three, Scene One.'

For a moment, Captain Slade's self-possession left him. This was war and he had been making that joke all through the summer.

'Well, well, we live and learn, eh?' His face was bleak with anger. 'So it's Shakespeare is it, sir? We *certainly* live and learn, don't we, if we hang around long enough?'

He went to extremes of self-abasement, disclaiming all knowledge of the world, stating his inability to do anything except, perhaps, knock back a few pink gins. He turned to his now uneasy family for corroboration. 'You see how we old chaps have to learn our lesson. Age bows to youth. I bow to you, sir.'

He began a slow, facetious bow to Dermot but had to take two quick steps forward before completing it. He was too angry to keep up the irony.

'I've been around a bit in my time,' he said, standing close to Dermot. 'It does no harm to get around a bit. Do you a lot of good if you saw some of the world before settling down on the ancestral acres. The East, for instance,' – here Mrs Slade looked apprehensive – 'I've spent quite a few years in the East. Funny people there. Get up to all sorts of odd tricks. Do some funny things there. In fact I'll show you a damn funny thing I've got in the study that'll—that'll—'

He choked and Dermot had a wild hope that he would be sick. But he recovered and went into the study next door, leaving the door slightly ajar. They heard him bumping about and swearing; it sounded as if he was moving heavy furniture around.

Mrs Slade put down her glass and stood up.

'I don't want to hurry you boys away,' she said, 'but time's getting on and you've a long ride home. I don't want Del's mother after my blood for keeping you both out late.'

She smiled, but the smile said *Go*.

'But hasn't Captain Slade got something to show us?'

'You wouldn't like it, Dermot. It's just for the family, something between us.'

She surged towards them, impelling them to the door.

Dermot said, 'I haven't said goodbye to Captain Slade.'

'I'll do that for you.'

Her eyes were suddenly awake, concentrating on Dermot. 'You're a sweet boy.' She seemed to say this out of a piercing afterthought, as if something in his face had reached her through the effects of a drug.

They heard Captain Slade shouting from the study. 'Hold on, I've found it! Don't go!'

'Go,' said Mrs Slade.

Dermot went out first. Behind him Delmege was saying goodbye to the girls; there was much whispering but he heard Doreen say, 'Bring an older one next time, it's more fun.'

They walked up the steep avenue towards the gate where they had left their bicycles. They had become strangers.

Dermot couldn't raise his eyes from the ground. He felt as if he had been immersed in filth. The drenched leaves above him splashed cold drops on his neck. As they approached the gate they heard a saxophone howling again.

They wheeled their bicycles onto the public road and in a few minutes Dermot saw the open fields leading to clear horizons. They rested again at the top of the hill. Below them, stretched between three counties, Lough Derg drank the evening light. The great lake seemed to hold all Ireland in its peace. Dermot drew a deep breath and looked far out to the island where the tall trees paced the water.

Oh God, he thought, time is daylight, nothing more.

Then he looked down at the trees that clung round the yellow chimney. In his mind the identities of the three women seemed to have coalesced, as if they shared one brain. But Captain Slade was separate; hungry and vampiric, he fed on them, darting his teeth into the soft flesh, rending and devouring.

Madame Lussac's Madness

*M*iss Scofield spread her wings in the abundance of bright air. Delicious, the coolness running through the downy underfeathers where the miraculous new limbs joined the body! The high rock on which she stood was firm; yet it felt free, as if detached from the earth. There was a gentle lifting of her weight. Stretching upwards on her toes she took a final look down and saw a green country quilted with fields.

She pressed her throat to the wind. Here it was, the moment of flight.

A burst of loud laughter fixed her to the rock. This harsh, derisive bellow quenched all private aspiration, and as she awoke she identified it with those two American boys staying in the house.

The small orchard was hot and still, and today there was even a feeling of the Midi, although Montfort-la-forêt was only eighty kilometres south of Paris. It was Sunday. For miles around, and indeed throughout most of France and Mediterranean Europe, the huge sour sleep of afternoon had crushed the variety out of life. Shut-eyed houses were resonant with snores and piggish grunts, in darkened rooms sweating limbs and torsos lay scattered over beds like the wreckage of a museum. Except for a very few old people here and there who feared the hazard of unconsciousness, it was as if the rural population had been gassed.

Miss Scofield had also sunk into the big sleep, but with a few thoughts still flying. She was wondering, for instance about Madame Lussac. Surely she wasn't mad? Enigmatic, yes, but surely not mad? Rich, very rich. Shrewd. Formidable. Respected. Managed her own money. Secretive, though. And when that young English couple were waiting for their train at Houdon, having spent only one night at Montfort, the husband had whispered, 'She's *mad*. She said that if we became French citizens she would pay me a thousand francs every time my wife got pregnant. Two thousand if it was a boy. My wife won't tell me what she said to her.'

They were deformed by haversacks, those two, and wore grey rumpled socks inside their sandals. They stood like hunch-backed trolls waiting for a trolls' train. As they were leaving, the raw-nosed thin young wife called over her shoulder, 'She's disgusting!'

Miss Scofield found that her neck was tense against the back of her canvas chair. Let the head loll forward a little. Relax. Then you can be yourself. People kept telling her this. During the past year small patches of dry skin had begun to show at her temples, and her brown straight hair, strenuously brushed at bedtime, never really shone as she would have liked. Before coming to France she had done odd jobs and looked after her mother. She had done some child welfare too, and had written a pamphlet on child nutrition.

It was now a little over ten months since she had joined the de Lammes in Paris. Charles de Lamme was a merchant banker. Three of their four children were grown up and Miss Scofield's special charge was the youngest son Antoine, aged eight. She taught him English and did her best to keep him out of mischief. Coming from her background of thrift, and imbued with her mother's pietism, she had not seen their like before. They were full of capricious animation, the de Lammes, headlong, meridional people, and they spent money in a way that Miss Scofield had only read about in books.

Their luxurious flat was in the Trocadéro district. Although punctual, meals were boisterous. Distinguished guests, including ministers and even royalty, went there in some dread, knowing that they might be shipwrecked in the storms of anarchic comedy that could sweep the table without warning. Plates were sometimes smashed. This was no place for the English monoglot, the sensitive or ill at ease. Yet M. de Lamme, faultless in mimicry, had the gift of nonsense to such a degree that even Miss Scofield, lifted momentarily from the prison of her shyness, had once thrown back her head and laughed in total liberation.

That one big laugh had kindled a sympathy between her and M. de Lamme. She found herself looking to him for protection. From what? She didn't know. But she knew that although these people were not unkind there was a precipitation in their enjoyment of life that cowed her. They made a great deal of noise, they ate hugely, and they were prolific, increasing the already wide network of cousinhood in fruitful marriages year after year. At weekends they got into several cars and tore out of Paris to this 'cottage' at Montfort (no cottage really but a house with a complex of outhouses and farms). They had yet another house by the sea at Arcachon where they lay in the sun and raced in boats. Miss Scofield had never seen such pleasure. Doubtless in bed – she skimmed over this thought very quickly – they were noisy too. They were attracted to the hard and shiny surfaces of life. Although they were exhausting people she had had the misfortune to grow fond of them. Like a stray particle of matter she had been drawn into their constellation and consumed.

M. de Lamme's mother-in-law, Madame Lussac, was unlike the others. At times, she seemed to be part of the same pattern, but she was in fact a different animal altogether, like a creature living in the depths of the sea, powerful and slow moving.

Was that laughter? Wide awake now, Miss Scofield wondered if it had come from the other side of the orchard wall. Those American boys! They were either too quiet so that you didn't know what they were thinking, or they were too noisy. Their name was Gruner. They had been sent to stay for a few weeks at Montfort while their parents were on a business trip with the de Lammes in the south. Here at Montfort, away from the loud flat in Paris, she would have had Antoine to herself, were it not for the two Gruner boys. Without them, this might have been the happiest week of her time in France as *jeune fille au pair*. *Jeune fille* at thirty-two!

She glanced at the book lying open on her lap, from which the observations of Jean Henri Fabre came with unscathed urbanity through the translation of Bernard Miall:

> *I see under what may be called the chin of the bee a white spot, hardly a twenty-fifth of an inch square, where the horny integuments are lacking, and the fine skin is exposed uncovered. It is there, always there, in that tiny defect in the bee's armour, that the sting is inserted. Why is this point attacked rather than another?*

It was unpleasant the way the Gruners got at you. They had a way of smelling out the things you would rather keep to yourself. Intimate things. And the questions they asked were somehow not nice. No self-respecting person with a proper sense of restraint and decency would ask such things. She was glad, for this reason especially, that her mother wasn't here.

But the prurience of the Gruner boys paled beside the atrocities of the praying mantis, and of insect life in general, that Miss Scofield studied unflinchingly. The butchery, the precision of it, was appalling, but somehow fascinating too. The horror of such behaviour was in its lack of volition. In that world, the rigid masks revealed no intention: conflict and massacre, and their attendant skills, were pre-ordained.

Some insects stung to kill, others only to paralyse. The philanthus embraced the bee like a lover, mouth to mouth, belly to belly. She groped and stung the bee at the one point where it would kill. Some people knew exactly where to sting you without having to learn. Like the Gruners. Their polite, serious manner of enquiry had menace; their sense of social smell was acute; they recognised your nest odour.

For Miss Scofield was not strictly speaking a *jeune fille au pair*; Madame de Lamme had found her by advertising for 'an English girl.' But she had worked hard at her convent school and had taken much trouble over her accent. The de Lammes introduced her to their friends as 'our jeune fille au pair', but her Christian name was not used, she was 'Mademoiselle Scofield'.

A sweet clear voice: 'Mademoiselle!'

Miss Scofield closed her book.

'I'm here, Antoine.'

Antoine opened the door in the orchard wall and came towards her. His resemblance to his father was so strong that it always startled her.

'It is very late, Mademoiselle, nearly five o'clock. Grandmaman Lussac says it is time for tea.'

He pulled her from the chair. They ran towards the house. An inner voice told Miss Scofield that soon, perhaps in two months' time, a boat would be carrying her to Dover.

She felt tired and hot. He was tugging at her hand.

'Not so fast, Antoine.'

He ran faster, faster through the orchard and she had to jerk her head and shoulders away from the low branches. She knew that if she laughed her strength would go. She threw her head back and ran until her knees buckled and she fell.

'Antoine, you are a dreadful angel, you will kill me.'

He pulled her to her feet. As they reached the house he said, 'Before we go in I must tell you something. There will be a battle tonight.'

'A battle?'

'You will see. There will be anger.'

'I don't like anger.'

'Grandmaman Lussac's cook will arrive from Paris this evening, perhaps very late.'

'But Madame Denise cooks for us all.'

'Grandmaman does not like the cooking of Madame Denise, so she brings her own cook. Each year Papa asks her not to do this because it makes trouble, and she says no, she will not, but after a few days she sends for her cook. Madame Denise is jealous and there is always a battle. Grandmaman does not mind, she lets them fight. It passes. Last year Madame Denise won. You will see, there will be much anger.'

'I don't like anger, Antoine.'

'Sometimes I enjoy it. I will protect you. They are only women.'

Madame Lussac and the two Gruner boys had sat in silence while Antoine was fetching Miss Scofield. The Gruners each wore glasses with very thick lenses. They looked like robots waiting to be programmed.

Although the Trocadéro flat was formal with elegant and uncomfortable furniture, here at Montfort the feeling was more reminiscent of a villa by the sea. The cloth on the long bench-table was made of plastic; rush mats and some well-worn rugs lay here and there on the tiled or wooden floors; there were wicker chairs and sofas, many cushions; the colours were bright. Yet this informality was tidily arranged. Nobody relaxed when the de Lammes were here. Miss Scofield had not seen one member of the family stretched on the sofa with his feet up. No one had read a book since she had arrived.

'*Voilà*,' said Madame Lussac as Miss Scofield and Antoine came in for tea.

Madame Lussac was in her late seventies. She was big, but not overweight. Her body, with its ample white flesh, seemed to fill a great deal of space, yet it was the right size for itself. When the de Lammes were present, her stillness was noticeable against the nervous and excited movement that continuously went on around her. But it was not inert; it had strength, and at Montfort, or at the flat in Paris, it seemed to generate more activity than was usual even in this family. It was particularly apparent in the younger men: they paid more attention to their wives, or to other women.

'Good afternoon, Miss Scofield,' the Gruner boys said in turn. Their names were Max and David. Max, the elder one, was eighteen.

'Did you have an interesting afternoon, Mademoiselle?' David asked, and Miss Scofield caught the sarcasm in the 'Mademoiselle.'

'Interesting?'

'I mean, did you read some more of your book?'

'Yes, I read some more of it.'

'Miss Scofield is studying insect life, Max.'

How did they know this?

'That certainly must be interesting, Miss Scofield.'

How rude their politeness was! If M. de Lamme had said that to her she would have felt warmed and flattered.

'I used to put in some work on insects when I first went to college,' David said, 'got around to moths and butterflies. Like the great peacock. He certainly is interesting. Do you know what his purpose in life is, Miss Scofield?'

'His purpose is to be a butterfly.'

'Yes, but what do you think he really lives for, what drives him?'

'Well, to…'

'To have lots of little butterflies, Miss Scofield?'

'To reproduce himself.'

She was angry with herself for blushing. They could make you blush about quite innocent things.

'*Ça, c'est intéressant,*' said Madame Lussac.

'Yes, ma'am, that's all he's interested in. If he doesn't get around to that he just dies.'

'*C'est naturel, ça,*' said Madame Lussac.

'You don't know anything, Dave,' his brother said, 'you're talking to Miss Scofield. She's an expert on this. It's the female that dies, isn't it, Miss Scofield? Please correct me if I'm wrong. Dave, do you remember Dad's collection of butterflies?'

'You tell us about it, Max.'

'He certainly had a most wonderful collection. He had a female great peacock too. One night he carried out a very important experiment. Do you know, Miss Scofield, the great peacock's so smart he can find his mate anywhere. No matter how far away she is, he'll find her, even in the dark. No one knows how. Dad thought he'd try to find out. So he caught a female and he put her in a kind of a cage covered over in muslin. Would you credit it, that night the room was filled with great peacocks, big as bats, all trying their darndest to get into that little cage. He cut off the males' antennae. He figured that maybe they work by smell, so he sprayed the room with disinfectant, and they still found her. But he didn't let any of them into the cage, and do you know what happened to the female? She laid her barren eggs and she just died.'

'*Voilà,*' said Madame Lussac, who had listened closely.

'Worn out from waiting, I guess,' David said.

'Fabre conducted the very same experiment,' said Miss Scofield, 'I wonder if you're not thinking of that? And so far as I know the great peacock is confined to Europe. I understood you have always lived in America.'

They had been to her room, looked at her books, gone

through her things. They had invaded her meagre privacy. She looked steadily at them for a few moments and they gazed back at her with the faces of astute codfish. Their personalities seemed to be identical, and opaque. They were like idols. The strong lenses covering their eyes collected the light and shone it back at Miss Scofield. There was something about them that she couldn't quite fathom. What were they? In what soil had they grown? Their tortuous thinking and the uncomfortable way it both drew and repelled you, their satire with its mixture of attack and retreat, were not of the Saxon world, and they had none of the ingenuous kindness that she associated with Americans. Nor had they the sensitivity of Jews. They were a puzzle, the Gruners, they seemed to have been smeared with the paste of several civilisations, absorbing none.

Later, they went outside and played a ball game with Antoine. While she tried to read, Miss Scofield found her attention wandering to their footsteps on the gravel as they ran round the house.

After she had taken Antoine to bed, she returned to the sitting room.

'*Voilà*,' said Madame Lussac, it is already time for my walk.'

Madame Lussac had very pale skin which she protected carefully from the sun. Even at the villa in Arcachon she remained perfectly white. She despised her own sex in general and Miss Scofield in particular, though she kept this to herself. The company of men delighted her. Her five years of married life had been passionate ones, until they were cut short by the death of her husband at Verdun. Twenty-five years later, her only son had been killed with the Free French in Syria.

Miss Scofield brought the old lady her stick and together they went out. For a quarter of a mile they followed a rough path to some farm buildings at the top of a gentle slope.

Here there was a stone bench. Madame Lussac liked to watch the sunsets.

As she walked beside her Miss Scofield felt a force coming from Madame Lussac. It was so strong that it seemed atmospheric, like the minutes before thunder. The sensation was oppressive; Miss Scofield felt that it could crush her. It was very simple, almost brutish, and appeared to manifest itself through mere proximity, as if it were a substance in the body. Miss Scofield wondered what influence this old woman had over the younger members of the de Lamme family and its branches, over all the many grandchildren, even over tenuously related cousins. They were excited and fractious in her presence. They would come to see her when they were staying at Montfort – married couples, or the husband or wife separately. They were nervous when they arrived, and so affectionate and attentive that their behaviour seemed sycophantic. Could it be avaricious expectation? Madame Lussac was reputed to be a millionairess. They often talked to her privately upstairs. Some left with jubilant faces, others were crestfallen. There was heightened emotion. And secrecy.

Miss Scofield gazed at the pink horizon as Madame Lussac's English unfolded itself with baroque splendour. Her grammar was faultless. She spoke relentlessly of her youth. Statesmen, officers in brilliant uniforms, ambassadors and pretenders to thrones moved past in a shadowy parade.

'What an interesting life you've had, Madame.'

Miss Scofield turned to Madame Lussac as she said this. The light was fading. Lustrous dark eyes peered at her out of a skull.

'Interesting, Mademoiselle? You may have your own judgement of what is interesting. I have had three things in my life: eighteen years of virginity, five years of passion, fifty-five years of celibacy. Can you talk of interest in my life when the manhood of France was destroyed fifty years ago? One million four hundred thousand Frenchmen killed, and all the children in their loins as well. Can they ever be replaced? I cannot tell you what a manhood we had, how proud and beautiful and strong it was. Such nobility and fire! *Quelles hommes!*'

Miss Scofield's bedroom was an attic in one of the outbuildings at the back of the main house. It was ventilated only by a skylight, so that although she could hear the crunch of feet on the gravel outside she could see no one. At night, of course, she could see the stars or the darkness looking back at her. As the skylight blind was broken, anyone could look in on her from the roof, even when she was in bed. She wondered if the Gruner boys ever slept; it seemed impossible that the eyes behind those unblinking lenses should ever rest.

At night, she could hear the boys' feet on the roof. It would happen about an hour after she had gone to bed. They would put on trainers and the game was, they said, that each climbed onto the slates at opposite ends of the building and tried to reach a point in the middle without being caught in the beam of the other's torch. It was a steeply sloping roof and they had to get round chimney pots. For several minutes there would be silence, and Miss Scofield would imagine them, still wearing their glasses, crawling like disc-eyed lizards towards her skylight.

She hadn't yet undressed and was lying on the bed with her shoes off. Half an hour ago, a car had arrived bringing Madame Lussac's cook and since then Miss Scofield had faintly heard the voices of the two women in the kitchen. There had been droning grumbles, outbursts of aggrieved self-praise, simultaneous tirades. Then – a high-pitched burst of rage. Something was thrown or dropped, some large and brittle thing had been smashed. When control was lost, when balance failed, Miss Scofield felt a creeping dread. This was a real fight below her. As she listened with closed eyes she imagined fangs bared, demons in the air around her. It seemed to her that a slender bright thread running perilously through the world had been severed.

Light footsteps on the gravel, the sound of skin on wood. Bare feet were pattering up the stairs to her room.

'Antoine! What are you doing here?'

'Please do not worry, Mademoiselle, it will quickly finish. It is always like this. We are used to it.'

'What on earth have you brought with you?'

'My bow and arrows. I have come to protect you.'

He drew the bow taut and released it.

'You shouldn't have come outside in your pyjamas. Your mother would be very cross if she knew about this. No slippers!'

'Please lie down again. I will sit on the edge and we can talk.'

She said all right but only for five minutes, and then he would have to go back to bed. A solemn look from Antoine made her smile. His head, with its closely cropped hair, was stubborn and courageous just like M. de Lamme's. She wanted to rub her palm over the crisp locks but knew that he wouldn't like this. He never liked to be caressed.

He asked her what she would most like to do if she was free, absolutely free.

'I can never think of such things. I think perhaps I should like to fly.'

'In an aeroplane?'

'With my own wings.'

'Impossible. A dream. I would like to be an engineer. I will build dams and bridges. I will irrigate deserts. I will bring water to the countries that need it. Your flying is a dream.'

He drew and released his bow again. Yesterday it had been a spear, before that a sling. Tomorrow? A pistol, a machine gun...?

'What is the most exciting thing you have ever done?' he asked.

'I've done nothing exciting.'

'Think hard, please tell me.'

'Once I rode pillion on a motor-bicycle.'

'Ah, that I have done with my cousin André. You have done it often, with a friend?'

'Only once, rather a long time ago.'

'With a man?'

'A boy – well, yes, a man.'

'Did you go fast?'

'So fast I could hardly breathe.'

'You were frightened at the corners?'

'No.'

'What is his name? Where is he now? He will be waiting for you with his motor-bicycle when you go back?'

When I go back, she thought.

'His name was Patrick. I don't know where he is now. We lost touch. No, he will not be waiting for me with his motor-bicycle. My mother will be waiting for me with her Morris Minor.'

'I am sad. You liked him?'

'Oh yes, I liked him.'

'Quite well?'

'Quite a lot, yes.'

'Please, what is the word you say in England to someone you like very much?'

'I suppose you say lots of things.'

'But there is a word. Say it, please. I have forgotten. It is a nice word.'

'Dear?'

'No, that is ordinary. Someone you like very much.'

'What about darling?'

'Darling, that is *it*! You would say that to a grown-up? You have called a man darling?'

'No, Antoine.'

'Not Patrick?'

'No.'

'Darling!' He bounced on the edge of the bed. 'Darling, darling! It is fun. Darling Mademoiselle Scofield! Papa calls Maman *chérie*. Once I heard him say *mon amour* and he stroked her cheek.'

'I suppose you love your Mother very much?'

'Oh yes, but not all the time. No one is ever quite right all the time. I would like different mothers for different times.'

'Who else would you like?'

'Oh, you would be all right, sometimes.'

Miss Scofield had a feeling of release. She had had this feeling before: riding on the pillion; running through the orchard with her head back; laughing at M. de Lamme. It was happiness.

The insects were gathering in the room. High up near the ceiling, from which a shadeless bulb was hanging, and around Miss Scofield's reading lamp, they whirled and collided and drew apart.

'I wonder if I should go across and see your grandmother?'

'Oh, Grandmaman, she allows nothing to disturb her. See, they are quieter in the kitchen now. It is always like this. I think Madame Denise has won again.'

'She is strong, your grandmother?'

'Yes. Sometimes we call her Grandmaman Reine.'

'You are all very fond of her?'

'She is something that is always there.'

'But your cousins, all your relations, they seem to – to love her very much.'

'She helps them.'

'Helps them?'

'Yes, when they have children. She gives them money, much money, when they have children. They get rich.'

'Why does she do this?'

'She says France is dying. When there are two men walking on the road, Grandmaman sees three. There is a ghost between them, she says, the one who was killed. She is full of rage at all the Frenchmen killed. She says we must have more life, always more life. I am sorry, I do not understand it well. You must ask Grandmaman. Or André. With five children, he has made the most money. I only know that she buys children. André calls it "fuckpay".'

'Antoine, that's dreadful language!'

'André knows English aristocrats. He is good at well-bred English conversation.'

'To hear someone of your age saying…'

'Don't be cross, darling Mademoiselle. I don't know what it means. It is polite English. André has cultured friends.'

'If I ever hear you saying…'

But Antoine had stood up and had taken an arrow from his quiver. He arched his back and drew the bow to its limit. The skylight was open, leaving a gap about eight inches wide. With perfect aim he shot an arrow into the dark sky.

He yawned. 'I am sleepy.'

'Yes, Antoine, you must go to bed.'

In a few moments his feet were on the gravel. She heard him whooping a Red Indian war cry. Then she was alone.

She lay on the bed with her fists clenched. On the pillion, as they roared through Epping Forest, she had taken great gulps of breath, her hair spilt on the wind. 'Lean with me at the corners,' he had shouted over his shoulder, 'as if we were one person!' She could feel his ribs under his billowing shirt.

The reading lamp threw a ring of light on the ceiling. In this bright circle, and around the naked bulb that hung a few feet away from it, the insects were still massing. She watched the sudden squalls of movement that brought them together dizzily, then scattered them again. It seemed that with each collision, these tiny units of life enacted a furious re-generation of themselves. She remembered that it was the termite whose whole existence was consummated in the nuptial flight. You grew in darkness to your full strength; you crawled into the light; your sticky wings unfolded in the thrilling unfamiliar air. They lifted you. You soared into joy.

He had not called, written or telephoned after that day on the motor-bicycle. She got up from the bed and stood before a long mirror. She cupped her small breasts in her hands, then released them, rubbing her palms slowly down the sides of her body as far as her hips.

A moth blundered into her face, drunk with light.

After she had undressed and brushed her hair, she got into bed and opened her book on insects which had for her the fascination of a detective novel. She read of the murderous weapons of the mantis; her long forelimbs were double-edged, articulated saws which could be clamped together, equipped with teeth and needles and a sharp hook at the end. To terrorise her prey she would assume a spectral form, opening herself like a fan, exposing her beautiful jewelled markings, the blazonry of death. '*Once within reach of the enchantress, the grappling hooks are thrown, the fangs strike, the double saws close together and hold the victim in a vice...*'

While the cooks were fighting in the kitchen, Madame Lussac had sat calmly at her desk, indifferent to the noise directly below her. She began her third letter:

My Dear Philippe

I write to entreat news of your family, and to learn whether it is growing happily as it should. The last time I saw you and Natalie with your three beautiful children your health gave me joy, and of course you know how pleased I am that your third child is a son. Natalie is such an attractive girl, is she not? Such glowing cheeks and womanly figure! I know, dear cousin, that you will give her all the ardour of your love. You are strong and vigorous and she has years in which to bear you many children, and be certain that in my affection for you I will not be ungenerous at any joyful news. France needs such strength as comes from people like ourselves. We must bind up her wounds and fill her with new life. We must give her all the lusty sons we can until she has to spill her precious blood again.

We have this English girl still here. I fear she is useless for our purpose – a grey, spiritless creature. She has not the desire to please men, as every woman should. Would you believe it, I sometimes have the opinion, though I am not sure, that she does not wear a brassiere. But of course with her it is difficult to tell…

Madame Lussac's thoughts drove her pen for many more pages. A fine network of pale blue veins covered the back of her white hand as it moved across the paper.

'A little girl called Delphine will arrive today,' Madame Lussac told Miss Scofield the next morning at breakfast. 'She is almost Antoine's age and in every way a suitable friend for him. I thought it would be nice if she spent a week at Montfort to keep him company. I will look after them both as Delphine does not speak English. It will leave you more time to yourself to continue your important studies of – what is it you are studying? You look tired, very, very tired. They have played together since they were babies, those two. One day, perhaps, who knows…?'

It was as if an iguana's tongue had shot from Madame Lussac's mouth and flicked Antoine away, out of Miss Scofield's reach. How would her presence at Montfort be justified if he were removed from her care? She also realised that without his company, her life would seem without purpose.

After lunch, as she carried her chair towards the door in the orchard wall, she felt, rather than saw, a golden brilliance a few fields away. A honeyed light shone from M. de Lamme's wheat which stretched into the hazy distance. It was the colour of a deer's belly. These tawny acres had something of their owner's nature, Miss Scofield thought, a quality of the sun, with its careless expenditure of warmth.

She sat back in her chair and closed her eyes. She could hear a far away sound of iron striking iron. It was repeated in coupled beats until it absorbed all her attention. This metallic pulse was thinned by distance, but she felt that at its origin there was strength. She had a vision of two men wielding sledgehammers, driving a thick post into the ground. They were naked to the waist and their torsos shone with sweat. Under the skin, muscles darted like fish. They struck and paused in turn, drawing back and round to swing their hammers in the shimmering light…

She drew herself back from the brink of sleep. They might ask me to stay on, she thought, because I'm useful. But I wonder if I should. If I stay with them I shall probably go on to another family later, and to another one after that. I'll be used up. These people are maddened by life. Even Madame Lussac.

She had come to realise that there were people who, although not stupid themselves, could bestow stupidity upon others. They could make a reliable thinking-machine seize up. Although she had laughed at M. de Lamme's antics and still found them funny, those lunches and dinners at the Trocadéro flat were ordeals for her. She would sit within the membrane of her own silence, as if overcome by catalepsy, or as though some vaccine had robbed her of articulacy. The high spirits, the energy in the voices, frayed her nerves; the healthy skin, the perfect teeth, the rich and glowing hair made her feel that she was withering.

But suppose that she went back to secretarial work in

London? In her last job, she had had to endure coffee breaks and sandwich lunches with the other girls who prattled on about the pill and about whoever it was who had got herself stuffed and had to have an abortion. She had sat tight with the almost guilty secret that she was a virgin. She had always thought that Mr Right might appreciate this one day. And in London too there were her mother's fragile and demanding sensibilities to be coped with. These were becoming a burden in her life, they were dragging her down.

What she needed was a great burst of light inside her.

She opened her book. Through the gauze covers of the cages in his laboratory, M. Fabre observed his female captives. *'The bellies of the insects grew fuller: the eggs ripened in their ovaries: the time of courtship and the laying season was approaching. Then a kind of jealous rage seized the females, although no male was present to arouse such feminine rivalry. The swelling of the ovaries perverted my flock, and infected them with an insane desire to devour one another. There were threats, horrid encounters, and cannibal feasts.'*

Miss Scofield would happily have married M. Fabre, that humane and courteous man who was such a close observer of the very small. She would have enjoyed helping him in every exacting task, tending his equipment, searching the hedgerows of Provence with him, recording his experiments. She imagined the peaceful diligence of their lives together after he had retired to Sérignan.

Across M. de Lamme's wheat, the shrunken sound of the hammers still floated to her in the orchard. The image returned to her of the shining giants as they heaved and struck.

She had been asleep for nearly an hour when she was woken by the voices of children. Antoine and Delphine stood before her, hand in hand. Their eyes were round and serious, they had stared at her in sleep. Delphine was a little younger than Antoine. Her skin was brown, almost swarthy.

From beneath dark lashes, the eyes of a grown up woman looked coolly at Miss Scofield. She was very composed, this child; already she looked like a successful businessman's wife. She seemed to be assessing Miss Scofield as an equal, almost as a rival.

Miss Scofield glanced down nervously at her freckled English arms.

'This is Delphine,' Antoine said.

'Hello, Delphine.'

'*Bonjour, Mademoiselle.*'

'She does not speak English,' said Antoine, 'but she will quickly learn. She is quite clever.'

'Are you a clever little girl, Delphine?'

'*Quest-ce qu'elle dit?*'

Antoine translated and Delphine looked contemptuously at Miss Scofield.

'Well, what are you going to do with yourselves?'

'We are going to get married.'

'When you grow up, you mean? That's very nice.'

'Now, this evening, after tea.'

'What do you mean, you silly child?'

She had never called him a 'silly child' before. They were immediately estranged.

'We are going to be married this evening under the staircase.'

'You're not to joke about things like that.'

Miss Scofield felt heat rising in her neck. Leaning forward she stared curiously at Delphine.

'What put such a foolish idea into your heads?'

'When you marry you have children. Grandmaman has promised ten thousand francs to my cousin Maxime when he has his first son. Now they have four daughters but not a son yet. Grandmaman wants them to hurry up. She telephones every week. We will have a son and get the money while we are young. We will buy a sailing boat for next summer at the villa.'

Miss Scofield wondered what was happening to her stomach. It had contracted as if she were crying or laughing.

'Look here, to get married you have to be grown up, and you must have a clergyman.'

'We would rather be married now. It would be more fun. If we wait until we are grown up Grandmaman might be dead and we would not get the money. I will be the clergyman myself.'

'Go back to the house,' Miss Scofield said, 'go away. Go!'

She watched them go, pressing her fingers to her temples to stop the headache that was coming.

At six o'clock, Miss Scofield went to fetch Madame Lussac's glass of lemon juice and water. Half an hour earlier, the children had slipped away quietly from the sitting room. Under the staircase there was a small area enclosed by wooden panelling and a door, a place crammed with broken, unwanted things. As she passed it on her way to the kitchen, Miss Scofield heard a muffled intonation. She crept back to the door and listened. She heard Antoine's voice droning. The sound was incantatory, the words were gibberish. She sensed ritual. Then Delphine's voice broke in, bringing argument and laughter.

Miss Scofield opened the door. There seemed to be no air in this tight space, only smoke. How could they breathe! On a tin tray on the floor charred paper was still smouldering. Incense! Two lit candles stood on the sill of a small window which could not be opened. Antoine was surpliced in an old yellow curtain which covered him like a tent. Delphine stood demurely beside him. The skin on her swarthy little arms had an almost voluptuous glow. On one of her fingers – the wrong finger, Miss Scofield noted – there hung a huge brass curtain ring.

'It is just over,' said Antoine, 'we are married but we cannot agree about the honeymoon, so we are going to different places. Delphine will spend hers in America and I am going to Africa. I will shoot lions.'

'I see,' said Miss Scofield. Then, 'How dare you!' She was shouting, she gave herself up to rage. 'How dare you! How dare you, after what I said! That filthy old woman!'

She glared at Antoine as if he had betrayed her. She rushed at him and tore the curtain from his back. Then she snatched the curtain ring from Delphine's finger and flung it in a corner.

'Go upstairs at once, both of you. Go up to bed and stay there. I don't want to see either of you again this evening.'

When they had gone she stood very still. She asked herself in astonished calmness why she had lost control. Over two children playing at marriage! She sat down on an empty trunk and found that she was crying.

'I was wondering why you were so long getting my drink,' Madame Lussac said as Miss Scofield brought her the glass, 'what is the matter? You look upset.'

'I had some trouble with Antoine and Delphine, Madame.'

'What have they done?'

'I found them playing a silly game under the stairs.'

'What was the game?'

Miss Scofield told her.

Suddenly, as if worked by a spring, a white, blue-veined hand shot towards Miss Scofield and gripped her wrist. With such strength! Miss Scofield wondered if she would ever break free of this vice. The swiftness of the movement had been primitive, like the seizing of prey. Madame Lussac's face was thrust forward, her lips were parted in a smile. Or rather, they had curled outwards. Miss Scofield realised that it was the first time she had seen Madame Lussac smile. There were scattered teeth. The lips were an old woman's on the outside, but on the inner side they were moist and lush, full and shiny like fattened worms. There was gummy youth in this mucosal sheen. The eyes were bright. Sensuality blazed in the ruins. This face was terrible.

49

Madame Lussac withdrew her hand.

'Is that what they were doing? Ha-ha-ha! They were playing a game, Mademoiselle. People have always needed to play, it is very important for them. Why does it disturb you?'

'I was brought up very strictly, Madame, very religiously. Perhaps excessively so. It's difficult to shake off, even if you want to. I've been taught to think of marriage as a sacrament, a sacred ritual. After all, it takes place in church. It represents a spiritual reality.'

'Ritual is a game too. It is all a game, Mademoiselle. It comforts. It helps to keep truth from the door, or whatever your saying is. Do you not understand that?'

'No, I don't.'

What an oddity you are, Madame Lussac almost said aloud. Miss Scofield was sitting up very straight. Madame Lussac looked at her reddened face, at the furrow between her eyebrows. Little beads of moisture were sprouting from the sides of her nose. This dew of outraged orthodoxy gave Madame Lussac such a spasm of boredom that she wondered if it was time for her to die. She had always felt that she could choose her moment. Really, this girl could make herself a little more attractive! *Quelle horreur!* Definitely, but quite definitely, no brassiere!

Madame Lussac wished that Miss Scofield was no longer in the room with her. The Gruner boys had taken guns out with M. Denise and she wondered if they had shot any rabbits. She was impatient for their return. When the time came for her walk she decided to go alone.

The Gruners did not return until long after Miss Scofield had gone to her room. She was sitting at her small table. The courtship of the mantis was in its final stage. The slender lover confronted the powerful female. He watched her patiently, both were still. Then… *the lover has seized upon a sign of consent, of which I do not know the secret.*

He approaches: suddenly he erects his wings, which are shaken with a convulsive tremor...

Miss Scofield heard the car arriving. The brakes were applied with unnecessary force, sending the gravel flying. She heard shouting and laughter; M. Denise was a drinker and evidently the Gruners had taken him to the bistro on their way home from shooting. The doors were banged, the horn was blown, uncontrolled voices were raised as the rabbits were brought in to Madame Lussac.

Miss Scofield felt the wretched chill of hatred.

She undressed in the dark, brushed her hair and got into bed. She lay on her back with her eyes open. Useless to try to sleep. She felt hot and irritable. The heat had spread from her neck and shoulders down to her thighs. She lay scalding in her thoughts. Through the she could see one cold star.

She got out of bed and pulled the cord of the skylight. She was surprised that it opened so wide; a thin person could quite easily have climbed in. She felt so hot that she took off her nightdress and lay naked on the bed. Soon she heard feet on the gravel again and when there was silence she knew that the Gruners were climbing onto the roof. She saw the flickering beams of their torches. A slate came loose and slithered to the gutter and she fancied that she could hear them breathing as they crept to the skylight. She did not cover herself but lay as if impaled. She lay still for a long time. She saw nothing but the star's cold light as it passed her on its witless journey.

Unexpectedly, Miss Scofield felt rested and in good spirits when she came down to breakfast the next morning. She had just read a sentence which had pleased her greatly: *At the end of the spring the capricorn, now in possession of his full strength, dreams of the joys of the sun, the festivals of light.*

The Gruners had gone. The telegram from their father, summoning them to the de Lammes' villa at Arcachon, lay on the hall table. M. Denise had driven them to the nine o'clock train.

'Montfort will be sad without those boys,' said Madame Lussac, 'they had such... such...'

Her voice faltered. She was looking out of the window as she spoke and Miss Scofield was shocked by her appearance. It seemed that at any moment the folds of white skin might abandon the skull from which they hung.

They ate their grapefruits in silence. Miss Scofield was thinking that from the Gruners' bedroom it would be possible to see the wheat shining in the distance.

'Now that the Gruners have gone,' she said, 'I wonder if there would be any objection if I moved my things across and slept in their bedroom?'

'Of course you may do so.'

When she had finished breakfast Madame Lussac decided to write some letters. She paused at the foot of the stairs. It was a long climb up these days; if Madame Denise wasn't looking she would take a little rest half way. *Enfin*, one had so many memories. She remembered the rumble of the guns. She had heard them when he was making love to her on his last leave. Fifty-five years ago! Neither of them had mentioned the guns.

When she reached her room she sat down with her elbows on the desk, resting her head in her hands. A thin little moan came from her great bulk.

'*Mon Dieu!*'

Throughout the morning Miss Scofield felt her estrangement from the children growing, as if they were plotting something and their secret had brought them closer together. They helped her to move into her new bedroom but they worked silently, with glances of complicity. When her things were in place, they left without saying where they were going. Two hours later, they came in for lunch with flushed faces and scratched hands.

'What have you been up to?' Miss Scofield asked.

'We have been preparing something,' Antoine said, 'but it is a secret until the evening. Grandmaman will not mind.'

Madame Lussac did not seem to have recovered her spirits since the Gruner boys had left. After tea, she asked Miss Scofield to read an English novel to her. Later she said, 'I will take my walk now, before dinner, and go to bed early. Let us go together. Bring me my stick.'

They walked up to the farm buildings and sat on the stone bench. Madame Lussac talked of the great lives of adventure she had read about, and what she would have done if she had been a man. But Miss Scofield's attention strayed and she was relieved when Madame Lussac at last stood up and they started to return.

It was Miss Scofield who saw the smoke first.

'Look!'

It was rising darkly, fatly, from somewhere between the orchard and the house, seeming to carry with it the voices of children. Miss Scofield quickened her pace.

'What can they have done? I think I had better run on ahead, Madame, the whole place may be burning down.'

'Stay with me, child.'

The smoke swelled and blackened. It made a cloud.

'Antoine!' Miss Scofield did not shout the name but whispered it to herself. She said, 'It seems to be rising from just under my bedroom window, Madame. Antoine may be in danger.'

'They are all right. Listen to their voices. They have probably made a bonfire.'

They cut through the orchard and arrived at the little lawn below Miss Scofield's window. Madame Lussac was right; the children had soaked rags in oil, collected old boxes and bits of broken furniture from the space under the stairs, and torn dead wood from the trees to make a fire. Dense coils of smoke gushed from the rags and sometimes a flame soared. Delphine and Antoine were performing a frantic dance. When the smoke swelled towards them they would not retreat but throw themselves into it with a loud cry. The cry sounded like a word but Miss Scofield couldn't quite catch it.

She saw that Madame Lussac was trembling.

'Are you unwell, Madame?'

Madame Lussac was laughing silently. Her body seemed to be shaken by some inward mime. She put a hand on Miss Scofield's arm.

'Let us sit down and watch. It is beautiful.'

They went over to a seat against the wall of the house and sat down. Antoine saw them and shouted to Miss Scofield.

'Come and play, Mademoiselle, it is fun! You have to embrace inside the smoke without getting burnt!'

'*Allez*, go and play, Mademoiselle, it is a game, a game! When you dance like that you are close to magic. Did you know that in the Samalsain dance in the Pyrenees, the attendants of the king and queen are still known as Satans?'

Miss Scofield started to walk towards the fire. She felt the heat scorching her face, her eyes ached and watered. The children now seemed to be dancing in the centre of the flames. She heard Antoine shout to her, 'Take care, Mademoiselle, you will be burnt!'

She took a few steps forward but she was choking and she knew she could go no closer. She went back to Madame Lussac, dabbing her eyes with her handkerchief.

'It's too hot for me,' she said, 'I don't know how they can stand it.'

'They are young. How old are you, Mademoiselle?'

'Thirty-two, Madame.'

'*Quoi*? Thirty-two? And you have not found a young man?'

'Excuse me, Madame, I need to bathe my face.'

And so Helen Scofield, who felt a long way from home

just then, went up to her room and bathed her face in cold water. She lay down, breathing painfully. The cries and laughter of the children came to her.

She took up her pen and writing paper.

Dear Mother

I think that after all I will come home at the end of the month. I cannot...

Useless to go on writing with her eyes smarting like this. She went to the window. The sun was setting. Madame Lussac seemed to have infected the air with a kind of fever. She had stood up and was performing a little parody of the children's dance, laughing and tapping her stick on the ground, provoking frenzy in the small figures near the fire. In this fading light they seemed as insubstantial as spirits.

She could hear the word now, shrieked out as Delphine and Antoine embraced in the smoke.

'Darling,' they were crying, 'darling, darling!'

Tristesse de Voyage

Only a few passengers had come off the ferry from Holyhead so it was a quiet morning at the Pier Hotel. The waitress had been daydreaming, recalling an afternoon she had spent with a bearded gentleman. Now her attention was fixed on the small boy with his father at the far end of the dining room. He was wriggling with excitement, sitting on his hands, kicking the table's legs.

The waitress went to serve them. The boy asked for porridge, bacon and egg, toast and – most specifically – for marmalade. The father ordered orange juice and a kipper for himself.

'And is it tea or coffee you'd like, sir?'

'Tea, Dad, let's have tea!'

'All right,' the father said, 'I think it's going to be tea.'

The father and the waitress exchanged a smile. The waitress brought the order to the kitchen.

She had never been out of Ireland, unless you counted a day trip to one of the Arran Islands on the old *Dun Angus*, the little boat bucking into the waves with the tourists being sick and two nuns, dark as cormorants, sitting in the stern. She had been out of Dublin only on rare occasions, one of these being a memorable drive in the Wicklow mountains with that bearded gentleman.

So the travellers who arrived and departed on the Sealink ferry at Dún Laoghaire seemed to her as alien as the seagulls that screamed in the morning sky as she went to work. Mrs Mulcahy's hotel was only five minutes walk from the pier, and when the waitress was serving breakfasts in the dining room from seven o'clock, she could tell whether these migrants were spreading their wings or folding them.

She had been leaning against a pillar near the door of the kitchen. The father and son, she had decided, were at the beginning of a holiday. She could see the blade of a paddle sticking out from one end of a canvas grip. In the boot of their car there would almost certainly be an inflatable canoe. How old would the boy be? Eight, maybe? Nine? He was neatly turned out. Who by? A mother? An aunt or governess?

'Now, sir,' she placed a pot of tea and another of hot water on the table. She left and returned immediately with soda bread, toast and bright yellow butter rolled into dotted pats. Finally came the bacon and egg and the kipper.

'Is there any marmalade?' the boy asked.

'Oh my!' She smiled into his freckled face and checked an impulse to ruffle his hair.

'Will you be all right now, sir?' She said this when she brought the marmalade.

'Oh yes, thank you.' The father looked up and they smiled again. His was a full, open smile, not the patronising grimace of some of the travellers but one of those smiles that happen like fine days.

She went back to the pillar. The father's voice wasn't quite English. You could understand him because he opened his mouth properly when he spoke. Some of the English, she thought, the posh ones, spoke as if they were being throttled. Protestant Irish, she would have said. Would he have gone over to England to bring his son home for the school holiday? She had been told that Protestants didn't like children and sent them away to England as soon as they could walk. And why was there no mother? They might be divorced, the Protestants went in for that too. Or could he – the thought almost startled her – could he possibly be a widower?

Others in the dining room needed her attention. During a lull in her work, she marvelled at how life had thrust her into a black dress with a silly white cap on her head, carrying bacon and eggs and kippers about. She had, of course, worn black clothes before; as a novice with the Carmelite nuns. She hadn't made it all the way; the bearded one had fixed that for her all right.

The boy was chattering with excitement, crumbs were flying into his father's face. The father's hair was darker than the boy's, almost brown, and was feathery over the ears. It needed a little bit of a cut, the waitress thought, but it was nice hair, thick, with just a touch of grey at the sides. His tweed jacket was beautifully cut and, even though he was sitting, she could see that he was a slim, tall man who would look good on a horse. He would be in his thirties, surely? If there was no wife what did a man like that do for female company? Who shared his bed, if anyone? Where was Mammy?

On that day in the Wicklow mountains her heart had thumped when he stopped the car and switched off the engine. The dark water of Lough Dan lay far below them, the slopes were golden with the bloom of gorse. He inquired if it wouldn't be more comfortable in the back. She said, 'No it is very nice in the front really Mr Duggan,' but later she found that they were in the back of the car and that Mr Duggan appeared to have asthma because his breathing had become laboured. He was rather a stout gentleman.

'Aren't you a lovely girl!' Mr Duggan said.

'Thank you, Mr Duggan.'

'For God's sake, don't call me Mr Duggan! Call me Dug, everyone calls me that.'

'Thank you – Dug.'

He was quite important in Customs and Excise, he told her. He wore a lovely dark suit and his white linen was gorgeous. And he wore cufflinks!

'I'm going to kiss you, Nuala.'

A warm, moist thistle was pressed to her mouth, withdrawn, and pressed again.

They had finished the kipper and the bacon and egg and were buttering their toast. The boy scooped a chunk of marmalade onto his plate. They talked of plans with their heads bent over maps and brochures. What were their plans, she wondered, what was at the heart of their lives? She felt a little ache of isolation. You cannot penetrate the experience of others.

Her eyes rested on the father. He was well built without being too muscular. His shoulders were quite broad and he was narrow-hipped. She liked the way he made his son laugh and wriggle with excitement. An embrace with such a man, she thought, would be tender and loving.

Mr Duggan had been reticent about his address and had asked her not to call him on the telephone because, he said, his housekeeper had a most unusual allergy which made her come out in a rash whenever she heard a bell ringing. Naturally, a busy man like him wouldn't want to be disturbed and it would be unkind to give the poor housekeeper a rash.

When he telephoned her again, he said would she meet him under the Ballast Office clock near O'Connell's Bridge? This was a romantic rendezvous, he told her, many a good thing had started from there.

He took her to the Pearl Bar in Westmoreland Street and gave her a glass of sherry which he assured her wouldn't do her any harm in the world. He wanted her to have a second one because, he told her, a bird never flew on one wing. Then he said wouldn't it be great if he could find a little flat for her where she could be independent of her mother and do what she liked? He winked.

'You mean until we find a house?' she said. 'A flat isn't much of a place to raise a family.'

Mr Duggan froze. He put down his glass. 'Let's not rush things, love.' He looked like a man who had had a bad fright.

Mr Duggan went out of her life and, after a little while, the Carmelites came into it. She adhered faithfully to the disciplines required of a novice. She fasted and prayed. One evening when she was alone in the chapel, she became aware of a presence behind her. It had arrived very quietly. It was Mother Mary Paul.

'You do not have a vocation, my child.'

'No, Mother?'

'You long for the world.'

'Yes, Mother.'

'Who, may I ask, is Dug?'

'A friend.'

'A note has come into my hands. It was forwarded by your mother. It says, "How about another frolic in the Wicklow mountains?" As an alternative it offers you a second thrash in the Pearl Bar and says you are still flying on one wing. And other things I prefer not to mention.'

'He was a nice man…'

'Listen to me…'

'His beard…'

'Be quiet, will you!' Mother Mary Paul stamped her foot. There was a hush.

'What do you desire from life, my child?'

'I want happiness. I want to care for someone. I'd like to have a family. Is it impure to want children, Mother?'

'It depends. There are different kinds of wanting. You know what I mean, don't you?'

'No, Mother, I don't think I do. Would you like to have children, Mother?'

'Don't give cheek,' Mother Mary Paul said, and turned away to hide a little smile.

They were folding their napkins, they would soon be away. Thoroughbreds galloped on their green acres, their lawns flowered. What would they think of her little bedsit in Marine Drive? Still, she was lucky in a way, lucky to be drawing her old age pension on top of what Mrs Mulcahy paid her. Mrs Mulcahy was good, she paid in cash and no questions asked, so she wasn't doing too badly.

She overheard the boy saying, 'Let's go, Dad. Ask the old girl for the bill.'

At the door, as the father was pressing a coin into her hand, she said, 'So yee're off for a holiday together?'

'That's right,' the father said, smiling. Such a kind smile it was.

'Just the two o'yee?'

'Just us,' the boy said, swinging the canvas grip.

'We have a lot of fun together, Tim and I.' The father put his arm around the boy's shoulders. The gesture was slightly too pronounced for confidence, as if affirming something that might be questioned. For the first time the waitress took a close look into the father's face – and got a shock. There had been a momentary slackness about the mouth, a drop of the jaw. Beyond the smile and the kindly eyes she had glimpsed a carefully hidden darkness. There was something there, a hurt or grief perhaps, that wouldn't heal. She felt anxious for them both.

A flash of likeness between them made her catch her breath. It had centred on no single feature, but was diffuse, an aura about their persons. It lasted only for a second, this genetic shimmer.

She was downcast as she watched them go. Scattered lights were going out in the rooms of her mind. That drive in the Wicklow mountains must have been – what? –

getting on for fifty years ago now. There had been other times with other men. All had told her how lovely she was, but none had wanted what she had most wanted to give, which was everything for ever.

A foghorn blasted from the Hill of Howth, a huge throat bellowing to the lost. It spoke to her of lives adrift and shores not reached.

THE QUICK AND THE DEAD

(In memoriam David Thomson)

'The imperfect tense indicates a continuing, uncompleted action, whereas—'

'You're getting a spot just to the left of your mouth.'

'—the preterite, or past perfect, refers to a finished—'

'It's almost ready for squeezing.'

'Please, Antonia.'

They were in a sunlit room at Brookford, the home of the Gillespie family in Co. Roscommon. The twelve-year-old girl composed her features into an expression of reverential interest, the sort of expression that could easily ignite into a giggle. She wore a faded blue skirt and a red jumper. Her elbows were on the polished table and she sat close to Maurice O'Loghlen, second-year Trinity scholar and itinerant tutor. The faint smell that came from her was of soap and recently washed hair. A little girl smell, he thought.

'Perhaps we should move on to the irregular verbs,' he said with a sigh.

His attention had also been wandering from the lesson. He could hear the sound of a violin coming from somewhere upstairs. It was Lorian at her morning practise. A difficulty had been encountered; a chromatic run-up leading to a prolonged trill, followed by a strong, definitive note in a major key. It was tried again, botched, then tried once more and triumphantly achieved. Lorian was Antonia's sister, aged twenty, almost exactly Maurice's age. He felt himself to be falling in love with her. Everyone in this extraordinary family, he now realised, did something artistic. Antonia was learning to play the piano, Lorian played the violin, the father, or the Major as he was called, painted landscapes with dogged perseverance, and the mother, the enigmatic Mrs Gillespie, sang German Lieder to Lorian's accompaniment. Enigmatic because she was given to long silences and, so Maurice had been told, had dealings with the occult. He felt drawn to her, but warily, fearing she might call up demons.

'Now Antonia, the verb *gehen*—'
'Boring old verbs.'
'—*ging, gegangen*.'
'Gingy gangen. Are you going to the war?'
'Probably.'
'Will you kill that man with the moustache?'
'First thing.'

The door was opened narrowly and the face of a balding man wearing thick-lensed glasses appeared.

'Lunch,' he said smilingly, and withdrew.

The balding man was David, an Oxford history graduate of twenty-eight who had been Lorian's tutor. When the tutoring job ended he had stayed on, seemingly with no likelihood of leaving. He had become a part of the family's biology as a kind of farm manager, a helper in their lives; sharing their crises, the deaths of their pets, their fraught emotions, for with the Gillespies everything was dramatised. He had been in love with Lorian for some time and it was strange for Maurice to have a rival for whom he felt nothing but affection. David's diffidence was misleading; he had a hesitancy of manner because every thought that came to him had to be true and carefully shaped before he could utter it. In the years ahead he was to become a writer of distinction.

Despite encroaching debts, the Gillespies lived with dauntless and eccentric optimism. In their time they had bred racehorses, one of which – a generation ago – had won the Grand National. But now the air was getting chilly and there was the unmentionable possibility of having to sell Brookford. The war was much spoken of in this Anglo–Irish family. Mrs Gillespie was English to the bone and the Major had served in the Indian Army Cavalry during the Kaiser's war. The English papers were delivered, sometimes two days late.

'What about you, Maurice,' the Major said at lunch, 'are you going off to face wounds and death?'

Although the question ended with a gentle laugh, it said, 'You must go.'

'I expect so.'

'You'd look quite nice in uniform,' Mrs Gillespie said, and Maurice looked down at his soup in confusion.

After lunch, the Major ambled off with his easel to do what he called 'a bit of a paint'. Arthritis gave his walk a curious distinction.

'*Sah ein Knab' ein Röslein stehen, Röslein auf der Heiden…*'

The singing stopped suddenly and Mrs Gillespie could be heard talking to Lorian. The phrasing was being discussed and Lorian tried out the accompaniment again. Maurice went in search of David who had been missing throughout the afternoon. He found him in the stables, leaning against a door, rolling a cigarette.

'Loitering with intent, David?'

'I'm trying to keep out of Mrs Gillespie's way for a while.'

'Why?'

There was a pause while David gathered the words.

'She wants to fasten a fried egg to the top of my head with sticking plaster.'

'Isn't that rather unusual?'

'She says it will stimulate hair growth. She read about it somewhere.'

'How long would you have to wear it for?'

'I don't know. A few hours probably. Perhaps a whole day.'

'Does it have to be a recently fried egg, straight from the pan?'

'She didn't say.'

'Because if so, the grease would run down your neck and face, wouldn't it?'

'Yes.'

'She's an attractive character. I feel drawn to her.'

'So do I, but she's strange. She used to attend seances in London. She knows what's going on in the next room. Her feelings for Antonia are obsessive even for a mother.'

David paused to lick the gum on his rolled cigarette. He seemed to be debating whether to say more.

'Obsessive?'

David shaped his hand into a claw which had fastened onto something. Then the claw tightened into a clenched fist.

'She'll never let her grow up. Antonia will be bonded with her mother until her mother dies, with an infant's helpless dependence. It isn't wholesome.'

'David, would you mind not wearing the fried egg when we go to the pub?'

'No, of course not.'

Once or twice a week they would go to the pub in Carrick where they romanced a barmaid called Maureen. The counter formed a boundary which made both sides feel safe, allowing their flirtatious banter to be more daring than it would otherwise have been. Carrick was two miles away and they rode there on bicycles. Once when Maureen had an evening off they sat in a dark corner drinking pints of stout, talking, as always, about the Gillespies. Maurice observed that the Major didn't seem to say much.

'Don't underrate the Major, he's a remarkable man, much loved around here.'

'Remarkable?'

'There have been wounds.'

'What do you mean, *wounds*?'

'Things have happened in this family that you don't know about. Mrs Gillespie used to spend winters in London, while the Major was away with his regiment. She moved in musical and occultist circles. The Major was wounded.'

'In a war, you mean?'

'No, in the spirit. He didn't show it. He stayed steady, and he steadied the others. They got through it, thanks to him. A remarkable man.'

'I wish you wouldn't talk in riddles.'

'If you look for Antonia in the Major's face, or in Lorian's, you won't find her there. She's different from the others, different even from her mother, though less so. Something different has come from somewhere.'

'More riddles.'

On their way back it was getting dark and David, because of his poor eyesight, rode with his right hand on Maurice's shoulder and Maurice brought him safely home.

Mrs Gillespie used to sing professionally in London and she still liked to have an audience. Sometimes Maurice sat and listened while she sang, with the adored Lorian at the piano. He watched more than listened, watched Lorian as her head and shoulders moved with the music. He realised that he loved even the little scar under her chin where the violin had chafed it.

In the middle of a song, Mrs Gillespie snatched up the music and threw it to the floor.

'I'm tired of these lyrics. Those German Romantic poets, they all wanted to die. I don't want people to die. You should never desire death.'

'I'd like my enemies to die,' said Maurice, who hadn't yet made enemies.

'Never wish such a thing! Enemies are more dangerous when they're dead.'

She stooped and picked up the music sheet.

'Now Maurice, you're studying French and German literature, aren't you? I want you to write something in German that I can sing. Write for me, please, a short poem that I can sing to this accompaniment. Take it away with you now. You can do it. Only please, no death.'

Maurice took the music, and by the evening had composed three stanzas in the manner of Heine, with exactly the same number of syllables as in his poem '*Du Bist Wie eine Blume*'. Mrs Gillespie stayed in her room all that evening but the next morning, before his lesson with Antonia, he handed it to her. 'It's the best I can do,' he said, 'poems are not easy. You can't tell them what to be. They tell you what they're going to be, if you're lucky.'

She read it through.

'It's a little mechanical, but the sentiment is pleasant enough. And it's clever of you to write a love poem that sounds truthful. At your age, one knows nothing of love, only infatuation.'

'I'm not sure about that.'

'Where's Lorian?'

'Practising, I think.'

She opened the door and called out.

'Lorian!'

No response. Maurice watched the veins swelling in Mrs Gillespie's neck.

'Looo-ri-aaan!'

The name rang through the house with awesome mezzo-soprano power. The dogs began to bark. Soon Lorian appeared. She moved as quickly and silently to the piano as a beautiful slave, Maurice thought.

'Lorian dear, play this accompaniment for me so that I can sing Maurice's poem.'

And she sang it with such passion that she gave it painful life, as if her soul ached.

One night in bed, Maurice read a story by Maupassant concerned with the subject of death. The story played on his mind for several days and macabre associations proliferated. David had told him that in the nearby Protestant churchyard of Ardcarne the bones of the long-dead worked their way up to the surface. You could pick them up and handle them. In the late afternoon of a day when nothing much seemed to be happening, he asked Lorian if they might go for a bicycle ride together.

'Yes, a good idea. Where shall we go?'

'I'm rather interested in old graveyards.'

'So am I, but don't tell Mother.'

'David says there's one in Ardcarne.'

'I know a much better one, at Kilronan a few miles away. We'll go there.'

'All right, but why should I not tell your mother?'

'She hates death in the way that one person can hate another. She regards being dead as an unnatural condition. To her, every death is a kind of murder.'

'Murder by whom?'

'Oh, goodness knows. Come on, let's ride to Kilronan.'

They sped down the avenue and out onto the main road. Soon they turned off onto a much narrower twisty road. Unusually, there was traffic and they went in single file with Lorian leading. She was wearing shorts. The sun did not often blaze over Roscommon and he contemplated the milky whiteness of her calves and thighs. He had not encountered such sweetness and warmth before, such care and concern, such vulnerability. She could conceal none of her thoughts. These things were not to be found in his life at home, nor among his rather raffish student friends.

69

'Will you be off soon?' she asked over her shoulder. 'To the war, I mean.'

'Yes. Most of my friends have gone now.'

'Are you brave?'

'I don't know. I don't think so. I don't feel very brave.'

'You might surprise yourself.'

Wisps of hair were floating about her neck in the breeze. David's love for her was deeper and more intense than Maurice's. He had surrendered more. There were bonds between them which Maurice knew he could not sever. They joined in the harvesting, David pitching and she stacking the sheaves in the cart; they had mourned and buried chicks that had been burnt to death in the incubator; most symbolically of all they had drunk together from the Healing Well a few fields away from Brookford.

'You're keen on David, are you?' he called out, trying to sound casual.

'David is a true person.'

'True?'

'A true person,' she said again, firmly. She glanced to her right. 'Look at those fat bullocks. Poor things, you'll soon be roast beef. We love you and we're going to eat you!' She blew them a kiss with her right hand which made her wobble badly on her bicycle. It was a blue and cloudy day. In a field on their left, at the other side of a dry stone wall, a young chestnut mare was galloping excitedly alongside them, her tail outstretched.

When they reached Kilronan church, they leaned their bicycles against a rusty gate and entered the graveyard. Lorian led the way.

'I want to show you a VIP's tomb.'

She stopped and pointed at an ancient tomb encrusted with moss and lichen.

'There lies Carolan,' she said, 'make obeisance in reverence and awe.'

'Who was Carolan?'

'O sublime ignorance! He was the last of the great Irish minstrels. He died in 1738. A really great harper.' She went up to the tomb and touched it, almost as if caressing it. It was then that Maurice put his arms around her, drew her to him and kissed her.

For just a few seconds she gave herself to the kiss, then released herself.

'Oh Maurice, oh dear-o—'

She laughed and tweaked his nose gently.

There were clinging weeds, long grass and thistles. They left Carolan's tomb and stumbled about among the dead, tapping on green whips of clinging weeds. They stopped when they came to a tomb which appeared badly awry. The stone panels had partly collapsed inwards, like a fallen house of cards. One of the corners at the bottom gaped darkly. The opening was only a few inches across, but dry leaves were just visible inside. Then, as they looked more closely, they saw something paler. Maurice got down on all fours and put his hand inside the tomb.

He gingerly drew something out.

'It's an arm bone,' he said. 'I think it's called an ulna.'

He felt about in the darkness again and eventually pulled out another arm bone, this one stained with earth and moss.

'Two arm bones.'

'We're doing something awful,' Lorian said.

'Do you want me to stop?'

'No.'

Maurice searched again. After a while, he felt something moveable. It was round. One of his fingers slipped into what felt like an eye socket.

'I think I've got the skull,' he said.

He manoeuvred it towards the gap and saw that it was indeed a skull. With some difficulty he eased it out into the open.

'Oh God,' Lorian said.

Maurice arranged the bones into a pattern on the ground. 'There, skull and crossbones.' Then he picked up the skull and handed it to Lorian.

'This comes to you with my love.'

She giggled nervously, then looked down at it solemnly.

'I wonder who he was. He might have played the fiddle for dancing at the crossroads. Or joked, and told stories.'

' "Alas poor Yorick" is what you're saying?'

'What shall we do with them? Can you put them back in the tomb?'

'Couldn't we bring them home, put them on the mantelpiece?'

'Not on the mantelpiece, but yes, why not bring them back? We can put them in the shopping basket on my bicycle. Use your jacket to cover them.'

They rode back to Brookford in silence. They went, not to the front, but to the yard and leaned their bicycles against a wall.

'Don't go in yet,' Lorian said, 'I want to get the all clear.'

She shouted across the yard.

'Where's Mother, David?'

'In her room with a headache.'

'Good. Hide them somewhere, Maurice. I wish now we hadn't brought them back. There could be trouble if Mother finds out.'

Maurice brought in the bones and put them in the bottom of a dark cupboard in the kitchen passage.

Mrs Gillespie did not come down for dinner. Lorian and Antonia left the dining room as soon as they had finished eating. The others were still sitting round the table when they heard an unusual noise. It sounded like wailing and chanting, with a dry, brittle noise in the background. Maurice and David went to investigate, and when they reached the hall they saw what was happening. The skull lay on the carpet in the centre of the floor. Lorian was dancing round it in bare feet, wearing a ragged old shirt. She looked beautiful, unaware of the two young men watching. She was wrenching her body into sharp, angular movements, as if under torture. Now and then she would whirl herself about with a wild shriek. Her dance was accompanied by percussion. An old army drum had been found and on this Antonia was beating a disjointed rhythm, using the arm bones as drumsticks. She too shrieked and wailed, and sometimes she twirled the bones around her head.

Suddenly all was silent and still, as if winter had come.

Mrs Gillespie had come down from her room and was standing motionless at the bottom of the stairs. Her face was chalky, lifeless except for outraged eyes. Even at this moment Maurice thought how beautiful Lorian was as she looked at her mother with deepening concern. Antonia stopped, arm bones in the air, poised for the next drumbeat. Mrs Gillespie stared at her.

'Drop those things.'

Antonia didn't move.

'Drop them. Drop them at once!'

The arm bones fell onto the drum with a clatter.

As if holding the tail of a dead rat, Mrs Gillespie took Antonia's wrist between a finger and thumb and led her to the stairs which they climbed quickly, wordlessly. Unnoticed by the others, David had crept upstairs to the lavatory which was always his refuge in times of crisis. It was next to the bathroom, and through the flimsy partition he could hear Mrs Gillespie spitting out orders.

'Scrub it! Here, not *there*! Scrub it. Scrub it again! Filthy dead things, you don't know what you were playing with. Now your left hand. Put it in the water. Wash your fingers and thumb. Hard! Now rinse both your hands. Don't touch those things again.'

David went quietly downstairs. Throughout the house

there was a feeling of forbiddance. Outside, the air was thunderous as he walked across the yard to the loft which was used as a granary. There he found Maurice looking out of a window, smoking a cigarette. It was getting dark. Soon they were joined by Lorian. They stood close together and spoke in hushed voices as if planning escape from a scene of crime. What was to be done with the bones? Re-interment at Kilronan was not feasible at this hour. Ardcarne was closer but visible to passers-by.

'There's only one option,' Maurice said, 'they'll have to be buried round here somewhere.'

'But where?' Lorian asked. 'If we bury them in arable ground they'll be ploughed up next year. Then the Gardai will come sniffing around. There'll be a murder inquiry.'

Until then David had been silent.

'I think I know. It's a horrible place, under those pine trees near the lake. No bird will nest there, not even the hens. The soil is spongy and receptive, like – I don't know what it's like. They won't be discovered there.'

'Will you and Maurice see to it?' Lorian said and left them.

Maurice went to fetch the bones and David to get a spade. Just as Maurice reached the house, there was a peal of thunder.

They walked down to the place of burial, Maurice with the bones under his jacket. David dug the black earth that seemed to move after he had put down a spadeful. Maurice had put the bones on the ground and was waiting. The sight of the bones made him feel wretched.

Lightning flashed, then there was more thunder, loud and close, an ancient and dreadful sound. Rain was now falling through the sparse trees.

'We're in a cheap horror movie,' David said, feeling that some frivolity was necessary. As he picked up the skull to place it in its new grave there was another flash which lit up the broken face in his hands. He and David looked at each other, appalled. David laid the arm bones beside the skull and started to fill in the hole.

Maurice trod the earth in firmly.

When they got back to the house all had gone to bed. The bones were never spoken of again.

★

The approach of Michaelmas term at Trinity, as well as the necessity to decide about enlistment, brought the end of Maurice's stay at Brookford into sight. It was time for him to go. David and the Gillespies stood outside the front door to wave goodbye, heedless of the rain. Mrs Gillespie said it would be nice if he came back when the war was over. The Major drove him to the station. On the way they said little. He was shy of the tall ex-cavalryman and had always sensed in him a quality which he was unable to identify. On the platform, as the train was coming in, the Major put an arm around Maurice's shoulders.

'Well, Maurice.' He gave a little chuckle and almost imperceptibly drew the young man closer to him for a second, then let him go. It was his way of saying goodbye. He turned and walked away with his slight arthritic limp. Suddenly Maurice realised that what the old man had was serenity.

Drizzle was falling over the fields of Roscommon as the train gathered pace on its way to Dublin. Maurice thought about the Gillespies and how strangely they had moved him. And about Lorian. Love, he decided, was not a fever, far more like rheumatism: a dull, pervasive ache which shifted when you tried to locate it, shifted among past events, through dreads and joys. It was not without fear. It was his habit to shake himself whenever he felt a cold coming on, as if to throw it off before it took hold, and he shook himself now.

At Mullingar station, his spirits began to lift. As the train was moving off again he had smiled through the window at an attractive girl carrying her luggage along the platform, and she had given him a great smile back, full in the face, emboldened because the train was moving. He told himself he had much to keep him busy. Dublin was full of girls and he had friends who were fun. And there was dear big Maeve O'Donnell of the medical school who was so nice she could never bring herself to say no; so obliging was she that she had become known as 'the college bicycle'. Alone in the carriage he laughed aloud. Yes, there were all those things.

And there was the war.

Van Tonder's Mistake

On a morning several years before the end of apartheid rule, Gert van Tonder had a bad feeling. It was no more than an inkling that providence might be planning some monstrous trick that was beyond the powers of human arrangement. This foreboding had been with him for some time, living discreetly in a corner of his mind, coming out in stealth to importune him whenever it chose.

Perhaps because of the Huguenot blood that had come from his mother, he was a cultivated man with an appetite for European traditions. He had read widely and his house was full of precious things: figurines, ancient coins and silver, antique furniture. His lined face, grizzled hair and tall, slightly stooping figure amounted to a presence that was courteous but recoiled from intimacy. In van Tonder's company, small talk died on the lips.

His only companion, though that is hardly the word, was his cook and housekeeper Frieda, who lived in a small, self-contained extension to the house. She was a Zulu woman in her fifties, big but without surplus fat. From this solid frame she sent forth authority, a moral strength which transcended colour and education. It was released from her as effortlessly as sweat. Even white visitors somehow felt in awe of her. She showed no emotion. In the three years that she had been with him, van Tonder had not seen her smile. She received his occasional extra kindnesses with indifference. He sometimes wondered whether, in her wooden silence, there was a hatred for all whites. He kept her on because she was reliable and was not a thief.

Van Tonder was a millionaire. He started as a farmer, had succeeded where many around him failed, and had later sold his farm and moved into industry where he had again succeeded. He came to feel that South Africa was no longer a good home for money. Over a number of years, by complex and painstaking means, he had circumvented the exchange control regulations and moved the bulk of his fortune outside the republic, leaving himself plenty to live on at home. He had transferred large sums to his two daughters who lived in Switzerland. From each of them he had received a short letter, more of acknowledgement than thanks.

He had been a widower for eleven years and was thought of as a good Afrikaner by his small circle of friends, although because of his reticence none of them felt that they knew him well. In the last few years, he had withdrawn behind ramparts of self-protection and had spent thousands of rands on an anti-theft system which was wired up to the local police station. Recently, he had had the spaces between his window bars narrowed to eight centimetres. He always carried a gun in his pocket. He feared terrorism, mass black uprising, extreme right-wing white violence by the AWB, a general collapse of order. These fears were not beyond reality. It was when he began to speak of assassination that his friends thought he was showing signs of paranoia.

Now, after breakfast, he was sitting on the stoep of his house in the affluent suburb of Bryanston where he had bought land many years ago at a time when a hectare could be had for little more than the small change in your pocket. It was more of an elegant veranda than a stoep, but because of his early farming days he still used the Boer word. Bryanston was far enough from the centre of Johannesburg to make him feel that he was not a town-dweller. His two big dogs were with him: Faust, the Alsatian, lay stretched on his side at the edge of the stoep, while the Doberman,

Riebeeck, sat, as usual, close to his master. Van Tonder would speak in English to Faust but, for a reason he had never tried to fathom, he would slip into Afrikaans with Riebeeck. Faust had charm, Riebeeck had none. Riebeeck responded to a caress no more than a weapon responded to the handling of its owner, and Riebeeck was van Tonder's weapon against gathering anxieties. For a while he had employed minders but had dismissed them after reading an article which told him that they were open to bribery. With care and patience he was training Riebeeck to be a killer.

Beyond the stoep there was the half-hectare garden of grass, trees and shrubs, and there was a large swimming pool. Van Tonder looked with distaste at his late wife's sculptures lurking among the shrubs. Theirs had been a cold marriage. She had been a conventional person which made it more surprising that her work tended to portray malformation. Near the middle of the garden there was a female bust with a single breast, centrally placed, a thing which required a smirking apology to visitors. Van Tonder observed with satisfaction that the dogs cocked their legs against it.

For the past year or so he had been feeling a little pain in his chest. It would come and go. He felt it now. He searched in his pocket for the heart pills his doctor had given him. He sometimes thought with curiosity about the crimson muscle that was obliged to throb from the beginning to the end of life. Years and years of throbbing. No matter what you got up to, whether you were good or evil, it would hurry the innocent, blind blood through the darkness of your body.

As a young man living alone on his farm in the northern Transvaal, he had fathered a child with an African girl. Driven from her home by some dispute with her parents, she had turned up looking for work two days after his previous servant had left. She was a Xhosa girl, doe-eyed and timid, probably not more than eighteen.

'What is your name?' van Tonder asked her.

'Rakiya, master, but my sisters call me Joy.'

Before he could check himself, van Tonder smiled at her.

'Joy? The last girl I had was called Sorrow. Why do they call you Joy?'

'I don't know, master.'

Timid though she was, she had returned his smile without misgiving. She was ragged and exhausted and her hair was covered in dust, and she was beautiful.

'Well, you can stay for a little while. The house needs cleaning and the floors scrubbing. I have a lot of dirty clothes to be washed and ironed.'

He led her to the back of the house.

'Look, there are my dirty clothes in that big basket. Soap on the shelf there just above you. Do you see that door across the yard? There's a camp bed inside. You can sleep there.'

He started to walk away, then stopped and turned.

'You look tired and hungry. You'll find some food in the kitchen. Have a rest before you begin.'

As the days passed, Rakiya washed and cleaned and scrubbed and tidied the place up. Van Tonder was surprised and touched when he found that she had put some wild flowers in a little vase on his bedside table.

There had been poor rains that summer, the grass on the veldt looked tired and the weals of red earth around the house had been baked hard. Van Tonder lived in parching celibacy. Sometimes he would watch Rakiya through the kitchen window as she went about her work in the yard. She was slender and graceful and it almost seemed that her ebony sheen came not from the light, but from a source within her body. When they met face to face she was too shy to raise her eyes to his. She feared him because he didn't speak, even to chastise her. Chastisement – either by parents or employers – had become so familiar that it provided the stability of a routine.

One night she crept whimpering into his bedroom during a violent thunderstorm. She was wearing only a slip.

Van Tonder switched on the light. 'What is it?' he asked, sitting up.

'I am frightened, master.'

Van Tonder knew the law, he had read the Immorality Act.

'Get in here. Take that thing off.' The orders were given gently. He drew the sheet over their heads and took Rakiya in his arms, while above them an angry clown was trying to smash the universe. Her trembling ceased and their embrace grew passionate. Van Tonder's climax coincided with a flash of lightning, followed immediately by a sound as if space had been shattered. They lay still together until the storm had passed. Van Tonder held her head close against his chest and in his hand her hair felt like the wool of a lamb.

Rakiya had become pregnant. Van Tonder's workmen lived in huts about two hundred metres away and he was certain that she had not left the precincts of the house. He did not deny parentage. She was given money and sent to a township where their child was born.

Word was brought to him of the birth. Secretly, driving at night in a small hired car so that he should not be recognised, van Tonder went to see his son who was suckling his mother. Rakiya looked up at van Tonder with eyes that concealed nothing. The orbs were so absolute in their giving that he felt diminished. Like his father, he had seldom given without some reckoning of the cost.

'What will he be called?' she asked.

He was silent for a few moments.

'Let him be called Lightning.'

There was a flash of white teeth, a bubbly laugh revealed a pink tongue.

'OK, he will be called Lightning.'

'He can have my name too.'

'Am I allowed to love my master?'

Van Tonder realised that she was teasing him. He smiled. 'I don't think there's a law against that, but I'll check.'

He bent down quickly and kissed the boy's forehead.

'Is der one left for me?' Rakiya asked.

'Yes,' he said, and kissed her tenderly.

He gave her as much money as he could at that time afford, and left. He did not visit again. They had both committed a criminal offence, entered in the statute book as 'Irregular Carnal Intercourse'.

He returned home with a smile on his face, repeating the name *Lightning van Tonder*. Before going into the house he looked up. There was a full moon in a broken sky. The clouds were as fat as sheep. It was all so startling, so magically improbable, that he wanted to run, or shout, or burst into song.

Some months later he got a cautious letter from a black solicitor giving him a P.O. address in case he 'might want to contribute to a small charity'. He began to prosper and through the years he sent money regularly and generously, not knowing whether or by whom it was received. From time to time an unsigned note would arrive, giving a changed address. After he had sold the farm and moved house several times, he was no longer accessible to Rakiya and her little son but continued to send the money.

For business reasons, in his later years. van Tonder belonged to the arcane and powerful *Broederbond*. He kept secret from the other members the existence of his coloured son. He did not tell them that he was an anonymous benefactor of the Market Theatre in Johannesburg where plays of black protest were performed. He kept secret also the fact that he was a generous donor, again anonymously, to African Self Help. In the *Broederbond* they treated him with respect because of his position in industry, but their respect was cool. Although none of them could have explained why, he seemed to have a different smell from the rest of the pack.

On the morning of his unease in Bryanston, van Tonder watched a weaver bird putting the finishing touches to the nest he had been building. For three days the bird had hurried to and fro with twigs and grass, pulling and pushing with his beak. This little architect had by now achieved an almost perfectly spherical construction. Van Tonder noticed that the grey loerie birds with the long tails that always flew among the trees at the far end of the garden had been absent for nearly a week. The virus of paranoia made their departure seem like an omen to him.

By midday he felt in need of company, a rare thing for him. He decided to drive to the Rand Club for lunch. When he got into the Mercedes he took the gun from his pocket and put it in a specially designed holster under the dashboard within easy reach of his right hand. He drove with the windows closed and the doors locked. When he arrived at the club he went to the bar, exchanged a few banalities, then ate at his usual table. Members seldom joined him at his table now; drumming up a conversation with van Tonder had become hard work. His silences and his manner of detached observation made him a difficult companion.

When he got home he shut the Alsatian in the lounge and went out onto the stoep. He clapped his hands.

'Now, Riebeeck, time for training.'

He started to walk across the garden. Riebeeck remained on the stoep, tense and still, a slight quiver of excitement on his flanks. After van Tonder had walked about twenty-five metres he turned and shouted, 'Kom!'

Riebeeck sped towards him silently. Van Tonder turned

again and walked on, the dog following close at his heels. At the far end of the garden there was an area hidden from the house by shrubs. Here, van Tonder had erected two iron rods connected by a crossbar at the top. From the crossbar there hung a dummy, filled out to give it human form, grotesquely dressed in old clothes. Its head was a football with a crudely painted face. Thick layers of tough leather had been glued around its throat. The ground was littered with pieces of leather and torn clothing. Van Tonder and the dog stood about twenty metres from the dummy. The dog was quivering.

'Kill!' van Tonder shouted.

With a growl the Doberman raced to the dummy, leapt up at its throat and tore at it in a frenzy, ripping away pieces of leather.

'Stop!' van Tonder shouted. The dog jumped down from the dummy and stood still.

'Kom!'

The dog ran to him silently.

The exercise was repeated several times. The dummy was unhooked and placed lying down in various parts of the garden, sometimes concealed from the Doberman behind bushes. The session lasted for half an hour.

'Good, Riebeeck!' van Tonder said when they returned to the stoep. He did not pat Riebeeck but got a piece of meat from the kitchen and threw it to him.

Van Tonder had just finished having his tea when the front doorbell rang. With his hand on the gun in his right-hand pocket and the indoctrinated Doberman close behind him, hackles raised and ears erect, he went to the door, looked through the spyhole and saw what he took to be the face of a young coloured man. It was a handsome, open face and it seemed friendly. Van Tonder opened the door on the chain and Riebeeck growled. The young man smiled through the narrow gap.

'Hi,' he said.

'Hallo,' said van Tonder, 'who are you? What can I do for you?'

'I am Lightning. I am your son.'

'You— What?'

'It is legal for me to visit you and I have papers of identity.'

He handed some papers through the gap. Van Tonder glanced through them. Then he looked intently into the young man's face. Yes, he thought, you are my son.

'You may as well come in,' he said, not quite believing what was happening. 'How did you find me?'

'That's a fairly long story. You are careful with the door.'

'These are bad times.'

Van Tonder pointed to the stoep. 'We can talk out there,' he said. It seemed to him that the young man walked across the room like a gazelle. He was unhurried, looking about him as he went.

After they had sat down van Tonder could think of nothing to say.

'How is your mother?' he asked formally, as if entertaining a white schoolboy.

'May I call you Father?'

'That is what I am.'

Without answering van Tonder's question Lightning looked at the extensive garden and the pool.

'You are a big boss?' he said, smiling.

'I'm hardly a boss at all now, I've almost retired. But I suppose you could say that I was once, well, yes, quite a big boss as you put it.'

They were silent for a few moments. It was van Tonder who was tense.

'I asked about your mother.'

'I didn't like to answer the question. Rakiya is dead. A stray bullet got her in the back at Sharpville. She had gone with a big crowd to the police station where they were going to make a protest about the Pass Law. It was a friendly crowd, laughing and joking, and they were unarmed. When they got close to the station, a policeman panicked and fired and then they all opened up with rifles and machine guns. Rakiya crawled home through all the wounded bodies. 'I was eight years old. I saw her crawling in through the door on her belly. She was panting like a dog. She said, "Stop the blood, little one, or you won't have a mother". I stopped it as well as I could with cloths and towels. At last a doctor came. She survived the wound but she was a cripple and she was always in pain. She was brave. She would try to cheer me up when I felt sad.'

'How did she do that?'

'She would say, "One day the white baas who is your father will come for us. He is a good man".'

'What is our future?' he asked abruptly.

'Our future is on Robben Island. It is waiting there in a little room.'

Van Tonder nodded. 'Which side will you be on?'

'I hope there will be no sides, but if there are I suppose I will have to be with the whites. The blacks don't like us coloureds all that much.'

Neither of them spoke for a little while. Then Lightning said, 'Father, I hope you will not be offended but I don't any longer need the money you have been sending. It has been a great help. It has bought me special education. I was able to hire a tutor and I could buy nice clothes.'

Van Tonder had noticed that the shirt and jeans looked expensive and felt pleased about it. 'You are welcome to the money,' he said.

'I don't need it any more.'

'As you wish.'

'There are charities for the blacks—'

'I know about charities. I will give it to them if that is what you wish.'

'I have a good job in the Western Cape. I work in a bank.'

'I hope you'll do well.'

'I will. I have your thought in my head.'

'That's probably true.'

The young man smiled. 'You gave it to me in a flash of lightning.'

Van Tonder was smiling too.

'So you know about the thunderstorm?'

'Rakiya told me about it.'

They talked for another hour or so and then Lightning said it was time for him to go. Van Tonder had to agree; if neighbours were to denounce him for entertaining a coloured person in his house his business interests could be seriously damaged. Neither of them spoke of another meeting. Van Tonder opened the front door. They were on the point of embracing but did not do so. They were strangely embarrassed as they shook hands. They were unable to say goodbye, it seemed like a silly word.

Van Tonder held the door open and watched the young man walk up the concrete path. When he reached the gate he turned and smiled. Then he waved and walked out of sight.

Van Tonder went back to his chair on the stoep. The little pain returned briefly. He fumbled wearily for his pills, then realised he had left them in the gents at the Rand Club. Looking up he saw a jumbo jet, a silver shark swimming serenely towards Jan Smuts airport.

'Hello, travellers,' he said aloud, 'welcome to this beautiful country.'

There was not a sound anywhere.

Rakiya.

He sat very still and quiet and allowed the tears to roll down his face. While he was sitting there, the hen weaver bird came and settled into the nest her mate had built for her.

When he looked at his watch it was seven o'clock. The light had that quality of cool bronze which meant it would be dark in twenty minutes. It was unsmiling Frieda's evening off, so it fell to him to feed the dogs. He went to the kitchen and prepared the food on two tin plates which he brought back to the stoep. He clapped his hands and said briskly, 'Apartheid!'

This was the signal for the dogs to sit in their appointed places at opposite ends of the step so as to avoid fighting. Each would sit patiently until his food was brought to him. Van Tonder found that he had forgotten the water and remembered that Riebeeck must have a garlic pill. Leaving the food on the table he went back to the kitchen. It took him some time to find the pills and then he had to fill the watering can.

When he got back to the stoep he found the dogs fighting with a ferocity which appalled him. Hunger and temptation had overcome apartheid and some of the food from one of the plates was scattered on the table. Van Tonder had always been fearless with animals but this fury in a domestic space alarmed him. He thought that if it went to a finish Riebeeck would probably kill Faust. He shouted and swore, kicked them and threw the water over them. Then he took a sjambok from the wall and lashed them with it. The Alsatian began to tire and by using his knees van Tonder succeeded in manoeuvring him into the lounge so as to isolate him. He was about to close the glass doors when Riebeeck slipped between his legs and the fighting began again. 'Fuck you, dikkopf!' van Tonder shouted, and brought the sjambok down hard on Riebeeck's back, which seemed only to increase the Doberman's savagery. Covering his genitals with one hand and using the sjambok with the other he managed to separate them at last. The Alsatian surrendered and went into a corner to lick his wounds.

In the silence that followed van Tonder had a feeling of

dread. It had arrived suddenly and crushed him. Seconds later, he felt a pain so bad that he knew something bad had happened. He gasped. The room seemed to darken and he had lost the feeling in his legs. He managed to move these wooden stilts towards a chair and crashed into it.

It was a few minutes after ten when Frieda came in. She looked at van Tonder, at his stillness, and saw that a trickle of pink froth had flowed from a corner of his open mouth. In his struggle to reach the chair he had overturned a small table and scattered a collection of Roman coins on the carpet. Frieda's eyes were expressionless. She studied the face that used to give orders with such remote courtesy.

How can they be so white, she thought, it isn't natural.

She went out onto the stoep where the light was still on. Bangles flashed on black arms as she cleared up the food.

'Come, Riebeeck, come, Faust, I will feed you now.'

The dogs came onto the stoep. Frieda clapped her hands. 'Apartheid!'

As she spoke the word a trembling started in her belly. It rose in her and made her shoulders shake. She threw her head back and sent a long, throaty laugh into the night.

LONELY HEARTS

*V*ictor Maguire's apartment was on the sixteenth floor of a block called The Statesman in the Hillbrow district of Johannesburg. Looking down from the window of his sitting room he could see the bowling green and, this being Saturday, the usual white figures were there. They were slow and deliberate in their movements, ripe people intent at one of the games of late life. To the left, and higher even than his window, there was the Strydom Tower where he had been occupied for the past seven weeks. Maguire was in the electronics industry, a senior salesman who did not knock on doors but did business in plush offices with government ministers and, sometimes, military commanders. He had been selling some very advanced equipment to the South African government and was now advising on its installation. His bonus – if the deal went through in its entirety – would bring him almost £200,000 when he got back to the UK. In the operations room of the tower there would soon be a cluster of controls which, if used in a crisis, would have surprising consequences many miles away. On closed-circuit television screens he had been looking at places as distant as Bloemfontein where bridges could be blown and mines detonated at the touch of a finger. This elderly government is frightened, he thought, and paranoia is my firm's bread and butter. We thrive on fear.

On Saturdays, he had noticed that among the ancient figures far below there was always a young girl. She did not join the game but sat chatting and laughing. She was a succulent little thing, with a piece of green silk around her neck. Maguire wondered what she could be doing with those old wrinklies. It was embarrassing really, this surge of the sap at fifty-two, and it was particularly troublesome in the adulterous heat of February. He went to the bathroom to put on a shirt and comb his hair. The hair was surprisingly dark and thick, one of the assets he hoped he could hold on to. He saw with satisfaction that the skin at his waist had not yet begun to fold over his belt. He could pass for forty-five, no problem.

On his walk to the garage where his hired Audi was kept, he enjoyed the tangy flavour of Hillbrow. Friends shouted to each other across the traffic; there was a bustle. He had come to recognise the permanent drunks who slept rough, some with bits of hay or straw clinging to their clothes. They did not stagger or sing but walked quietly about with wild faces, as though some psychological disaster had happened. Apartheid of a modified kind survived within this boiling pot, but there was an almost European feeling, something of the vitality of Soho, even of a back street in Naples. The day was not too hot and Maguire felt well. He had come a long way from the time when, as a young door-to-door salesman, he had worked for Slumberjoy selling vibrating mattresses. He would sit in a car in prosperous suburbs watching a house until he saw the husband leave for work. Then he would move in with his brochures. In response to his rather swarthy good looks, and the discreet but suggestive patter about the mattresses, housewives tended to melt and sometimes parted with more than their money. He closed his eyes for a second and smiled. The vibrating mattress had been a killer all right.

He drove to the offices of the *Evening Star*. Before handing in his advertisement he read it through again:

> Help! Lively forty-five-yr-old w/e tail slim sensitive cultured gent visiting from UK yearns for plump broad-minded lady 30–45. Dinners, outings, fun. Funds no problem. Photo would oblige.

He deleted 'broad minded'. It was not good salesmanship to put everything on the table at once.

Maguire now had a free day. He lunched in the centre of Johannesburg, then spent the afternoon shopping. He drove back in reflective mood. At this age, one was rather out of the market for girls. One could no longer beckon with the eyes, one had to take trouble, spend a bit of money, make a strategic approach, and that was where salesmanship came in. On these foreign trips he had always rewarded himself with what his friends in City bars called a bit on the side. Indeed, it was what you were expected to do, and your marriage would be none the worse for it. Better perhaps, although Maguire had doubts about that. Sex had never been high on Hilda's agenda and was now given grudgingly as an unavoidable duty, or dispensed like pocket money when the day came round. He wondered if it was because they were childless that she had recently started a gymnastic regime to keep herself occupied. He had been alarmed when he came home one evening to find her exercising with dumb-bells. She now attended a keep fit centre twice a week from which she would return slicked with sweat. Her life had begun to be driven by what she called 'functions'. On Thursdays, she would put on a white overall and look menacing behind jars of jam at the WI. She was active in church affairs and had been made treasurer of the Parish Church Council. She was showing signs of aggressive ambition in the local Conservative Association. Oh God, how could a man be blamed for wanting a little bit on the side? Mind you, he'd been indulging in these little indiscretions on business trips for most of his married life. Sensible wives didn't ask questions and no harm was done.

It was dark when he got back to Hillbrow. A neon glare came from shop windows and there was the usual throng of people. At the end of the main street where he would turn off for The Statesman, a paunchy police officer was draining a glass of lemonade down his throat while chatting to a man standing beside him. The officer took no notice of a shapeless heap of clothes on the pavement a few yards away. From it, a dark stream of urine was worming its way to the gutter. Indifferent feet were passing over it. Maguire felt a little stab of loneliness. What he needed was a bit of company.

Two days later he collected a batch of letters from the *Star* and brought them back to his flat in some excitement. The writers of the first four he opened all gave their weight in kilos, as though he had advertised for groceries. One informed him that she had seven dogs, three cats and twenty pigeons and that if he was an animal lover they had a future together. Another was a born-again Christian who thundered on about redemption. Two more were equally unpromising: Maguire was not looking for bridge partners. The last letter he opened held his attention:

Dear lively UK visitor

So you're well-endowed and you're going to do a lot of good to a plump lady and all you want is dinners, outings and fun? I wear pointed shoes and I could give you a toothache in your endowment like you've never had before. I know your type. You just want to get your dick in a few times and then scarper back to your wife when your business here is done. I'd like to look after you with a hot iron.

Goodbye, fuckpig.

Definitely not yours,

KP

Maguire was intrigued by sales resistance and respected it. He had to admit that the letter had style, vocabulary, and an imaginative quality unexpected from the conservative white society of Johannesburg. Regretfully he dropped it in the bin.

One of the devices had failed to detonate during a test run. This was beyond Maguire's competence to remedy and the firm was sending out an expert to reprogramme the computers. His work was therefore in temporary suspension and his stay in Johannesburg would be extended by several weeks. He had time on his hands. Each day he went to the *Star* offices to harvest replies to his advertisement. By now, he had received twenty-three and, after eliminating the nutters – the volleyball enthusiasts, the scuba-divers and other unsuitable candidates – he settled for someone called Tina Brewster who was 1.57 metres tall and weighed seventy-six kilos. He rang the number she had given. A no-nonsense voice told him that she had come to South Africa from the UK twelve years ago with her husband and they had divorced. She was thirty-eight, had a son at Witwatersrand University and now worked in an accountant's office. They arranged to meet the following day.

Feeling a little foolish, Maguire stood at a corner with a folded newspaper under his left arm and the agreed scarlet handkerchief sprouting from his breast pocket. Tina identified him immediately and approached him without shyness or affectation.

'Tall slim gent?'

'Yes.' His salesman's antennae were working hard to get her measure in the first few seconds.

'What do we do now, slim gent?'

'We could start by having a drink, I suppose.'

'Right, you're on.'

'There's quite a nice bar a short distance away. We could try that.'

Maguire felt the warmth of attraction spreading through him. He had struck lucky, first time. There was a gung-ho quality about her, a come-what-may feeling. He got an impression of courage. He imagined her as a Brownie. Did Brownies still exist?

'You're not bad looking,' she said, looking up at him without smiling as they walked along. He felt drawn to her gruff, down-to-earth manner. It immediately implied intimacy. In the next twenty minutes she told him that he needed a haircut and that he should have his trousers pressed. Over drinks, she explained to him that divorced women in South Africa found it almost impossible to make new friends because wives never invited them to parties fearing they might steal their husbands. The Lonely Hearts column was their only course.

'And you're divorced?'

'Yes, I preferred divorce to cutting his throat.'

'So there's no one in your life now?' Maguire made his inquiry sound casual.

'Oh yes, there's Samantha.'

'Samantha?'

'She's my cat. She's Siamese. She's gorgeous.'

'Not much satisfaction in that, though, is there?'

'Better than nothing. And you, you have a wife?'

Maguire said he was technically married but hardly ever saw his wife.

They went to his flat and Maguire, the seasoned seducer, didn't apply any pressure but listened sympathetically as Tina talked about her life. In the evening he took her to an English farce at which they held hands. After the theatre they had a drink in a hotel bar and then he ordered a taxi for her. They arranged another meeting. As she was about to step into the taxi he held her to him and kissed her lightly on the lips. He let her go but said nothing, apparently too overcome to speak.

Some would say that Maguire was a bit of a creep.

The next morning he got a letter from Hilda who told

him that last week she had put in two and a half hours on the rowing machine. She and Christine, the church organist's wife, were rowing a million metres for Comic Relief and she asked, would he sponsor them for £1 a kilometre? She had been neglecting her fast-twitch fibres and this had led to muscle loss and fat deposition, but now that she had joined *Intashape* the problem would be remedied. Maguire sent a cheque for £20, wondering what fast-twitch fibres were. Though his wife had chosen athletic celibacy, it certainly was not for him.

'You're so clever with the ladies,' Tina said.

Maguire demurred modestly.

'Do that again, slim gent.'

He was happy to oblige. Later, just as Maguire was about to achieve the purpose of his advertisement in the *Star*, the telephone rang. Thinking it might be the Minister of Defence he answered it and heard instead a distressed African woman's voice. 'For you,' he said, passing the receiver to Tina. As she listened she gave little cries of anguish. 'Oh no! Oh God! I'll come straight back.'

She scrambled out of bed, clawing Maguire as he tried to restrain her.

'What the hell's going on?' he asked.

'That was my maid. It's Samantha. She's got out. She's in season. She'll get raped. That suburb is crawling with Toms. I want to breed from her.'

'She'll be all right. Come back to bed, forget about her.'

'I can't do that to Pusskins!'

She was hopping and darting about the room like a blackbird, snatching up bits of clothing.

'Ring for a taxi, slim gent.'

Maguire was stowing his waning and now redundant erection into his pants. Once he had done this he ordered a taxi.

'I'll have to get you out the back way without Reception seeing us, they're very strict about that sort of thing and there'll be trouble if they find out you're here. Do up those buttons.'

They travelled down in the service lift, wedged in with a large hamper of dirty linen. Outside they found the taxi waiting. She quickly kissed him on the mouth before getting in.

'Let's keep in touch,' he said, 'I'll call you.'

In the morning, Maguire reviewed his situation. He looked through the letters again. None of them exactly fitted his requirement, although he quite liked the sound of one who called him 'Blue Eyes' before signing her name. He still felt very drawn to Tina.

The heat continued. Beyond the bowling green, which was empty on weekdays, there was a small park with amusements for children. There the grass was littered with sleeping blacks, night workers, Maguire guessed, who were not allowed to live in Johannesburg but were too tired to go home to Soweto before their next shift. The thunderstorms came every afternoon, bathing the city and suburbs in warm rain. In places, the blossom that had fallen from the jacaranda trees made a blue carpet to walk on. Maguire was much travelled, his senses assailed by almost continual novelty, yet he was aware of a special atmosphere in Johannesburg and there was some of the tension he had felt in New York. It was a dangerous place, a city, it seemed, living in barely controlled anger, with violence always just below the surface. Recently, two drivers – well-dressed professional men – had shot each other almost simultaneously in an argument over a minor traffic incident. Both had later died.

They were in the service lift again, travelling up. Maguire was carrying a large cardboard box.

'You're holding it the wrong way up,' Tina said, 'the

holes should be at the top. Poor Samantha!'

When she was taken out of her box, Samantha sat on the floor and glared resentfully at Maguire. He thought her face had an unpleasant expression, overly critical, self-righteous and snobbish. A bitch-cat, he thought.

'I'm not happy about bringing that animal in here. It's against the rules. They're very strict in this building.'

'She isn't "that animal", she's my gorgeous Samantha!' Tina picked her up and held her to her cheek. 'Booful Pusskins,' she said, and put her down tenderly. Maguire had taken off his shoes and was starting to undo his tie. He was wondering about Samantha's lavatory arrangements. Tina asked if her Pusskins could have a saucer of milk as she always had one at bedtime. Maguire found there was none in the fridge.

'I can get some from the machine on the landing,' he said. He went through the narrow lobby and opened the door of the flat. As he did so he felt something furry brush his ankles. A shriek came from Tina.

'She's got out! Oh my God! Catch her! She must not get out into the street. Go on, man, run!'

Maguire hesitated. He was barefoot. Tina, now stripped to her bra and tights, dashed past him onto the landing.

'Samantha, Pusskins, come to Mummy. Come on, darling!'

'For God's sake get back inside, you're not supposed to be here. I'm paying for single occupancy.'

'Will you please catch Samantha!'

In his socks, Maguire found the tiled floor slippery but attempted a slithery rush at Samantha. She retreated a few yards and then sat looking at him with a sarcastic expression. When he moved again she scampered to the far end of the landing, then disappeared round a corner. Maguire went in pursuit, and came across a middle-aged couple who had just come out of the lift.

'Excuse me, I wonder if you've seen a Siamese cat called Samantha. I'm trying to catch her.'

The woman spoke. 'She didn't give her name. She ran into the lift just as we were leaving it. Then the doors closed. If she's pressed the right button she'll be on her way down.' This humorist turned her back, took her husband's arm and walked proudly away. Maguire felt anger rise as he watched powerful buttocks moving contrapuntally above fat thighs.

Tina had joined him. She had put on her top but still wore nothing over her tights. They tore down the sixteen flights of stairs. As they reached the reception area, they could hear Samantha snarling and hissing. Then the manager came out of the lift with the cat struggling in his hands. He was a formal man who always wore a dark suit and tie even on hot days like this. He handed Samantha to Maguire who quickly passed her to Tina. Blood dripped from the manager's clawed left hand. He wrapped a white handkerchief around it.

'Is this your cat?'

'Yes,' Tina said, fearless in her tights.

The manager tried to pretend she wasn't there. He addressed Maguire.

'Mr Maguire, sir, it's against the rules to bring animals into the building.'

'Yes.'

The manager's left hand was evidently still bleeding. The handkerchief had turned a brilliant red. It made him look incongruously festive.

'Mr Maguire, sir, I take it your visitor will have left by eleven o'clock? It's a house rule, you see. And, sir, we like lady visitors to be properly attired.'

'Very well.'

For a second time Maguire saw Tina into a taxi. She was clasping Samantha to her bosom. There was no kissing.

Maguire returned to his flat, took two sleeping pills and went to bed.

The expert from the UK had gone home, leaving only a few minor problems to be solved. Quite soon a minister would arrive at the Strydom Tower to press an inaugural button, thus annihilating a dummy bridge improvised in a field thirty miles away. The end of Maguire's work was approaching. After a brief visit to the London office he would be on a train to Motsford in Sussex for a fortnight's leave in the parochial scene he abhorred, and he still hadn't had his bit on the side. Now he wanted Tina badly; if only he could have her without bloody Samantha. Strange how such a down-to-earth woman could be so soppy about a detestable cat. It was while he was thinking this over that his telephone rang.

'Am I speaking to Mr Maguire?' It was an English voice; slow and a little ponderous, with a touch of northern accent.

'Victor Maguire speaking.'

'Is it going nicely, Victor?'

'I'm afraid I don't recognise your voice.'

'The name's Piercey, John Piercey. Everything going smoothly?'

'What do you mean?'

'You and Tina having a nice time? Picnics? Looking at old churches? Going out to tea, potato cakes and muffins? I used to love muffins.'

'You know Tina Brewster?'

'We were going strong, like. We had a super row a few weeks ago, then we made it up. Then Victor Maguire comes on stage.'

Maguire remained silent. He was beginning to visualise a youngish, very large, balding muscular man with a square head.

'It takes a lot to get me aggravated,' Piercey said.

'I've no wish to break up a relationship.'

'It would be unfortunate if you did – for everyone.'

'I'm just a visitor here, looking for a little companionship, feeling a bit lonely.'

'Please don't make me cry.'

'I don't want to upset anyone. I'm willing to get out of your way if that's what you want.'

'I was hoping you'd see it like that, Victor. It wouldn't be at all nice for anyone if we fell out. I'd like you to enjoy your visit here, I really would.'

The telephone clicked and the conversation had ended, leaving Maguire thinking very carefully. He didn't relish the idea of a brawl, and the last thing he wanted was scandal. As a very successful man he was vulnerable to trouble of that kind. He had had a few near misses. There had been an awkward situation with a minister's wife in Ankara...

That evening he rang Tina at home and asked if she knew a man called John Piercey.

'On and off, yes.'

'What do you mean, "on and off"? Is he part of your life?'

'Yes and no. He comes and goes. Sometimes he meets someone else and forgets about me for a while, then he comes back again. He's made over the benefits of his insurance policies in my favour. It's no big thing for me.'

'I think it is for him. He might punch me on the nose.'

'No, he only uses knives.'

'I'm serious. I think perhaps we ought to cool it. I'm rather high profile with the government here. I'd be at risk if we had any sort of drama or scandal.'

'I'd miss my slim gent.'

Their conversation continued in a falling cadence. There was a long diminuendo, a winding down, until at last Tina said, 'Oh all right, bugger off then,' and put down her receiver. Maguire was much relieved. He had never had any difficulty in dropping people. It meant no more to him than flicking a fly off the back of his hand.

He was setting off again in his Audi, this time towards the suburb of Randburg to keep a tryst with Anne, the one who had called him 'Blue Eyes' in her letter. She was, she had told him, plump with brown hair and a ready smile. She enjoyed movies, quiet evenings at home, long suppers by candle light, and she had a son whose age she did not mention. So far so good, Maguire thought, but wished she had sent a photograph. He had misgivings. On the telephone, she had told him that her husband had left her for a young secretary two years ago. 'The story is almost too banal and predictable to tell,' she had said with a brave little laugh, 'I prefer fiction to real life, it's much more believable.' Maguire had sensed intelligence, and intelligence was not what he was after. But she also sounded vulnerable, and the vulnerable were attractive to Maguire.

As he drove along, he thought with some curiosity about these communications through the advertising columns between people who had not met, like mating calls among the blind, an imperious urge for togetherness. What do we all want? he wondered. It was surely something more than sex? It was the spectre of everlasting aloneness that drove people to huddle. Huddle and cuddle, huddle and cuddle – he made up a little tune and tapped it out on the steering wheel.

It was beginning to get dark when he found the house in a not very prosperous-looking street. On some flagstones outside the front door, an old Labrador and a cat were sleeping beside one another. The sound of quarrelsome pigeons came from a dovecot attached to a gable of the house. The grass would soon need mowing. The Labrador got up and walked stiffly towards him wagging her tail.

Unusual for a Johannesburg dog, he thought. He looked warily at the cat and decided it was less bitch-faced than Samantha. The slightly ramshackle appearance of the whole place did not give an impression of poverty, rather a contented unworldliness on the part of the owner. The door was opened and Maguire was looking at a smiling woman.

'Victor Maguire,' he said.

'Hallo, I'm Anne.' She held out her hand. Her smile seemed to convey sympathy; it was also self-deprecatory, as though they were in a regrettable situation which was partly her fault. Maguire wished again that she had sent a photograph. She was not fat but her body seemed to have surrendered in the battle for shape. It had sagged. From unwantedness? Her face, though, was beautiful, full of trust and humour, and this made him uncomfortable. She might have been in her late forties.

He had followed her into the house and they now stood in a smallish room. Although it was not yet quite dark outside the curtains were already drawn. Maguire noticed a pile of school exercise books on a table. Was she a teacher, perhaps? On a sofa he saw Coetzee's novel *Waiting for the Barbarians*, and a book of poems by Cavafy. There was a cosiness about this untidy place. Maguire also had an impression of something he didn't properly understand. It had something to do with a combination of vulnerability and courage.

'This is Malcolm,' Anne said, nodding towards a corner of the room behind Maguire. He turned round and saw a small boy of about eight. He was sitting very still at a table which was brightly illuminated by a reading lamp with a green shade. Maguire was aware of intense concentration. On the table there was a large array of miniature soldiers, an army complete with cavalry and artillery. The terrain was realistic with grassy mounds, trees and ditches. The uniforms, Maguire noticed, were nineteenth-century French, with a number of redcoats opposing them.

'I ordered them from the UK,' Anne said, 'they cost a mint. We lived on bread and soup for weeks afterwards, didn't we, love?'

'S'right, Mum.'

Mother and son seemed very close, Maguire thought.

'I'll get you a drink,' Anne said.

'That's very kind.'

Maguire was engrossed with the soldiers. His voice sounded absent.

'What's the battle?' he asked.

'Waterloo, Sir.'

Maguire was momentarily startled by the 'sir'. He drew up a chair and sat down next to the boy.

'I see you've got the Prince of Orange with Wellington there.'

'Yes. How did you know he's the Prince of Orange?'

'By his uniform. They're very accurate, these models.'

'He was brave, wasn't he?'

'Brave, but very young and rather hopeless. He lost Wellington three battalions. Made them advance in line. They were wiped out.'

'The battle hasn't begun yet. Napoleon is reviewing his army. It's eleven o'clock.'

'From where you're sitting I take it you're fighting Napoleon's battle?'

'Yes, I want him to win.'

'I'm afraid he lost.'

'I can make him win, Sir.'

Maguire looked carefully at the arrangement of the soldiers.

'It's nicely set out, Malcolm, but one or two things need putting right.'

'Where, Sir?'

'Your artillery's in the wrong place, much too far back.

Napoleon assembled eighty guns on that ridge, just there, to bombard Wellington's centre before attacking. Then he sent five divisions forward. Look, you've put the Imperial Guard much too far forward. They were right at the back, about here.'

'They were in the battle, weren't they, Napoleon's heroes?'

'Yes, but at the very end, his last throw of the dice.'

Obediently Malcolm moved eight pieces, each representing ten cannon, to the centre, and moved the Guard to the rear.

'Good, Malcolm. Now, Marshal Grouchy... you've put him much too close to Napoleon's main force. He was several miles to the right, out there, with his corps of 33,000 men, pinning down the Prussians. And look, here you need to leave a space for Ney to get through with the cavalry. At about 3.30 he charged with 5,000 horse along a front of only 700 yards. They were slaughtered.'

The boy listened in wonderment as Maguire made the battle unfold before him.

'It's almost like you were there, Mr Maguire.'

'When I was your age,' Maguire said, suddenly feeling elderly, 'I thought of little else but Napoleon's battles. I knew them by heart.'

'And still do, evidently,' Anne said, smiling and handing Maguire his forgotten drink.

When the time came for him to go, a faint breeze rippled the grass as they stood in the small front garden. For a few moments he felt out of his depth, uncertain what to do or say. His original purpose now seemed embarrassingly louche, almost in the dirty raincoat category. What new purpose could there be? He saw that Malcolm looked flushed and excited, his eyes bright and slightly dilated.

'Will you come again, Sir? We could fight another battle. I have more soldiers.'

'You never know.'

'Your eyes aren't blue after all,' Anne said, 'they're grey and they give nothing away.'

On an impulse that surprised him, Maguire bent forward quickly and kissed her on the cheek.

'Goodbye,' he said.

'Goodbye, my dear.'

On social occasions Maguire was blokeish, an easy smiler who jollied people along. In Green's Champagne Bar in the City he usually had a group of drinkers around him, and often they were laughing. But, like most predators, he had no really close friends. Being popular wasn't quite the same as being liked. He didn't expect to be liked, or even trusted. What he wanted from life were transactions; with those, you knew where you stood; you won or lost, and most of the time he had been a winner. Driving back to The Statesman after his time with Anne and Malcolm, he felt troubled in a way that was new to him. The look of trust in Anne's face had disturbed him. He had been conscious of a little pang when she called him 'my dear'. The look in Malcolm's eyes when saying goodbye had troubled him too. It was a look almost of adoration. Maguire was beginning to feel protective. He wanted to cherish the boy, to care for him, to advise him. What had this mother and her son done to him? He had gone to Randburg with lecherous intent, but something quite different had happened. He felt as if he had lost a layer of skin. It was strange how the boy had revived a long-neglected enthusiasm for Napoleon and his battles which he had studied with a schoolboy's obsession. Looking further back in time, he found dark little thoughts growing in the rank corners of memory. Maguire was an orphan. He remembered how his adoptive parents had grown cold towards him when, to their surprise, they began to have children of their own: a son and, soon afterwards, a daughter. He supposed now that some clever fertility specialist had done it for them. 'Our own flesh and blood, those two,' he had overheard the father say one afternoon when they were playing on the grass. The coldness had grown slowly. It was not unkind, just a creeping indifference that seemed inevitable, like the approaching end of summer. He drew apart from the others and spent more and more time in his attic room with his soldiers. With Napoleon he fought at Wagram, Austerlitz, Marengo, Borodino, until their campaigns brought them to Waterloo.

There had been a small ceremony in the control room of the Strydom Tower. Several ministers were there, including the Minister of Defence. Champagne was drunk. Maguire received congratulations on behalf of the firm. He told some good stories and made even the dourest of Afrikaaners laugh. His time in Johannesburg was almost at an end.

After the party, he walked back to The Statesman feeling as if he had lost some of the substance of himself. This always happened at the end of a business trip. He thought gloomily of the days he would spend in Motsford before returning to the office, the perfunctory kiss from Hilda at the station, their almost asexual proximity whenever she was not rowing or pedalling at the fitness centre. Hilda. The name, he thought, went with girls' boarding schools, hockey and cocoa at bedtime.

The girl at the reception desk called out to him that there was a letter.

'That's the only one today, Mr Maguire.'

'Thanks.'

It was a typed envelope with a Motsford postmark. Hilda *never* used a typewriter. He brought it up to his flat, poured a drink and opened it.

It was an unsigned one-liner, typed in italics.

Your wife is getting it every night, wham, wham, bammity bam.

107

Maguire put down the piece of paper very gently and took a deep breath. He took another. He moved to the window and stared out fixedly. All seemed as before. The Strydom Tower was still there, and the bowling green below. Traffic roared by as usual. He was beginning to feel apprehensive, little alarms were exploding in his head: fear of not mattering to anyone, of meaning nothing. Behind the brio of his manner, Maguire had the psychology of a castaway. Survival was his dominant theme.

He sat down again and looked at the dreadful italics. He began to feel angry, and that was familiar and comforting. Who on earth could that muscular giantess have dropped her knickers for? Not that weed of a vicar? Surely not that old queen who had the antiques shop at the end of the village? The names of several members of the Parish Church Council came to him but were soon dismissed for their improbability. Or some sweaty hulk she had met at the gym? Could a flash of pale thigh have aroused the overweight press-ups addict she had told him about? And who could have written the note? Could it have been her lover jeering at him in tumescent pride? How could Hilda have done this to him after nineteen years of marriage, looking him in the eye and talking about her fast twitches while all the time romping in the sheets behind his back? You could trust no one, absolutely no one.

Maguire had not telephoned his wife to warn her of the time of his arrival. He took a taxi home from Motsford station. He had the house keys and was pruriently half hoping to catch her *in flagrante*, yet dreading to do so. He found the house empty. On the landing, as he was bringing his luggage upstairs, he was confronted by a giant medicine ball. Dumb-bells of various sizes and weights lay in a row on the floor beside it. A complex machine with much elasticated ribbon did not reveal its function.

Almost disappointingly, the days that followed Maguire's

return were free of drama. His questions, burdened with irony and cunning, sailed past Hilda. She brought him up-to-date on church matters, and on the goings-on at the Conservative constituency office; she described at length an unexplained skin eruption on a friend unknown to him. They clung to matters of daily routine. The italic message slept in his wallet. Several times he had thought of placing it in front of her but had not done so. Gradually, its importance receded and he began to think of it as a practical joke.

After he had been at home for about a week, a letter arrived from Johannesburg. It had been forwarded from *The Statesman*.

Dear grey-eyed man

I have been half expecting to hear from you, but of course my expectations have never been realistic. I have never imagined anything but the good. You will have noticed when we met that I am no longer alluring to men. I am out of the biological game. There are other things: I read, I teach, I help the blacks. I answered your notice in the paper for Malcolm's sake. The boy needs a father again. He's a born hero-worshipper, and you have stepped into the role because you are tall, quite handsome (as if you didn't know it!) and you know all about Napoleon and his battles. Every day I am asked, 'where would Mr Maguire put these soldiers, Mum? What would Mr Maguire do about this, about that? When will Mr Maguire be coming again?'

And so, Victor, couldn't we three be good friends, always and ever? I would never ask you to live in the house – just to be around for us both. I shouldn't be telling you this because I think you may be a little conceited, but after only one meeting I feel quite fond of you, though in a way that a man perhaps might not understand. You are a salesman and have made your mark with the government here. You would easily find employment. Think of this beautiful country, the glorious light. We would make expeditions to the Drakensburg and munch sandwiches together in the

Giant's Cave. So come and live here, dear Mr Maguire, and be content.

Affectionately,

Anne

After he had read the letter Maguire had feelings which were entirely unknown to him. That was the effect this woman seemed to have on him. She and her son knew little of his success and wealth, yet they liked him. The armour he put on every day had been pierced. If he had looked carefully for words he might have said that what he had felt was a kind of benign electric shock.

He wrote a letter to Malcolm saying that each of them was on his own campaign, and that the demands of campaigning made it difficult for friends to meet. He would be supporting Malcolm in all his battles and would Malcolm please write to him whenever he needed advice – about anything. He should study the battle of Marengo which was exciting because Napoleon lost it in the afternoon and won it back again in the evening.

When he had finished the letter he read it through, thought it rather false and patronising, but sent it off. He enclosed a short illustrated book about the uniforms worn at Waterloo.

The next few days were unremarkable. Hilda attended a meeting of the Hardy Plants Society. She had a birthday; Maguire gave her a beginner's manual on unarmed combat. Anne's letter was still unanswered. Could he possibly heave himself onto a completely new track, get divorced and go to live in South Africa? He thought carefully about all the things he would miss: the camaraderie of Green's Champagne Bar, the excitement of big deals, soaring into the sky on Concorde.

One morning when he was shaving, negotiating the

tricky area of the upper lip, he took a step back from the mirror and made a decision. I'm too far down the road for a change of that kind, he thought, I am what I am, a damn good salesman. I am finite. There's nothing more in me to give to anyone.

He had been at home for nearly ten days. One fine morning of gentle sunshine in early spring, he was strolling to the village when he answered a call on his mobile. It was Morgan, the director of overseas sales, divorced and with a roving eye, who sometimes stayed with the Maguires and knew what their marriage was like. He was a quiet, courteous, mischievous man who, behind a smiling face, had never wished anyone much good. He and Maguire had a civil but wary relationship.

'Well, Victor, enjoying the domestic scene again? I know how valuable your time at home must be after so long away. Sorry to break in so soon but opportunities are always at the door. "Onwards, onwards" is our motto.'

'No problem.' Maguire went on walking.

'The Kuwaitis are showing interest in our pylons. You know about our beautiful pylons?'

'I read some of the bumf on them you sent round to my office last year.'

'They were at the experimental stage then. They're really rather special. As you probably gathered, they're not as innocent as they look. They have important defence potential. The Kuwaitis would like to have some of them along their border with Iraq. We're hoping to get the Saudis interested too. It would be a chance to get something in ahead of the Yanks. Should be no difficulty with the export licence. It would be a big order. Nice bonus goes with it. You're the only one who can handle a job as big as this. Are you on, Victor? I mean, I hate dragging you away so soon and all that.'

'Don't worry.' Maguire wondered why Morgan always piled on so much flattery.

'Well, get up here as soon as you can. You'll need a lot of briefing on this one. You can stay in the directors' flat, of course.'

'I can be there tomorrow.'

He started to pack that evening.

To his surprise Morgan insisted on driving him to the airport instead of using a company car. On the way they talked about how to handle the sale to the Kuwaitis. Then Morgan asked if Hilda was upset about his going away again so soon.

'Not really,' Maguire said, 'she's been married long enough to a salesman to know what the life's like.'

'It means a certain amount of, er, deprivation for you both, of course.'

It was almost a question. Maguire didn't answer.

'By the way, Victor, something I forgot to mention. You know what these Arabs are like. No booze, no women, OK?'

'No problem.'

'Are women a problem in your life, Victor?'

'No more than in yours, I would say.'

'You've said all your goodbyes, I suppose?'

'Yes.'

At the terminal Morgan stayed close to Maguire until he went through to passport control.

In Johannesburg, Malcolm was setting out his soldiers with great care. Maguire's letter lay on the table before him, a letter he would always keep. The battle of Marengo was about to begin.

THE OMEGA POINT THEORY

*A*licia Landamore couldn't have foreseen precisely the kind of violence she was soon to encounter. She had always been a bold individual but now, in decrepitude and getting a little deaf, she had begun to feel uneasy about the things she saw on television and read about in the papers: the chilly tide of youth, the push from behind, the expensive boot. In the village, only last week, poor Mr Taylor had been left bound and gagged in his shop.

Painfully she got out of bed, grasped her two sticks, drew back the curtains and looked out. After last night's storm there was a silence like held breath. The climber rose had reached almost to the window and its leaves wore the gaudy jewellery of raindrops. A large lawn stretched before her down to the sunk fence, beyond which she could see her drenched fields. Under the copper beech to her left snowdrops glittered in defiance of the long winter. Close to the beech there was a big squat yew; shorn of its upward growth some years ago it had spread its skirts in matronly abundance. Next to the yew there was that mysterious tree, a sycamore perhaps, that seemed to sprout white fire when the wind blew from the west. Over the gazebo a golden dragon stood on the top of a tall pole, staring at the weather.

It was eight o'clock. Or was time a cosmic illusion? Alicia had read Physics at Cambridge when scientists were peering into Heisenberg's uncertainties, before the infant quantum theory had grown into the monster that no one properly understood. After postgraduate studies she had obtained a lectureship and when she published a short book, *Quantum: A Universe of Options*, she was thought by her colleagues to be heading for distinction. But then a young man in naval uniform had turned up. This led to marriage, motherhood and, eventually, widowhood. When she got engaged, her gay professor told her with a curling lip that she had chosen to enter what he called the 'vortex of reproduction' and shook hands with her in silence before turning away. But she had kept her eye in and had contributed to scientific journals until she was in her seventies.

As a lecturer, she had taught a young American called Alan Teppel whose ability disturbed her. He seemed eerily familiar with problems that she still found challenging. After she was married and he had returned to America, she followed his career closely and they had kept in touch. In his forties he became Professor of Mathematical Physics at a Californian university. Late in life he published his last book, *Immortality: Thoughts Beyond Physics*, and sent Alicia an inscribed copy. He said that, because we are living in the childhood of the universe, which would last for another hundred billion years, we can see only a small part of reality. Drawing his argument entirely from physics, without reference to any formal religion, he foresaw a resurrection for every individual during the last moments of time. For this to happen it would be necessary for consciousness to have spread throughout the universe by the time of its maximum expansion. With computer power yet to be developed we would have to create emulations of ourselves to travel the huge distances and seed the cosmos with intelligence. God, in a transcendental form, existed only in the far off future, at the Omega Point, where all things intersected. From mathematics Teppel had construed eternal life.

After she had read about a third of the book Alicia sent him a postcard.

Thanks for the book, Alan. Are you off your head, dear?

Love, Lilla

In the bathroom she took off her nightdress and looked bravely in the mirror. She saw an ancient lizard with skin like brown wrapping paper.

She put her face close to the mirror and spoke to her reflection.

'Horrible old woman!'

When she was dressed she stepped carefully onto the stairlift and pressed a button. The little chair trembled and purred. The rotation of small cogs and a smooth progression of tiny gears conspired to bring her downstairs. Her descent was slow and ceremonious. She thought it would be fun to fly a little flag on the chair, the Cross of St George, perhaps; and music was called for: one of the Brandenburgs, or the opening bars of Vivaldi's *Gloria* would have done nicely. On her way down she tried to clear the strange weather in her mind. There was a fog in there, but areas of bright recall, wispy sequences of half-remembrance, appeared intermittently. She forgot most things now although, almost freakishly, she had not forgotten her Physics. And she had never been able to forget the terrible last sentence her sister Edith had spoken a few minutes before she died.

Mrs Rigby, the cleaning lady, was in the hall. She was a large person. Gauntleted in rubber gloves and with a long mop tilted at the ceiling she looked rather like an un-horsed jouster. Light poured into the room behind her so that she was hugely silhouetted. For a moment Alicia felt apprehensive. Who was this?

'Morning, Mrs Landamore.' The Yorkshire voice was reassuring.

'Good morning, Mrs… er…'

'Rigby, luv.'

Mrs Rigby lunged at a cobweb.

'You remember that young girl you had before me, the one who left without a word, not taking her wages?'

Alicia said untruthfully that she did.

'She's been taken in by the police for questioning.'

'Oh my goodness! Why?'

'Thieving, or so they think. She's taken nowt herself, mind. They think she's working for someone else, taking note of what she sees in houses. All them she's worked for have reported summat missing a while after she's gone. She's a pair of eyes for someone into big crime, I'd say.'

'Are Mars and Minerva safe, Mrs Ringbell?'

'Safe as houses. I've just given them a dusting. Your son, Mr Robert, has given Minerva a pretty hat and Mars has a hunting horn. You'd think he was blowing it, the way it fits in his hand.'

'They're my most treasured possessions. I wouldn't part with them for anything.'

'Speaking of Mr Robert, he told me to ask you to tidy up those what d'you call 'ems – dividends, is it? – lying around in the study. The accountant's been on to him, says you're not paying them into the bank.'

'I must see to that.'

The two lead statues of Mars and Minerva stood at the end of a passage that ran from the front hall to a glass-panelled door opening onto the lawn at the back of the house. Minerva, long-skirted, left hand on hip, held a slender rod in her right hand. Mars stood proudly gazing to his right, a spear in his left hand. Both wore helmets. Since the time of Queen Anne they had stood as sentinels on pillars outside the front door until they were stolen. Alicia had worked tirelessly to retrieve them, telephoning antique dealers and police stations, sending emissaries abroad to pose as buyers at auctions, advertising in newspapers. Eventually they were found and, after much wrangling between Alicia, Sotherby's and the innocent buyer of the stolen goods, returned to Thorsby Hall.

Alicia went to see if there were any telephone messages. Teppel rang several times each month and sometimes he would dictate equations into the answering machine so that she could write them down and work on them. Today there were none. After she had sent the postcard thanking him for the book but questioning his sanity, she reminded herself that he was an internationally respected physicist who should be taken seriously. As she read on she felt drawn to the elegant way in which he dealt with free will, and when she looked at the appendix for scientists she felt her atheism melting. The postulates and equations were beautiful and she had found that if a theory was beautiful it was quite likely to be true. She had never been credulous and had always thought that the supernatural narratives in the New Testament read like unpolished science fiction, but now she began to feel at ease with this mathematical God, Lord of quantum and quark, waiting somewhere in the future.

She looked at a photograph of her husband beside the telephone. He was standing in heroic pose, wearing the stripes of a lieutenant commander. There was a pale misty background and she sometimes wondered if, Cheshire Cat-like, he would melt into it. His eyes were on far horizons, gazing across empire, ruling the waves. There had been a few times of hope and glory: during a period ashore he had made her pregnant with a son. But she wasn't sure how much love there had been. High principles were not in themselves lovable. She remembered a tight-lipped man, his reserve sometimes broken by unaccountable rages. He had left her the house and more than enough money to live on. She gave much of the money to charity. Volcanic eruptions, tidal waves, earthquakes, civil wars and famines all sent her in search of her cheque book.

After Mrs Rigby had gone, the house was silent, except

for the grandfather clock in the hall. Tick-tock, hurry, it's getting late. That evening the land around Thorsby exhaled a mist, a viscid nastiness covering the garden, the fields beyond. Swollen birds were roosting in the chilled air. Soon the whole flat vale of Pickering lay under a shroud.

Alicia poured a strong whiskey.

'Evil is winning,' was what Edith had said, before going into a coma from which she did not return.

'You lost your nerve, poor love, that's all,' Alicia had said, as she watched the ashen face, the dregs of the spirit going.

Rat-tat. The knock came at about two o'clock, just as Alicia was settling down for her afternoon snooze.

Rat-tat-tat. The second knock came a little too soon for good manners.

'Shit,' Alicia said, and picked up her sticks. When she opened the door a moustached man of middle age and heavy build stood before her.

'Mrs Landamore?'

'Yes.'

'Delighted!'

Alicia's arthritic hand was seized in a clammy grasp.

'Name's Blunt from Exodust. I've come to take a gander at the parquet flooring.'

'The parquet?'

'Yes, you rang a few days ago, said you'd like to try our rejuvenation treatment.'

'Did I? I suppose I must have done. I don't remember doing so. I have difficulty in remembering things.'

'Happens to the best of us. *Anno Domini.*'

'Annie who?'

'Time, the old enemy. Can I have a look at the flooring? Back hall I think you said.'

'Very well, if you'll follow me.'

Alicia led the way, exercising her hand as she went. Blunt followed, small eyes in a fat face darting about, memorising.

'Do you believe in God?' Alicia asked over her shoulder.
'Oh of course, yes.'
'Have you met him?'
'Haven't had the pleasure, ha ha!'
'I sometimes think he may be in pain.'
'Dear oh dear.'
She pointed to a wooden bowl on a small table.
'Those mushrooms were picked by John the gardener this morning. Mushrooms are beautifully designed, if you look closely.'
'I love mushrooms.'
'Without love we're lost, finished, down the plughole. We're a violent species. It's all gone wrong.'
'Right.'
When they reached the hall Blunt looked about him, not paying much attention to the floor.
'You wanted to look at the parquet, Mr Blump.'
'Yes, well, you've got quite a bit of distortion there. Some of the blocks are rising. We'll impact those down for you. We'll inject a fluid that will give some protection against changes in temperature. All done by machine, of course.'
While he was talking, Blunt had noticed Mars and Minerva standing by the door onto the lawn. They held his attention. Alicia saw that he was taking a very small camera from his pocket.
'Are you going to take a photograph, Mr Thump?'
'Just my little hobby, if you'll bear with me.'
'You can get Mars and Minerva in from here.'
'You mean the statues? Beauties, aren't they!'
'They're most favourite things. They're extremely rare, done by a Dutch artist who worked in this area in the 1690s. They're worth thousands.'
Blunt raised his eyebrows.
'Well, whaddya know!'

'I beg your pardon?'

'I think I've seen enough now, Mrs Landamore. Nothing we can't put right. I'll be sending my lads round with the machine one of these days. Bye for now.'

He clicked his camera shut, strode back the way they had come and let himself out.

When he reached the dual carriageway to Malton he pulled into a lay-by and rang a London number on his mobile.

'Garth? Blunt here. I've checked out Thorsby Hall. The old girl's as doolally as they come. Asked me if I'd met God. Listen. The statues are just inside a door you enter from the lawn at the back of the house. I'm sending photographs today. The girl I put in there says that door's never locked in the daytime. The old woman goes to church every Sunday. That's when you'll do the job. Park your van in Thorsby Lane which runs along the edge of the property. There are trees growing right up to the house. They'll give you cover. You'll need a wheelbarrow which you'll find in a toolshed at the bottom of the lawn.

The job should take you about an hour. Check the lay-out for yourself next Sunday. Bring Andy with you. Make a note of the time she leaves for church and when she gets back. You should be able to do the job Sunday week. Don't try to contact me. And remember, if it goes wrong you're on your own, the boss knows nothing. All right? Bye for now.'

Looking out of the window when it was almost dark Alicia saw that the copper beech and the yew were stirring in a gentle breeze. It was a leisurely movement, like the heaving and swaying of subaqueous plant life. When would her roses start to bloom, her bulbs feel the touch of spring warmth? They, and Teppel's equations, were the motivations in her life now. She marvelled at the aliveness of things. Was the Omega Point God emerging out of the cosmos? She found that she had gooseflesh. She recalled the

119th psalm. 'Give me understanding,' she murmured, I am a stranger upon earth.'

Sometimes when she awoke in the night she would try to reassure herself about the balance of Teppel's mind.

She went to church on Sundays rather as an anthropologist might visit a remote tribe. The vicar was an ageing intelligent man called Mark Griffin. Occasionally, sodden with tea after a round of pastoral visits, he would call on Alicia, knowing that she would give him a good strong drink, laced with a theological grilling in which he was well able to hold his own. The church, she had told him, must marry faith and science. 'What we need is a raging appetite for the truth,' she said, stamping her foot and spilling a little of her drink. Griffin felt an exasperated affection for her. Although she gave generously to the church, she caused disruption during services, breaking into his sermons with remarks about quantum theory, and had once said 'Rubbish!' in a loud voice when he was preaching. She disturbed the atmosphere of worship by reciting her own version of the Creed:

> I Believe in the Singularity,
> In Hydrogen and Helium,
> And in Love Almighty.

Because of this behaviour, Griffen had insisted – with the bishop's support – that she sat at the back of the church in the pews occupied by disabled people and mothers with rowdy infants.

The front of Thorsby Hall was on the main road. Alicia always declined lifts and on the Sunday after Blunt's visit she set off as usual on the slow and painful walk to the church, glancing affectionately at the sturdy little stone houses as she passed through the village. In the church, heads turned to watch the dotty old lady who lived in the

Hall making her way to her ghetto of the infirm in the back pews. She was unaware that as she left the house she was being observed by two young men from behind a corner of the hedge on the other side of the road.

Garth had started his stopwatch just as Alicia closed the door behind her. He was tall and thin and a stiffness in his bearing gave him an automatous appearance. There was something strait-laced, almost sacerdotal about him. But for his shaven head and the little ring in his left ear he might have been an ordinand, or the curator of a museum.

'We'll let her get round the corner,' he said, 'then we'll take a walk.'

'Right.' This was Andy, shorter than Garth, with stubble on his face and dark, greasy-looking hair which hung down over his collar. With his hands in his pockets and his hunched shoulders he looked as if he were standing in the rain, although the day was fine. He had done a menial job at the London Zoo before taking up with Garth. Unlike the puritanical Garth he enjoyed a bit of cannabis now and then. He was a born admirer, one of life's permanent assistants, obedient, waiting for an order. That was his nature. It was the card he had been dealt.

'We was nearly caught the last job we done,' he said.

'We *were*.' Garth took pleasure in correcting grammar.

When Alicia was out of sight they crossed the road and entered the yard. Garth walked in a peculiar way without swinging his arms which gave him the air of an unfinished robot. They went through a white door and onto the lawn where they stood looking at the back of the house.

'It's Queen Anne,' Garth said, 'it has what the French call *petit grandeur*.'

'You was at public school an' all, wasn't you?'

'Yes, for a while.'

'Was it great?'

'It raised me above the level of the pig-ignorant, that's all.'

'Howja get into this work, then?'

'To what work are you alluding?'

'You know, nickin' things.'

'My stepfather was a cretin who drank all his money. He beat my mother and he used to beat me, until one day when I was strong enough I let him have it so hard the doctors had to stitch him together again. I left home after that. I wanted a certain lifestyle. I have standards.'

'Right,' said the adorer.

Garth's eyes took in the toolshed at the bottom of the lawn.

'The barrow's in there,' he said, pointing, 'that'll be your first job when we get in here next Sunday. You'll bring the barrow up to that door with the glass panels, see?'

'Right.'

They went up to the door and peered in through the glass panels to see where Mars and Minerva were standing.

'There they are,' Garth said, 'that's what we'll be coming for.'

'Where will they be going?'

'Only the boss knows that. Amsterdam maybe, or Dublin.'

They went back to their posts at the corner of the hedge. After what seemed a long time, Alicia appeared round the bend in the road with another hundred yards to go on her two sticks.

'They tend to grow crooked like that,' Garth said quietly, 'it's the uneven distribution of weight. One hip always goes.'

When Alicia reached the door Garth stopped his timer.

'An hour and twenty minutes, just over. That'll give us time to spare.'

'Should be a doddle.'

'No job's a doddle until it's done.'

The following Sunday morning they were in position at

nine o'clock, ten minutes before Alicia was due to leave for church. Garth started the stopwatch when she appeared. When she was round the corner he said, 'Let's move.' As soon as they reached the lawn, Andy ran to the toolshed and Garth waited until he returned with the wheelbarrow. Then they entered the house.

'We'll take a look around,' Garth said, 'we've got time enough. Some nice things here. This is what I mean by lifestyle.'

In the front hall there was an eighteenth-century spinet made of satinwood. There were exotic birds, their flight frozen in glass cases. On the walls there were oil portraits, water colours of hunting scenes, and snarling heads of leopards and tigers, the trophies of Alicia's father-in-law. Over the fireplace the huge head of a bison glowered, the stuff of nightmare.

Garth helped himself to a chocolate from a bowl of sweets on the spinet. When he had finished it he licked his lips and Andy was reminded of a cobra he had seen in the reptile house at the zoo, a tongue darting in and out of a prim mouth.

Then they heard Alicia's key turning in the lock.

When she had arrived at the church she had found it empty. A notice in the porch had informed her that because it was the fifth Sunday in the month there was a benefice service in a village six miles away up in the moors. After a few minutes rest she had set off to walk home, wondering if there would be a message from Teppel on the answering machine.

When she opened the door she found Garth and Andy in the hall. There were a few moments of silence. Garth took another paper-wrapped chocolate from the bowl on the spinet. Instead of opening it he played with it, tossing it in the air and catching it. Andy thought this was very cool.

'Hello, Grannie.' Garth had a fixed smile on his face.

'What are you doing here?'

'Just a social call, Grannie.'

Alicia took a good look at them. She found no friendliness in Garth's smile. Her legs and back were aching from the walk home. She advanced on Garth with her sticks, too angry to feel afraid.

'This is my house. Please leave at once.'

'Now Grannie, that's not a nice thing to say to visitors, is it?'

Alicia felt an old woman's powerless rage.

'Who are you, you peculiar bald person?'

The smile left Garth's face. 'That wasn't polite, Grannie.'

Alicia started to move towards the telephone.

'Where are you going, Grannie?'

'I'm going to call the police.'

'That wouldn't be sensible. Not sensible at all.'

He now stood in front of her, blocking her path.

'Let me pass.'

'Feel free, Grannie.'

He stepped aside and as she passed he kicked one of her sticks from under her. She tried instinctively to support herself by putting her hand out to him but he backed away and she fell to the floor face down.

'That was silly of you, Grannie, old people should be careful. They must be punished when they're careless.'

He kicked the left side of her body in the area of her kidney. A little moan came from Alicia, that was all.

'And they must be taught manners too. Here's something from a peculiar bald person.'

Another kick, a harder one this time, then another. And several more.

'No!' The word came from Andy's constricted throat.

'Look!' Garth shouted, 'she's done it, she's messed herself! Look, man, look!'

It was the first time he had shown any emotion. He seemed unnaturally excited.

Andy was looking down at Alicia. 'Poor old biddy,' he said, and turned away.

'Poor old biddy?' Garth's face was furious. There were little darts of white skin above his nostrils. 'You haven't got the iron, never did have. You haven't got what it takes. That's why you'll always be a number two, a no-hoper doormat.'

He spat. The telephone rang. There was the sound of a car pulling up outside.

Without a word they both ran past Mars and Minerva, out of the door and through the trees to the parked van and drove off in silence down Thorsby Lane with Garth at the wheel.

When they were on the motorway Andy said, 'I need the toilet. I need it bad.'

They stopped at the next service station.

'Be quick,' Garth said, 'and I mean quick. I'll be at the pumps, filling up.'

Andy ran into the service station and, for the first time in his life, struck out for himself. He found a telephone and rang 999.

'There's an old biddy lying on the floor in Thorsby Hall, Pickering area. She's been roughed up. She's bad, real bad, dying maybe. Get there.'

He slammed down the receiver and left the building by a back door. He ran across a car park, then across two fields and a railway line and stopped when he reached a country lane. There, hands on knees, he vomited.

Detective Sergeant Dring had almost finished going through Alicia's papers when the superintendent arrived. He was a tall, spare man of sardonic humour. Dring was in the study.

'Found anything interesting, Sergeant?'

'Not really, sir. There are no prints, except a smudged

one on a door handle. There's a son I haven't been able to contact yet, but I've been through the house with the cleaning lady and she doesn't think anything's missing. Some of the papers go back a long way. It seems she was a scientist once. There's a whole stack of letters from an American bloke, mathematical stuff, something to do with a general resurrection in the dying moments of the universe. I feel it's all a bit beyond me.'

'Well, that's a feeling you'll get used to, Sergeant. Anything about a getaway vehicle?'

'Nothing much. A woman living opposite says she saw a white van parked in the lane the last two Sunday mornings. Any news of the old lady's condition, sir?'

'I rang the intensive care unit this morning. They said that with the rupture to her kidney and all the internal bleeding she should have died hours ago, but there's still a pulse. She just won't go out.'

'From what the locals say she was a tough old nut.'

'Is. There's still a pulse.'

The superintendent looked round the room carefully. His eyes focused on the telephone.

'Anything on the answerphone?'

'Yes, an American voice. I think it's the mathematician. Most of it's double Dutch to me. Equations, the physics of the infinite, something called an omega point. There's a bit at the end in something like plain English though.'

'Let's hear it.'

Dring fiddled with the rewind key, then they heard Teppel's voice.

'...close to the final stage when the universe is in a highly energetic state and its radius is very small. And now, Lilla, I'm going to say something unscientific. Be careful about the doctrine of negation. It can be intellectually seductive and it often wears the mask of reason but it isn't all that smart. If you live in a shadow so large that you can't see the edges of it you take the shadow to be the whole of reality.

The universe gets stranger almost by the minute. If I look away from it I find it's different when I look again. In our discipline as physicists we search for the seed of it and we imagine that we have found it in the singularity and the fireball. I have a troublesome intuition that goes beyond that. I feel that we may count for something, that we're recognised – by what I don't know. It isn't comfortable, it makes my scalp tingle, but it's not negation. It may be that the line we draw between natural and supernatural is quite mistaken. Don't misunderstand me, I'm not a mystic, I'm a scientist all the way like you. Take care of your old bones, Lilla, you're a very special friend. Until we speak again, goodbye.'

Dring switched off the machine. 'What do you think, Sir, a nutter?'

The superintendent was silent. He looked at his watch.

'Time to be getting along. Check on that white van. If any other thoughts enter your powerful mind let me have them.'

He turned away abruptly and left. Dring gave his back two fingers.

Andy had thumbed his way to Holyhead from where he crossed to Dublin. There, in a seedy restaurant north of the Liffey, he got a job in the kitchen. Garth was lying low somewhere in a silk dressing gown, eating chocolates and planning a lifestyle. Unknown to him, an observant person had noticed the white van and could remember most of the registration number. He had not yet responded to the appeal by the police for information from the public. The little pulse still fluttered in Alicia's body. She had been barely conscious when she was taken to hospital and placed in intensive care. In a drip-fed dream she was walking in the garden. It was winter but the dead leaves made no sound beneath her feet. At the goldfish pond she looked for her reflection but the water was blank. Then she was looking in a mirror which showed the gaunt features of a crone. With her right hand she tore off her face. It made a crackling noise and she flung it to the floor. A younger face was looking back at her. She tore that off too, then the next one and the next, until she saw a girl's face, with full red lips. It was smiling and kissable and the eyes were tender. After that her brain was too deprived of blood to dream. The chemistry of dying was at work. When her son Robert returned from a business trip he authorised the removal of the life support system.

At the funeral, Mark Griffin gave an address in which he spoke of a spirit which could not be daunted. A few days later Robert put the house and its contents on the market and moved in with his girlfriend in London.

In Alicia's garden, her bulbs felt the warming of the earth. The tiny leaves of her rosebuds swelled moistly in their green wombs. Mars and Minerva, mute and indifferent, stood undisturbed in Thorsby Hall. On the agent's advice the shutters had been closed and it was twilight in the rooms. All was quiet except for the ticking of the grandfather clock. Mrs Rigby still came in to wind it, every eight days. On one of these occasions she answered the telephone and heard an American voice. Without preamble it began to talk excitedly about resurrection. She listened in bewilderment for a few moments, then replaced the receiver. Some poor nutter, she thought, the world was full of them.

When she left the house she locked the front door behind her and stepped briskly into the spring sunshine.

The Red Dress

Nine-year-old Martin Ross sat beside his unknowable father in the back of the Daimler limousine. A short distance ahead of them was the hearse carrying his grandmother's coffin. His mother had died just over a year ago and the old lady was following close behind her. She had been a Catholic in this Protestant family, although Martin had never properly understood how that came about. They had left Dublin at ten o'clock and were already passing through Roscrea, travelling across Ireland to the family vault not far from the wild coast of Co. Clare. Martin's mother had declined the hospitality of the vault but Grannie Ross, on being told that it was getting rather crowded, had insisted on being placed in it. 'Turn out the concubines and put me in,' she had said, making plain her opinion of some of the other occupants. The estate in Co. Clare had been sold; the old house, The Grange, stood empty, its paintwork peeling, the outbuildings haunted by the wind.

'How are they buried in the vault, Dad, are there holes in the floor, or what?'

'On shelves,' replied his father, the unknowable one.

On shelves. A library of the dead. Martin pondered this.

'Will you be put in there too, on a shelf?'

'No, I'll lie with Mum in Enniskerry.'

So he would lie with Mum. Martin saw them both under a duvet, deep below ground.

They had something to eat in a roadside café and then, at about two o'clock, they turned off the main road into a narrow lane which became a rough track. Martin's grandmother was getting a bad jolting. He tried to imagine what she looked like; a yellowish white thing perhaps, bouncing about in its box. Soon they were swaying and lurching across an open field towards the ruins of Clare Abbey. Here Martin's great-grandfather had erected his family vault, a solemn undistinguished structure rising from the ancient stones. Martin saw a number of his father's former workmen standing about, awaiting their arrival. He recognised Mick Slattery, Dennis Calnaan the herd, old Paddy Keane the bearded keeper, and another Calnaan, also called Paddy, whom he had always especially liked.

The coffin was placed on the grass. Then the door of the vault was opened with some difficulty and several of them crowded into it. Paddy Calnaan took Martin's hand and brought him in with him. There was a cheerful feeling among the men as if they were meeting old friends. Martin saw the coffins lying on broad shelves, as his father had told him. Paddy Calnaan did the honours for Martin, effecting introductions to the dead, banging the coffins with his fist.

Thump. 'That was your great-uncle George Ross, a fine horseman.' Thump. 'There's his wife. She lived happily eighteen years after him.' Thump. 'That's your grandfather. He used to frighten the life out of me, God rest him.' Thump. 'And there's his mother, your great-grandmother. She was a holy terror. Up at six every morning to see to the running of the house.'

They went outside and Martin saw a priest wearing a white surplice talking to his father. It was a damp, misty day. They knelt in a circle around the coffin and Martin felt moisture on his knees. The Catholic prayers sounded strange in his ears; it was strange for him also, in the polarised Ireland of the time, to see his father, a proud Protestant, kneeling on the grass with his hat off, his eyes cast down, getting wet. There had been a Requiem Mass in Dublin and now the prayers were short. When they were finished, the coffin was lifted and Grannie Ross was slotted into her place on one of the shelves in the vault. The door was closed and locked with a great key which Martin's father put in his pocket. He issued an invitation to those around him to join him in the pub in Clarecastle a little over a mile away. Three of the men squeezed into the car with Martin and his father. Their damp clothes smelt strongly of the smoke from turf fires which Martin found familiar and comforting.

In the pub his father bought stout, and whiskey for some of the older men. Pipes were filled with Clarke's Perfect Plug. There was much reminiscence and the volume of voices began to rise. Martin moved among the men without shyness. When he went up to Paddy Keane the old man put his arms around him for a moment and they both laughed. His father stood smiling and nodding, looking friendly, yet remote, almost as if he were elsewhere. The gardener Shea, a stocky figure in a ruined hat, got drunk and Martin saw him bend low to kiss his father's hand. The hand glistened with saliva from his lips and Martin noticed that his father didn't bother to wipe it off.

Father and son slipped quietly away. After supper in a hotel they were driven back to Dublin in the hired limousine and during the long journey Martin slept with his head resting on his father's shoulder. It was late when they arrived at the flat.

'Dad, can Catholics do magic?'
'No, there is no magic anywhere.'
'The priest was sprinkling water about.'
'It's a faith. Respect it.'

In a rare show of affection he ran the palm of his hand down the back of the boy's head.

'Just the two of us now. Martin.'
He gave an odd little chuckle.
'Off to bed now.'

In bed Martin went drowsily through the day. All the living and the dying. It was very strange. It really was wild, quite wild.

★

Letters from Ireland usually came from almost forgotten, even unknown relations. This one was different. It came from Joseph Clancy and Sons, Building Contractors, Monumental Sculptors and Funeral Furnishers.

Re Family Vault. Clare Abbey

Dear Mr Ross

Re the above, when passing by recently, through interest I dropped in at Clare Abbey to inspect the above and to my dismay regretted to find that raiders had attempted to break into the vault. Having failed to crack lock said raiders forced and broke off top hinge from hanging stile of door and from there have got no further as yet. This outrage on your respected ancestors is bad and your esteemed father would have been greatly distressed at an attack on the vault. I would be happy to repair same and at all times you know where to find me awaiting your instructions.

Sincerely yours,

Joseph Clancy

Martin and Sheila were sitting at a large round table in their Islington flat when the letter came. It was Saturday morning. Sheila was rubbing at a stain on her skirt with cotton wool. Martin had a clipboard on his knees. He had been trying out some sketches with a crayon, hoping to get something right; the page was covered with rough drawings of a small human figure performing strange antics. He had his own company now, making television graphics. He himself did most of the animations, where animations were required. He aspired to enter the American cartoon market and acquire fame of Walt Disney magnitude.

'Some yobs have tried to break into the family vault in Clare,' he said, after he had read the letter.

'Oh really?'

She was dedicated to the stain, rubbing and rubbing.

He flicked a piece of fluff off her shoulder and fondled her neck.

'Fair wench of Gloucester,' he murmured.

Sheila smiled and went on rubbing her skirt.

To outsiders, they seemed an unlikely couple, Irish Martin with his media background and Sheila, the daughter of a county family in Gloucestershire, a product of Volvoland and wellies, hunt balls and charity fetes. They had met at a reception given by the woman's magazine she worked for as assistant fashion editor. She was employed mainly because she knew smart people and this made it easier for the feature writers to get interviews. She could be fun but had a liking for decorum which was slightly at odds with her generation and contemporary London. Although her parents were not very old, they had deep and enduring prejudices which seemed to have been formed before the First World War; Martin put the date at around 1912. None of the family had been to Ireland; they thought of that country as an offshore fragment of Europe populated by turf-digging Paddies and gangs of friendly murderers. Yet somehow they managed to be likeable and Martin was fond of them. They felt affection for him too, as though he were an exotic trophy acquired by Sheila, to be exhibited at family gatherings. Before she had brought him home to meet them after they had decided to marry she asked him if he wouldn't mind having his hair trimmed just a tiny bit to please Mummy, and, so as not to give poor Daddy a shock, would he mind awfully not wearing his earring that weekend? Despite the robust hunt balls and the shooting parties her mother felt that a gentleman should not accept more than two drinks – ever. Although not a heavy drinker himself, Martin found the company of media drinkers stimulating and often in the early days when he was making his way they had given him profitable television work. Sheila had had only moderate success in weaning him from the wine bars.

Perhaps because he was an animator with a cartoonist's way of seeing things Martin had a habit of visualising people in extreme, definitive postures, with exaggerated facial expressions emphasising their character or situation. His preferred role for Sheila was as a dignified young woman arranging hyacinths in a vase in the drawing room of a large country house, her face melancholy and a touch severe. Or perhaps graciously presiding over a tombola at a fête. Or, more adventurously, being ravished, naked, in a wood. Often she figured in a rural scene by Constable. But usually she was arranging the hyacinths. They had been married for two years and had postponed having a family until they could buy a house outside London. Two things had bound Martin to her. He had never understood his remote father but had trusted the man absolutely. Could there be trust without understanding? It seemed to him that there could be. He had found this dependability in Sheila. She was an anchorage which, although restrictive at times, had become indispensable to him. The other attraction was an intriguing anarchy which he suspected lay deeply buried in her. There were signs of this whenever they made love. On these athletic occasions a startling change came over her. Mummy's lamb, who deplored any deviance from seemly behaviour in public, became so fierce that Martin sometimes felt alarmed. In the mornings, when he arrived in the office love-bitten and scratched, he had to tolerate rib-digging jokes about thorn hedges; if he stripped for a swim further lacerations were sometimes visible. When the action was over it was as if it had never happened. She appeared to have no recollection of it. The hyacinth face would return. She would walk about the room humming to herself, arranging small objects, dusting, patting her hair into place. It was not unlike epilepsy, Martin thought. He had read somewhere that epileptics had no memory of their fits. But it was not epilepsy, just Sheila who, although outwardly conventional, stopped at nothing once she had stepped out of her clothes.

'It would make a nice little trip for us both,' Martin said. They were having lunch in their local pub.

'What would?'

'If we hopped over to Ireland for a few days, just to see to that old vault. It would be an opportunity for you to meet my relations. There are twelve of them in there, stacked up on shelves.'

'Have you any living ones?'

'There are one or two.'

'How do you know they're not dead?'

'The banshee hasn't been in touch.' He had the solemn face he used when not being serious.

'I'm never quite sure what those things are.'

'The banshee is a female spirit who wails when there's going to be a death in the family. They stand that high, more or less.' He held his hand about three feet above the floor.

'What sort of noise do they make?'

'Something between a shriek and a howl. It's quite loud. Like this.'

She saw him take a breath.

'Don't you dare! If you make that noise I'll leave.' She had half risen from her seat.

When they got home Martin made the banshee noise at full power and Sheila stuck her fingers in her ears.

A few days later he had bought their tickets to Shannon.

Sheila looked very serious. 'Mummy says I ought to stock up with things like toothpaste, aspirin, elastoplast and so on.'

'For God's sake, we're not paddling up the bloody Amazon in a canoe, we're going to a modern European state with the fastest growing economy in Europe!'

'All right.'

'They have electricity there, water comes out of taps.'

'All right, all right.'

In secret, Sheila bought toothpaste, aspirin and elastoplast, as well as anti-diarrhoea tablets and a manual on first aid. She hid them in a shoebag. 'Better safe than sorry,' was what Mummy always said.

When they arrived at Shannon airport they hired a small car and drove to Ennis, where they checked in at the congenial Old Ground Hotel. The staff in this happy place were supervised by the manager, Mr Reagan, a rather shy, smiling man in his early sixties. Like Sheila he had a high regard for decorum, but when he saw Martin signing the register he felt compelled to burst forth.

'If it isn't Mr Ross, formerly of The Grange!'

Martin turned to him and smiled. 'Yes, that's right.'

'I remember your father coming in here, and you with him as a boy. Very quiet, very courteous. A lovely gentleman.'

'It's kind of you to say that.'

'It's the God's honest truth, Mr Ross.'

Mr Reagan felt he had already gone too far and discreetly moved away. During these exchanges Sheila had stood statuesquely still, wearing the 'hyacinth face'. Mummy had told her to be careful in Ireland.

After they had unpacked, Martin said he would get the key to the vault. Since his father's death it had been in the safekeeping of Mr Joseph Clancy, the funeral furnisher who had written to him. He left Sheila in the bar-lounge, a comfortable room with large windows that overlooked a lawn dotted with shrubs and a few flowers. It was late summer.

When he came back about an hour later, she accused him of smelling of whiskey.

'Old times and all that. Mr Clancy is a very hospitable man.'

They drove out to Clarecastle which was not more than a mile and a half from the town. Down the narrow lane they went, then into the field, as Martin had done with his father, following Grannie Ross in the hearse.

'It's almost twenty-four years since I've been here,' he said as they got out of the car.

Then, 'Oh my God!'

Further damage had been done since Mr Clancy had written his warning letter. The door had been forced open. One hinge had been broken so that the door hung skew-eyed, giving access to the vault through a narrow gap. Through the darkness, he could see the sheen of a coffin, that of his great-grandfather Martin reckoned.

'Bastards!' he said, 'come on, let's have a look, meet my folks.'

A short flight of steps led up to the door. With difficulty they managed to open it a little wider. Martin went inside.

'Come on in,' he said, 'make yourself at home.'

He wondered why he was making silly little jokes. They stood in silence looking at the coffins. Grannie Ross was still where they had left her, all seemed in order. Until, when his eyes had got used to the dim light, Martin saw something odd in the darkest part of the vault. This was where his great-grandmother lay. The lid of the coffin had been prised up from the seal and slid a little way across, leaving a gap of a few inches. With growing astonishment he could see what appeared to be a hand, resting elegantly on the edge of the coffin. It was not bare bone but mummified, as though his great-grandmother was wearing leather gloves. It was shiny. Martin held it for a second, then released it.

He turned to Sheila 'Did you see that?' She nodded.

'Obviously the local lads come here at weekends and shake her hand. They do it for a dare. Poor Isabella Ross, what an indignity for you! And you were known as the Holy Terror.'

He went up close to the coffin and peered inside. He could make out a shrouded form. They must have gone to some trouble to get the hand out. The shroud had been slightly opened where her head was. It was too dark for the face to be visible but he could just make out a gleam of whiteness.

'False teeth,' he said, 'beautiful white false teeth.'

It was not cold and dreadful in the vault but warm and friendly, almost benign. The floor was thick with dead leaves, blown in from a beech tree, making a soft carpet. A cloud moved and there was sunlight on the floor.

'It's rather nice in here,' Sheila said. She seemed at ease. She stretched. To Martin's surprise she lay down in the strip of light and stretched again.

'Our summerhouse,' he said, and lay down beside her. They were still and quiet for several minutes. They could just see a branch of the beech tree. A sparrow came and perched on it for a few moments, its tail twitching up and down, then flew away. Martin took her hand. He glanced at her sidelong. The 'hyacinth face' was still there but the eyes said 'come on'.

'Shall we?' he said.

'We shouldn't really.'

Long ago, he had learnt to interpret those three words as 'yes'.

'I'd better try and shut that door.'

'No, I don't want to be shut in with these people.'

He lay down again beside her. And so it happened. This

time it was unusually tender and slow and loving and Martin got away without a scratch or a bite.

They walked back to the car in contented silence, Martin wondering what Mummy would have said.

Back at the hotel Sheila said she was going to the loo and Martin said she would find him in the bar.

He ordered two Jameson's.

When she came back she sat down and smiled at him. She seemed very relaxed and Martin felt in good spirits. They sipped their drinks in silence for a while.

'I'm enjoying this trip,' Martin said, 'we'll have one more. It's only a short walk to Clancy's and he isn't expecting us until quite late.'

'We shouldn't really.'

They had missed lunch.

Mr Clancy lived in a plain stone house in Stanmore Park, a prosperous suburb of Ennis. He looked very like what he was, a citizen of some consequence in a provincial town, plump and unhurried in speech and movement. White skin contrasted with his dark clothes. He was doing very nicely in a trade as old as civilisation: the adornment of death. He supplied tombs, gravestones, inscriptions, crosses, mounted pictures of the deceased, and the curious things with glass covers containing messages that were sometimes to be seen on graves. There was hardly a grave within several miles of Ennis that had not received his professional attention. This emperor of the dead was smoothly accomplished in dealing with the bereaved; unctuous in manner, he was never at a loss for the appropriate word, eager to oblige in every small way, to agree with every opinion offered. He was very, very persuasive. He could slip a drink into your hand almost without your noticing. Writing cheques in his company came close to being enjoyable.

When Martin rang the bell it was Mr Clancy himself who opened the door.

'Mr Ross!'

'Mr Clancy, this is my wife, Sheila.'

'Welcome to Clare, Mrs Ross, it's an honour to have you with us, and a pleasure too. Come inside, won't you?'

They entered a large room in which the air was heavily laden with the scent of flowers. Lilies, perhaps.

'Sit down now Mrs Ross and rest yourself.' Indicating an armchair, Mr Clancy allowed himself an appraising glance at her figure. Martin was already in a luxurious chair, leaning well back. He felt light-headed. Mr Clancy poured Jameson's.

'Mrs Ross, I'm going to take the liberty of removing something that's become attached to your jacket.'

Mr Clancy removed a leaf. A dead leaf it was. He held it up.

'I've never known autumn come so early. Dear oh dear, time moves on apace, we have but a short span. It must have been a sad occasion for you, Mrs Ross, there in that old vault with your husband's departed ones all around you.'

'No, on the contrary, I enjoyed it.' Sheila used her social voice, then blushed when she saw Martin leering over his glass. Mr Clancy talked continuously, providing seamless transitions from one topic to the next.

'This is rather strong,' Sheila said, putting down her glass.

'It's the goodwill in it you're tasting, Mrs Ross, the goodwill makes the Jameson's taste a lot stronger than it is. Isn't that so, Mr Ross?'

'You're right, Mr Clancy.'

'You must see a lot of changes in Ireland, Mr Ross?'

'Yes, it's prosperous and busy, but the people don't seem to have the time for each other that they used to. The Ireland I remember has gone.'

'It's with O'Leary in the grave, Mr Ross. Your man Yeats, the great William Butler, never wrote a truer line than that.'

The subject of the vault returned and Martin gave instructions that the entrance be bricked up permanently to avoid further intrusion. He told Mr Clancy of his great-grandmother's hand, of the indignity inflicted.

Mr Clancy rolled up his eyes.

'There's our heathen youth for you.'

Under the cover of the shocking episode of the hand, Mr Clancy had in some sorcerous way refilled the glasses without encountering protest. Sheila was sitting primly on the edge of her chair. She was very red in the face and hadn't spoken for some time. Martin began to be worried about her colour. The flush had spread from her cheeks down to her neck where the skin had taken on a mottled appearance. She could never have drunk so much whiskey in her life, he thought. He wondered if she had done it out of loyalty to him, not wishing to let him down before his Irish countrymen. He hoped she wasn't going to be sick.

At last, when their drinks were finished, and after many more reminiscences, Martin made a move to go. Mr Clancy protested but was overruled. Sheila asked if she might go to the ladies and, on being told the way, walked carefully to the door. While she was out of the room Mr Clancy brought up the little matter of an advance on the work to be done on the vault because times were hard, God help us, and Martin wrote a eurocheque.

They walked back to the hotel arm-in-arm and because of the whiskey their progress was as slow and careful as that of a very elderly couple. In a passage off the front lobby there was a row of glass showcases displaying expensive jewellery, clothes and other items. Martin and Sheila stopped in front of one of them. It contained a dress worn by a faceless plastic dummy, designed to attract the predatory male eye. They stood and stared at it, trying hard to focus. It glared back at them, threatening and hypnotic, garishly illuminated. It was vermilion red, buttoned down the front with a deep frill round the neck and down to the hem, made of the finest Donegal wool cloth. It was straight but figure-skimming, close-fitting, buttoned and frilled from neck to hem. An awful dress, but to their bleary eyes a vision of splendour.

'It looks about your size, love,' Martin said.

Sheila nodded but did not speak.

'Let's have it, darling, something to remind us of our trip.'

Sheila nodded again and said nothing, rendered mute by Mr Clancy's generosity.

Martin bought the dress at reception. It was carefully parcelled up and they brought it to their room. They didn't unwrap it. Sheila sat in the only armchair and Martin lay down on the bed with his clothes on. He fell asleep immediately.

When he awoke it was a quarter to one. He had slept for nearly four hours. He saw that the parcel containing the red dress had been opened, the wrapping and tissue paper lay scattered on the floor. The dress was nowhere to be seen, nor was Sheila. Was she trying it on in the bathroom? She wasn't there. Martin brushed his teeth, took two paracetamols and splashed cold water on his face. He went out onto the landing, not knowing where to look for Sheila, and started to make his way to the lift, intending to go to reception. A breathless, running man collided with him at the corner. He was the night porter who didn't know who Martin was.

'I'm sorry, sir. Have you seen her by any chance?'

'Who?'

'There's a lady in a red dress who's run amok. She has no shoes on. She ran past me a minute ago, going like the hammers of hell. She said she was a banshee. We're worried about her.'

They heard a ghoulish shriek which seemed to come from the floor above.

'That'll be her,' the night porter said, and ran to the stairs. Martin, feeling bewildered, made for the lift. At the bottom, as he was getting out, he heard a long wail of inconsolable grief, ending in another shriek.

In the lobby he found a man talking on his mobile. He was the house detective and seemed to know who Martin was.

'Are you looking for a lady in a red dress?' Martin asked.

'I am indeed, Mr Ross. I nearly caught her a few minutes ago on the top floor but she got away.'

'Did she say she was a banshee?'

'No, she said she was a whore of Babylon.'

The night porter joined them. A few minutes later the manager Mr Reagan appeared, looking self-conscious in embroidered bedroom slippers and a pinstripe suit he had put on over his pyjamas. Martin hadn't yet disclosed that the person they were looking for was his wife.

'Have you tried outside?' Mr Reagan asked the night porter.

'Not yet.'

'If she starts running through the streets of Ennis we'll have the Gardai to contend with. It'll do the hotel's reputation no good at all.'

At that moment the four men got a severe shock. The lobby where they were standing had a large plate-glass window overlooking the gravel at the front of the hotel. The blind had not been drawn. It was dark outside. In the black square of glass a scarlet figure appeared suddenly. It was an attractive young woman and her face was close to the window. She put her thumbs to her temples and wiggled her fingers, made a horrible grimace and scampered away into the darkness with a shriek.

'Holy shit.' It was the night porter who said this.

'That was my wife,' Martin said.

The others looked at him with what he thought was a mixture of sympathy and embarrassment.

Mr Reagan spoke now, with greater formality than the night porter. 'Clearly Mrs Ross is not quite herself just at the moment. It could be the weather. I'd say there's a storm coming. Women are often affected by that. Try to apprehend the lady lest she injure herself. Do it with courtesy, the Rosses are an old and respected Clare family. Proceed along opposite sides of the car park and you might catch her in the corner next to the annexe.'

After searching for something suitable to say, Mr Reagan retired to his office behind frosted glass. Martin sat glumly on one of the chairs by the dark window. What was the appropriate action for retrieving a wife running loose in flaming red? He wondered what could have got into this nice steady girl from Gloucestershire, his 'rose of the shires' as he sometimes called her. Surprisingly he had no feeling of panic, perhaps because of his instinct that her indestructible common sense would somehow restore the situation. The hotel was silent now, no more shrieks or wails. He pulled a notepad from his hip pocket and began to doodle. He drew a sequence of a crazed female figure with golliwog's hair and splayed limbs, leaping and jumping and turning somersaults. After a while, the night porter and the house detective returned like dejected terriers, damp from the oncoming rain. They hadn't found her, which was not surprising at all: unknown to them, Sheila had got back into the hotel through a fire exit at the side of the building.

After several minutes of aimless discussion Martin decided to take a look outside. He went to get his jacket from the bedroom and found her sleeping peacefully under the duvet. The red dress lay crumpled on the floor like a recent atrocity, its horror still fresh. So as not to disturb her, he went to the bathroom to tell Mr Reagan on his mobile that all was well. Then he went back to look at her. She was resting deeply, sleep had taken her far away. The hyacinth face had gone and had been replaced by something almost childlike. He looked at her, at the strangeness of sleep, for quite a long time.

He gently drew the duvet over her shoulders so that she should not feel cold when she awoke. Then he undressed and got in beside her. He was glad to have her there, close, although mysteriously absent. He could hear rain falling hard on a corrugated iron roof outside. There were gusts of wind. A piece of the roof was blown loose and fell clanking onto concrete. Lonely sounds. His thoughts floated over the Clare landscape he remembered from his boyhood. The grey mountains of the Burren were being lashed with rain now, along the coast waves were smashing against rocks, shutters were being fastened against the storm.

THE TALE OF THE YELLOW WOLVES

(As told by Reuben C. Twite)

I do not think of my parents with affection. I recall only their wintry minds, their dwindling presences, the sickness of the house as it was when they died within a few months of each other. They were both of them Jehovah's Witnesses. From dawn till dusk they knocked on doors, spreading tidings of the Lord. The three of us prayed aloud three times a day. On Sundays we attended two church services. Perhaps because of that early surfeit of prayer and church, I now have little impulse towards religious faith. Yet I am inclined to think, or rather, the thought will not leave me, that there must be *something* not wholly accounted for by either theology or science. I wonder what it is up to. I wonder also whether it is benign. Probably you have read or heard of near-death experiences, of how beatific these can be, transcending earthly turmoil with their peace and joy. The immanence of bliss signified by a light at the end of a tunnel appears to be a frequent phenomenon.

I had my near-death experience in Geneva. I do not want another. I do not want to meet the yellow wolves again.

At the age of twelve, after the death of my parents, I went to live with Aunt Leah. Leah was the name she had adopted for herself because her husband, an immigrant Jew from Lithuania, was called Jacob. You will find them both in the twenty-ninth chapter of Genesis. At school I developed an interest in photography which suited my somewhat solitary temperament. I was given the use of a darkroom and there I spent many hours experimenting with my negatives. On leaving school I had become so proficient that I was selling photographs to illustrated magazines. Soon, I was earning a modest living as a freelance photographer specialising in portraits. I rented a small studio in Maidstone and my clientele began to grow, though only at a provincial level. After two years I summoned enough courage to write to a society photographer enclosing some samples of my work and asking for advice on how to improve my situation. He was a man so famous as to be almost a national institution. The noble and the rich flocked to him for their portraits. I shall call him X as he is still alive, beaten only by advancing years. I told him how I admired his skill, his genius for catching the living moment, his eye for line and shadow. How I crawled in order to progress! For many months I got no response and had almost abandoned hope, when one day I received a brief note inviting me to go and see him. Imagine my joy when it transpired that he was willing to take me on as his assistant with immediate effect. Initially my tasks were humble: to service his cameras, arrange lighting, receive his visitors, pour their drinks, deal with correspondence. Gradually his clients began to regard me as their friend. I mixed with the celebs, the highest in the land. You would be surprised if I were to tell you of the young ladies of fashion with whom I was on informal terms. Once, by taking a small, adroit step to the right, I insinuated myself into a photograph of Lady Thatcher before X had noticed. There we both were, smiling. I secretly saved the negative and had it printed and framed. It stands now on my mantelpiece and attracts respectful comment. By such little ruses one ascends life's ladder. Throughout this period I observed X's methods closely, took note of his exposure times, of how patiently he sought the best angle to achieve the impression of movement in stillness, and how he seized the moment to pounce, so to speak, when the subject had been lulled into unawareness.

X's energy began to decline with age. As he sank I rose. Increasingly I took over his clients, often with his consent, sometimes, I confess, in secret. Life is a battle. I opened a studio of my own in the West End of London and was soon making a considerable amount of money. I was just young enough to start a new career. I went on a television course in which my progress, although hesitant at first, turned out to be so commendable that I easily secured a job as a cameraman. Allow me to inform you that cameramen, if blessed with a little acumen, have many opportunities for financial gain. The openings for moonlighting are almost unlimited. Not only did I moonlight within the profession but also, unknown to my employers, I retained my photographic studio in Maidstone, leaving its day-to-day running to a paid assistant. All in all I made a good deal of money; so much that, with the addition of a substantial legacy from Aunt Leah at the age of forty, I was able to leave regular employment. Oh, the bliss of it, to be a gentleman at last! I purchased a farmhouse in Kent, just off the Pilgrims' Way, with several acres of land. To go riding in the country had always seemed to me a gentlemanly occupation and, after attendance at a riding school, I purchased horses and a groom. I would go riding in the mornings, carefully at first for I am not at ease with animals. Soon I permitted myself to progress from a trot to a canter, even to a little gallop, though I found this rather alarming. My breeches, like my suits, were made by a London tailor and I don't mind telling you that I cut quite a smart figure on my grey mare Belinda, a pretty but idiotic animal.

One day I invited two acquaintances (I choose that word because I did not then have friends) to come riding: a young gentleman and his ladyfriend. We set off happily enough in parkland close to the house, proceeding under a line of tall beech trees. As we rode quietly along a fateful decision entered my head: fateful because it initiated a series of events which would culminate a long time later in my pivotal Genevan experience. I decided to try a little gallop on my own in the open field away from my companions. This would involve pulling on the left-hand rein to induce Belinda to go into the field away from the trees so that we could start the gallop. I urged the others to go ahead, saying that I would join them at the far end of the field, pulling on the left-hand rein as I was speaking. Unfortunately, the young gentleman gave a cheerful shout, dug his heels into the flanks of his horse, and the two of them set off at a fast gallop, throwing up dirt behind them. This excited the usually placid Belinda into following them against my wishes. I am a stubborn man. I pulled so hard on the left-hand rein that her head was wrenched away to the side while her herd instinct impelled this stupid mare to follow the others. Thus she was galloping sideways at a fair pace. We were still in the wooded part of the field and in a few seconds Belinda and I arrived at a painful compromise: we hurtled into the trunk of a beech tree. I heard a sharp smack as my face hit the bark. I fell off. There was a funny feeling in my mouth. I cupped my hand and my upper teeth fell into it like a collection of dice. In due course I went to a private dentist who told me that the roots were too severely damaged for crowning and I was fitted with an upper denture at considerable expense.

This upper denture was to lead indirectly to what was perhaps the major undertaking of my life, but first I must relate an interlude of some importance. I had been examining my manner of living with detachment and had decided that it was too solitary. At forty I decided to enter into matrimony. There were a number of social clubs in Maidstone which I visited in the hope of finding a partner. I soon made the acquaintance of a young lady called Miss Hoggis. It transpired that her main concern was nature study, with a focus on the wildlife to be found in the neighbourhood. She was the author of a weekly column in the *Maidstone Courier* which I began to follow. To my surprise, she aroused my interest in the garden slug and its peculiar method of reproduction. She wrote an interesting piece on parasites and their place and function in the chain of life. But it was after her masterpiece on frogspawn that I decided to bring things to a head. Miss Hoggis and I took tea at the Bull Hotel where I discovered that she was of a serious and thoughtful disposition. I informed her of my desire to enter into a permanent commitment and asked her if she would be willing to entrust herself to my care. To my delight, she answered in the affirmative and at that moment, although Miss Hoggis was not what you would call pretty, I felt quite a strong attraction to her. I felt that no secret should exist between two people embarking on such a course and decided that this was the occasion to confide to her that I wore an upper denture. Imagine my joy when she blushed and confessed that she wore a partial upper denture which she had never told anyone about. There was a bond between us.

I have always believed in the wisdom of pre-marital co-habitation for a period; it seems sensible to assess one's initial impulse amid the commonplaces of daily living before taking any irrevocable action. When I made this suggestion to Miss Hoggis she agreed with an alacrity which again surprised me. We neither of us, in our rapture, could have perceived the rock upon which our joint venture was to founder.

The rock proved to be my steadfast adherence to a practice. For most of my life I have had the strong conviction that a plentiful supply of blood to the brain is essential for a happy and successful career. Since in the daytime we adopt a vertical, or near-vertical posture, it follows that the supply of blood is curtailed by gravity, and when we are asleep our prone position means that during the night the blood to the brain is not properly replenished. I therefore, at some time in my twenties, got a carpenter to make for me a footrest which would lie across the end of my bed; thus while asleep my feet would always be some fifteen inches above the level of my head. When I explained this to Miss Hoggis she agreed to comply with the requirement of a footrest, although her face, I thought, registered some doubt and perplexity.

So it was that we embarked upon what was virtually a conjugal existence. Occasionally, at times that I thought appropriate, we had intercourse, which I felt sure would be enhanced by the raised position of our feet. It was quite pleasant, although it always took Miss Hoggis a long time to achieve, how shall I say, 'contentment'. Indeed at times I had the impression that she was suffering a measure of discomfort. When eventually she expressed some uncertainty about the footrest, in the most tentative manner, I assured her that in time she would get used to it and that she would receive incalculable benefit from it. She remained silent.

Several months went by in apparent harmony. I made the various decisions that were necessary from day to day and was careful to give an impression of firmness so that she would perceive me as a person whom she could respect, and on whom she could rely. When we walked the streets of Maidstone she would take my arm and in general fell into step with my wishes.

There was never a word of argument between us, until one morning Miss Hoggis telephoned for a taxi and told me she had an appointment with a physiotherapist because of pains in the backs of her legs. I had the distinct impression that there was some resentment in her manner. Her demeanour lacked the usual anxiety to please me. I said nothing. When she returned from the therapist I thought there was something odd about her gait as she walked from the taxi into the house. She said in a rather tense voice the therapist had told her that as a result of the footrest the muscles of her calves and the backs of her thighs had become severely stretched and that the condition would take a long time to correct, if, indeed, it were not permanent. He furthermore told her that, in order to restore normality, it would be necessary for her to always walk with her knees slightly bent, thus relieving the strain on the muscles. I observed that she had gone red in the face. Then, to my dismay, she said unpleasant things to me. She said I was a crackpot, which was insulting as well as most unfair. I remonstrated strongly with her and tried to assert my authority. To no avail: Miss Hoggis raised her voice. She used coarse language, terms which I never thought I would hear pass a lady's lips, and which I shall not repeat. Finally, she telephoned for another taxi and went to the bedroom. When she emerged with her small suitcase, the taxi was arriving. Then she uttered a phrase which until then I had only heard used in male company and walked to the taxi with her knees bent. Good riddance, I thought.

The major undertaking which I have mentioned happened in this way. After Miss Hoggis and I had parted in that distressing manner I began to resume my attendance at social clubs and other gatherings. In time, I succeeded in accumulating a circle of quite congenial friends. I frequently dined at their houses and would return their hospitality in restaurants. It so happens that I am extremely partial to toffee after supper. On one of these social occasions in the house of friends, I had a most embarrassing experience with my denture which became lodged in a toffee so firmly that I was unable to speak and had to repair to the toilet. As time went by I observed that other people who wore dentures suffered similar, or worse, discomfort when eating sticky sweets. Gradually an idea of truly momentous proportions began to form in my mind. I would revolutionise the toffee industry. My plan was simple and bold. I would invent a new brand of toffee which would not coagulate in the mouth, thus relieving denture-wearers from embarrassment. No longer would they be rendered speechless by a soggy concentration of matter cleaving to their palate. If manufactured to the correct formula the toffee would remain in a slightly fluid state, while still possessing enough consistency to enable people to enjoy it at leisure. Almost immediately I had a name for it: *Easychew*. I decided that I had sufficient capital to form a small company to manufacture and market the product. All I needed was a chemist with some experience of the trade. After considerable thought, I remembered someone who had been at school with me, and with whom I had kept in touch in a desultory manner. He had graduated in Chemistry and, through sheer ability, had risen to eminence. He was one of the top chemists in the land and until recently had been in charge of the laboratory of a firm of international repute. His name was O'Mahoney. For some reason connected with his remote Irish ancestry, he preferred to be known as 'The O'Mahoney'. Owing to dubious accounting methods the great firm had been brought low and was now in liquidation, leaving The O'Mahoney exploring the possibility of a lucrative contract in the United States. After much persuasion, and by offering to pay him more than I could comfortably afford, I induced him to work for me. I explained to him my purpose of manufacturing a type of toffee which was less adhesive than usual and would dissolve more readily in the mouth. He understood perfectly and set to work.

I sold my horses, built an extension to the stables, and thus had a laboratory. The O'Mahoney brought a number of staff with him and among these was a young female assistant chemist. I mention her in passing because she was to play a passive but crucial role in the unfolding of events. She was a Miss Goodbody. There were times when I wondered in what way Miss Goodbody assisted The O'Mahoney. Admittedly, I once saw her watching a temperature gauge. Occasionally, when they were both bending low over some process, their heads seemed to be very close together. Sometimes they stood in silence staring out of a window. In short, I never saw Miss Goodbody *doing* anything. I had offered The O'Mahoney accommodation in my house, hoping to have the company of a man of his status for conversation in the evenings, but he declined politely, saying he preferred the privacy of a small flat he had rented in Maidstone. I did not inquire about Miss Goodbody's lodging arrangements. The staff also included local people recruited through an agency.

In due course, the first consignment of *Easychew* was ready for the market. We ran an advertising campaign, including several television commercials. Imagine my joy when reports began to come in from the shops and market researchers, informing us that demand was far in excess of supply. Denture-wearers were chewing with a confidence they had never previously known. We were hard pressed to get the next consignment ready in time to satisfy our customers. Within a year we were prospering beyond all my dreams, even becoming a threat to the dominance of national names. So rapid was our advance that I was contemplating offering shares in the business to the public. *Easychew* in the FTSE index – the prospects seemed without limit!

And then – problems. They began at a personal level which I can only describe as sordid. We were obliged to rush through a consignment with extra haste to satisfy our very first overseas order. Timing is of extreme importance in the making of toffee; if the treacle is allowed to get half a degree too hot or too cool the product will suffer catastrophically. On this occasion the gauges on our vats had to be watched late into the night. To ensure accuracy, and to save expenditure on overtime, The O'Mahoney and Miss Goodbody kindly undertook to stay on and monitor the gauges themselves. That night I did not feel ready for sleep at my usual bedtime, and at a late hour I decided to take a look round the laboratory to see that all was well. I was thoroughly shocked when, on passing from a corridor into the main room, I observed that a rug and some cushions had been placed on the floor and I could scarcely believe what I saw. A couple were engaged in – how can I put it delicately? – activity of a most intimate nature. Indeed I will be blunt: Miss Goodbody was prone on her back and The O'Mahoney, the distinguished chemist, was lying on top of her. I refrain from further detail. In retrospect, I have to say that I behaved in the most dignified manner possible. I said, 'Mr O'Mahoney, please attend to your professional duties.' I then turned on my heel and left the room, slamming the door hard behind me to express disapproval. The next morning I sent for Miss Goodbody and, with a few stern words, dismissed her. The brazen young woman did not even blush. I then sent a polite but firm message asking The O'Mahoney to come to my office. When he entered I asked him for an explanation. He replied that anthropologists had been studying the matter for many years and there were illuminating books I could read. He went on to say that it was mainly biological and chemical. Indeed chemistry was most probably at the bottom of it. But there was an emotional, even an intellectual dimension, which made it a psychosomatic problem. And you had to take into account nature's purpose in the business. He smiled and glanced down at his fingernails. Then he gazed out of the window. I was at a loss how to proceed. I realised that I was in The O'Mahoney's power. His formula for *Easychew* had introduced new and enticing flavours unknown to other manufacturers and they were the basis of our success. He had repeatedly refused to write down the formula, saying that it was safer in his head and to keep it there would remove the tiresome procedure of taking out a patent. I told him that I had felt it necessary to terminate Miss Goodbody's employment, whereupon his manner changed. He at first looked dismayed, then glared at me with an aggrieved and sullen expression.

It was after this that serious problems for *Easychew* began. My dismissal of Miss Goodbody had aroused The O'Mahoney's relentless hostility. Although I did not realise it at the time, he embarked on a course of revenge of the most malicious nature. By making subtle alterations to his formula for the toffee he brought about a series of disasters which for a time were unexplained. For the next consignment he introduced an effervescent agent which caused the toffee to bubble, so that out customers had brown froth pouring from their mouths and in some cases down their necks and onto their collars. Many a dinner party ended in distress and one of the tabloid newspapers succeeded in snatching a photograph of a leading politician in this embarrassing condition. I was obliged to make an apology in the press, pointing out that it was due to an unfortunate error in the manufacturing process which would not occur again. We were just managing to weather this storm when The O'Mahoney struck a second time. He introduced a coagulant into the formula which made the toffee set rock hard after it was placed in the mouth. Because of this I suffered a humiliating experience. One morning a jiffy bag arrived in the post. It was addressed to me and marked 'personal' in red ink. On opening it I found that it contained an upper denture with a large piece of toffee which had set like concrete on the teeth on one side. It was accompanied by an anonymous note containing obscene instructions. The sales of *Easychew* began to fall, and I was apprehensive of how matters might turn out. It should be remembered that at this time I still did not suspect The O'Mahoney's destructive motives. I complained to him most emphatically and asked him what was going wrong, but on these occasions he remained uncommunicative; indeed he was sullen. Meanwhile I had an unpleasant interview at the Board of Trade where I was accused, in so many words, of false advertising: a serious offence.

After several months *Easychew*'s falling sales reached a plateau and I was beginning to think that once again we were climbing out of trouble when The O'Mahoney struck his third, outrageous blow. As an accomplished chemist he was exact in his measurements, knowing just how far he could go without causing serious injury. For this masterpiece of mischief he introduced an explosive substance into the formula, not strong enough to inflict damage on the palate but strong enough to be memorably unpleasant. It could have put us permanently out of business. It worked in this manner: the explosive agent remained dormant while wrapped in paper, and was harmless even when unwrapped. However, as soon as the customer, aglow with anticipated pleasure, passed the toffee between his lips, the warmth of his mouth brought about an explosion.

The occasion on which this was manifested could hardly have been more damaging. Members of the press were present. As I have implied, our fortunes were recovering, indeed they had almost become buoyant again. It seemed that a publicity campaign would help us finally to turn the corner with a flourish. I informed various contacts in the press that *Easychew* was about to offer an improved formula which would bring joy to our many customers and be a revelation to even the most demanding of toffee connoisseurs. I decided that a public launching of the formula would be a good idea, and I prevailed on a prominent figure whose name was on everyone's lips to, as it were, perform the ceremonial opening of the first piece of toffee based on the new formula. He would then, as promised, pronounce himself overcome by the delicacy of the flavour, and declare himself to be a devotee of *Easychew*.

We hired a large room in the City for the occasion and I invited members of the press to attend. Some of our staff were present, including The O'Mahoney and, to my astonishment, Miss Goodbody, wearing a dress which I thought was revealing beyond the bounds of good taste. The central figure who was to sample the symbolic toffee is still very much in the public eye so I shall not mention his name but refer to him simply as the Important Person. We sat around a long oval table. I had arranged for Strauss Viennese waltzes to be relayed from a loudspeaker. I made a nice little speech introducing the Important Person and saying that I felt *Easychew* was entering a new phase of excellence. Good fortune attended upon us all. I received applause. Then came the moment when the inaugural toffee, tastefully wrapped in scarlet paper, was ceremoniously presented to the Important Person by a liveried footman. He unwrapped it and, with a smile for the cameras, passed it between his lips when, to my horror, he experienced an explosion which dislodged his teeth. I understate. It blasted the Important Person's upper denture out of his mouth and onto the table in front of him where it slid across the polished surface into the lap of our accountant, Mr Simon Ague, of *Ague and Ague*, who returned it with an expression of distaste.

It would be difficult to describe the shock felt by all. Apart from an unseemly shriek of laughter from Miss Goodbody whom I could happily have strangled, we were silent. The Important Person replaced the denture in his mouth, rose from his seat and quietly left the room. I found him in the toilet where I abased myself with apologies. He seemed dazed. I need not go through the tedium of relating the process of appeasement that was necessary in order to dissuade him from taking legal action. It involved a number of expensive dinners and outings, not to mention a promise of a year's free supply of *Easychew* delivered to his house, which he hastily declined. He was eventually pacified and the situation gradually settled into relative calm.

I knew that there would have to be a reckoning with The O'Mahoney who, by the way, had slipped unnoticed from the room before the toffee was presented. As I have already explained, I was in his power to the extent that, without his unwritten formula, *Easychew* would lose its hold on the market and sink into obscurity with the resultant loss of my fortune. On the day after the explosion I had him come to my office. I told him that matters had reached such a point that *Easychew* was in danger of extinction as a result of recent accidents and that I needed an explanation, as well as some assurance that such mishaps would not occur again. The O'Mahoney was silent for a few moments, then cleared his throat. He told me that matters had been difficult ever since he had been deprived of an assistant. He did not look me in the eye but stared out of the window. In a flash I realised that for some time he had been trying to frighten me into bringing back Miss Goodbody. I do not enjoy surrendering but that was what I had to do. I asked if Miss Goodbody was still in Maidstone.

'Yes, the poor girl is working at the *Fox and Rabbit*.'

'She has a job there?'

'As a waitress. Even as we speak the poor girl is no doubt serving a Ploughman's Lunch. It is always on the menu. Day after day.'

'Was she useful as an assistant?'

'She had an elfin grace among the test tubes and pipettes.'

Elfin was not a word I would have used about Miss Goodbody. Her proportions above the waist were generous, to say the least. I let it pass.

'Would it be a help if she were to come back as your assistant?'

'Ah yes, the poor girl.'

And so I offered to reinstate Miss Goodbody and our conversation ended.

Two days later, in response to a message from me, Miss Goodbody came to my office. A jangle of beads and bracelets warned me of her approach. When she entered I informed her that, if she desired it, she could return to her post as assistant to The O'Mahoney. Whereupon this peculiar young woman dropped to her knees with a cry of 'Oh, Mr Twite,' seized my hand and kissed it. I said, 'Don't be silly, Miss Goodbody, get up at once, please.' As she rose to her feet she informed me that she was a Druid and had insights denied to other people. She said she could see an amber-coloured aura around my person which showed evidence of wounds to my psyche that needed attention. She asked if I would come to her in private for a healing session. I wondered to what further liberties this might be the prelude and told her not to be silly and to report to the laboratory the next day and assist The O'Mahoney.

During the bad time after the coagulant I had engaged a PR firm to restore our fortunes. After the explosion I resorted to them again, when our need was even more urgent. I reduced the price of *Easychew* to a point where our profit margins were seriously threatened. These measures, and the fact that harmony had returned to the laboratory, resulted in a gradual recovery in sales. By the end of the year we were on our way to regaining our dominant position in the toffee industry, so much so that two years after the Important Person's teeth were blown out we had our own stall at a trade fair in Cologne. On the advice of the PR firm the stall was laid out in the form of a gigantic box of *Easychew* into which we invited prospective customers to sample the product. We travelled separately to the venue. The O'Mahoney turned up in a white linen suit and an outsize Panama hat, smoking a very large cigar. And Miss Goodbody! A furnace of orange-coloured hair raged on her head and I observed that what appeared to be a bone-pin pierced her nostrils transversely. She wanted to advertise the toffee by walking about offering a box of *Easychew* to customers while clad in a bikini, a garment shockingly unsuited to the peculiarities of her figure. I forbade this and tried to keep her out of sight as much as possible. Despite her alarming appearance, our stall was a success and we left the fair having gained an improved foothold in the European market.

I had arranged that after the fair I would fly to Geneva and spend a few days with my cousin and his wife whom I had not seen for some time. His name was Stanislas. He was chief accountant for an international firm of stockbrokers which had offices in Geneva, London and New York. He prospered and, like me, was a cautious man. He and his wife Sybil lived in the Rue Hoffmann. They were childless, although she had a child by a previous marriage. Their flat was sumptuous and quiet, and so tidy that it was lifeless. Indeed the neatness was eerie and a sure sign that she had nothing to do, except, perhaps, pick up an object, look at it and put it down again. She rarely spoke but seemed to float, wraith-like, from room to room. She was the coldest person I have ever encountered; so unnaturally cold that if she walked close by you I swear that the air she displaced felt chilly. The woman frightened me.

It was when I started to pack before going to the airport for my flight to Geneva that I began to feel out of sorts. I thought little of it at first; a slight chill, perhaps. I took an aspirin. I felt cold, then hot. I experienced spells of increasing dizziness. There was sometimes a burning sensation in my stomach. During the flight, I realised that I was very ill. I was sweating profusely and felt nauseous, and there were moments when I had double vision. At Geneva airport I took a taxi to my cousin's flat. The door was opened by Sybil. 'Ah, Reuben,' was all she said, although we hadn't met for several years. She led me to my room. At the door she stopped and said, 'You are ill.' I nodded. I went to bed immediately. My condition worsened. Stanislas looked in on me, then called a doctor.

When Dr Schwartz came, he and Stanislas had a short conversation outside my room in which I presume Stanislas explained who I was and what my symptoms were. Dr Schwartz was German. Or perhaps Austrian. I do not know. When he entered my room I could see that he was very large. He had trouble with his English.

'Ach, poor Herr Twit.'

Ill though I was I was able to inform him that my name rhymed with 'white'.

He felt my pulse and took my temperature. He shook his head.

'You hef feefer. I vill tek bloot from you. And wasser, please.'

He took blood from me with a little syringe, and then I obliged him with a specimen of my water. 'For test,' he said, 'I come bek ziss afternoon.'

I dozed on and off. At some point the ghostly Sybil entered, placed a glass of warm milk beside my bed, and silently departed. I fell into a sleep in which I had wild and frightening dreams. Where did these dreams come from? I am not a wild man.

I was awake when Dr Schwartz came again. Stanislas was with him.

'Herr Tweet, you are most unveil. I tseenk you hef burst.'

'I have not burst. My name is Twite, not Tweet.'

'In here.' He tapped my abdomen. 'In here I tseenk you hef little burst. Maybe big burst. In here sumsing ist los.'

He looked at me closely for a few moments.

'I tseenk you are poisonous.'

He turned and spoke rapidly in German to Stanislas. Stanislas spoke to me.

'Dr Schwartz thinks you've sprung a leak, Reuben.'

'A leak?'

'In your intestines. It's septic. Dr Schwartz says it's poisoning your bloodstream. You're seriously ill. You must have an operation.'

After they had left I must have gone into a coma, for I have no recollection of being taken to hospital in an ambulance. During a few moments of consciousness, I was aware of someone bending over me, asking questions in a quiet voice of a person standing next to him. I now know that he was the surgeon. An anaesthetic was then administered.

When I regained what I suppose I must call consciousness I was weightless, without pain or sickness. The thing that we call 'the self' was present, although inactive. I was aware of my situation, but was not participating. Please believe me when I say that I saw my body lying on the operating table. Several figures were bending over me. Someone left the room in a hurry. There appeared to be urgency and some anxiety, but I was unmoved by this.

The scene faded and then I found myself in a dreadful landscape, an arid, featureless plain all around me. I walked, but felt nothing with my feet. Clouds were scudding across the sky, moving unnaturally fast. I was not conscious of the boundaries of past and future. The plain stretched to horizons I could not see. After a while, I noticed faint signs of movement far away, no more than a slight stirring, either on the ground or in the air just above it, at that stage little more than a fuzziness in my vision. It seemed to be coming closer, very slowly. Soon I realised that the movement was made up of smaller individual movements; an agitation was growing. As it came closer I saw that a living presence was all around me. Closer still and I saw that it was made up of a multitude of wolves. They were not like ordinary wolves but had a yellowish colour which grew brighter as they approached. They came from all quarters; whichever way I looked they were there. They came silently, without baying or howling, their bellies close to the ground. Their eyes, like their coats, were yellow, and didn't leave me for a second. Soon these beasts were all around me. They were unspeakable.

How can I tell of the unspeakable? I began to feel terror, not only because of their silence, but also because of something more frightening: their intelligence. They sought intimacy in a way that I found appalling. Their power of understanding gave them insights into my most private thoughts and feelings. Nothing was hidden from them and I felt that their scrutiny, although intense, neither approved nor condemned. It was scorching. I gained the impression that these wolves had no autonomous will but were the instruments of a greater entity, agents with awesome powers of inquiry. They were searching and reducing me bit by bit. All the illusions I had cherished about myself, all my little defences had been swept away. I was, you might say, spiritually naked. In short, they understood me.

Just as a moment was approaching which I felt I would not survive, I found myself in a hospital bed, feeling very drowsy. I was aware of a nurse standing on my left and on my right were two male figures, one of whom was the surgeon. I thought he was looking at me with something like awed curiosity. He had thin lips and spoke English almost perfectly.

'Welcome back, Mr Twite.'

I managed a weak smile. 'I had a dream.'

'What is it like on the other side, Mr Twite?'

'The other side?'

'You were very seriously ill with uraemia. You slipped away from us. You were dead for over two minutes. A little longer and you would have suffered brain damage.'

'Dead?'

'No respiration, total cardiac arrest. You were clinically dead.' He gestured to the figure beside him. 'It was my assistant here who resuscitated you. It was touch and go.'

I tried to smile my gratitude. The assistant bowed formally and I remember finding that rather comical.

'How could I dream if I was dead?' I asked.

The surgeon smiled with his thin lips and bent low over my bed.

'Make of it what you will, Mr Twite. Make of it what you can.'

I spent a convalescence of several weeks in my cousin's flat in the Rue Hoffmann. I grant that they were patient and attended to all my tiresome needs. (Tiresome needs? Before the wolves came it would never have occurred to me that I might be tiresome.)

On my departure, however, a dark thing happened. Sybil said something which still makes me shiver. She and I were standing by the door of the flat. Stanislas was already in the car, waiting to take me to the airport. As always Sybil spoke in a voice scarcely above a whisper.

'Be careful, Reuben, be very, very careful. We don't want the yellow wolves to come again, do we?'

Please bear in mind that before writing this down I have never mentioned the yellow wolves to anyone. How could she have known about them? From what unthinkable springs of knowledge did she drink?

All my life I have lived by rules. Some might say they were petty rules, but they shielded me from the storm of life, its unforgivingness. I knew where I stood in every situation, and where others stood. If I stayed within my boundaries nothing could go wrong and I would always be in control. Now all these structures have been smashed by the yellow wolves. My assumptions, my pretexts for moral indignation, the newspaper I liked so much because it bolstered my political allegiances, a thousand cosy comforts which got me safely through each day have been dissolved. I have been opened up most painfully. I feel undressed. In the past there had been moments when I could have allowed myself to feel vulnerable, and perhaps it would have been better if I had done so. One of those moments had been when I first took Valerie Hoggis in my arms. I had such a strange feeling of otherness; the contact of our naked bodies, her heartbeat, her breathing, they made me feel responsible for her. For just a few seconds it was she, not I, who mattered, and that was new and disturbing. And good, as if a window had been opened. If only I had kicked away the footrest then!

When I got back to England I found that *Easychew* was flourishing under The O'Mahoney. I have to say that he was honourable. He had kept strict accounts and I was not out of pocket. He and Miss Goodbody are getting married. Miss Goodbody lives for passion and that has a kind of honesty. The O'Mahoney, like his formula, is a mystery. I wish them happiness. We shall soon be all three of us living under one roof, almost as a family. The house is big enough for them to have a separate flat and Miss Goodbody says she is going to heal my psychic wounds.

I seldom go out now. I have developed philosophical interests, a style of speculative thinking which I never used to indulge in. I read a great deal and am much concerned with psychology. Carl Jung has become a friend. He says somewhere that one of the worst things that can happen to a person is to be totally understood by someone else; then there is nothing left that is your own. I agree. I do not want to be understood.

    I want a small, safe place.
    Those wolves.
    I am afraid.

Field Work

Beirut in the early 1960s. The spitting, the gobs of phlegm, the taxis and their blaring horns, the dogged pursuit of pleasure. And the pimps, 'Hallo sir. You like big tits, little tits? You like boy? You like very nice massage?' Anything could be arranged here. A little laundering? A discreet assassination? No problem. Tony Whidbourne was glad he would soon be leaving for Jerusalem.

He had lunched with Marcus Dodds, the Professor of English at the American University; a pink, fresh-faced man who had given him some useful leads. Whidbourne was looking for the footprints of the late Arthur Babington, the Arabist who had been active in Middle East politics during the twenties and thirties, and in various other ways after that time. He had left thirty volumes of diaries written on ricepaper which Whidbourne had been commissioned to edit, interspersed with explanatory comment. The diaries recorded much, though by no means all, of Babington's activities in Egypt and elsewhere. As well as the diaries there were documents stamped SECRET. These were reports on the riots in Cairo when Lord Allenby was High Commissioner during the British Protectorate in Egypt and Babington was working in military intelligence. He should not have kept the documents and they were an embarrassment to Whidbourne who preferred to stay out of dark places. He had known Babington as an old man a few years before he died, but had gleaned little from him in conversation other than an impression of extreme wariness, bordering on paranoia towards the end.

Whidbourne was accountable to two conflicting powers: his publisher and Babington's very elderly surviving sister Amelia, a widow who lived in Sloane Street. They were in conflict because Amelia wanted a sanitised version of her brother to be given to posterity, whereas the publisher Engelman, who loved money more than literature, wanted every blemish recorded. 'Dirt sells,' he had told Whidbourne, 'put it in.' And Whidbourne had encountered hints, some of them conveyed merely with facial expressions by people he had spoken to, that there were things in Babington's private life which Amelia would prefer to be suppressed. There were rumours of a brothel in Beirut; there had been talk of Arab boys, too. She would have been busy with her blue pencil.

And so, at intervals during his travels in the Middle East, Whidbourne was sending bowdlerised accounts of his inquiries to Amelia, while offering encouraging and potentially scandalous details to Engelman. Engelman would prevail in the end, he thought, because money usually prevailed. Deplorably that was how it was, and Whidbourne wrote to live. Engelman had given him a generous advance.

When passing through the customs at Beirut, he had met a nice young American called Steve and on the evening of their arrival they had a drink together in the hotel bar. Steve told Whidbourne that he had just graduated in Archaeology from Tulane University. Whidbourne asked him if he had ever met the renowned American anthropologist McKelvie. Steve looked startled.

'You mean Alister McKelvie, the famous one? Sure I met him. He was Visiting Professor when I was at Tulane. I never attended any of his lectures, we were in different disciplines, but I met him on the campus a few times. A weird guy, really weird.'

'Weird, was he?'

'Sure was. He was focusing on cannibalism at the time, cannibalism and human sacrifice. He talked of nothing else. His last book caused a stir. Got him into quite a bit of trouble, academically speaking of course.'

'I read in a newspaper that he's working somewhere in Jordan just now.'

'Could be, he gets around. If you're heading for Jerusalem you'll almost certainly run into him. He'll be staying at the American Colony for sure.'

The American Colony hotel was where Whidbourne had booked a room.

He was anxious to track down McKelvie. While researching in London he had found a review by Babington of one of McKelvie's books. It was so hostile as to amount almost to a personal attack. Later he had found among Babington's papers a denunciation of McKelvie's character which appeared to be motivated solely by vehement dislike. It was typed, unsigned, on a separate sheet of paper, without allusion to its context. He would have liked to know what had passed between them.

The next day he went back to the American University. Dodds gave him a pass to the university library where he sat at a desk skimming through McKelvie's latest book, *The Small Divide: A Bridge from the Primitive to the Modern*. Embedded in the research and the erudition, he thought he detected signs of incipient dottiness. There was an almost unwholesome emphasis on human sacrifice. When he dealt with the subject of cannibalism, it seemed that McKelvie came dangerously close to recommending the practice in civilised societies. By implication he seemed to say that it was not immoral to eat someone provided that you had been on good terms with him. After a couple of hours Whidbourne closed the book, reflecting that a late obsession had damaged other reputations before McKelvie's.

It seemed that the aircraft cleared the mountains outside

Beirut with only a few feet to spare. The man sitting beside Whidbourne expressed the hope that aeroplanes in the area were properly serviced. He said also that he didn't know why all passenger planes didn't have backward-facing seats. He had sat tense and still before and during take-off. Taking a discreet sideways look, Whidbourne saw that this rather pale, middle-aged man was sweating, and sensed his fear. They got talking and Whidbourne tried to cheer him up by reporting to him details of the brothels of Beirut which one of the pimps had shared with him.

'He told me that the girls are very patient. They don't mind waiting until you're ready for it, and they don't charge you for the waiting time.'

The man nodded slowly with raised eyebrows, feigning interest. After they had talked for a while and discovered some shared interests they exchanged cards and Whidbourne learned, with some embarrassment, that his companion was the Rev. Paul Kaufman, an Episcopalian minister from Boston. He asked Whidbourne if he would be interested in sharing a car with some others for a visit to Petra when they got to Jerusalem. Whidbourne said he would. Kaufman told him he would be staying at the American School of Oriental Research.

The pilot banked and altered course. On the right there was a distant gleam of snow on Mt. Hermon, on the left Damascus sweltered in the hazy plain.

Whidbourne broke his journey at Amman, where he had an appointment with a retired Jordanian teacher who had known Babington during the Arab–Israeli war. The man looked weary and ill. He didn't like the Americans or the British and gave the impression that he thought Babington was spying for the British. His parting words were, 'History is made by unhappy countries.'

Whidbourne went back to his hotel and wrote up his notes. He felt troubled by his conversation with the gloomy teacher and to cheer himself up he hired a car with driver for a trip to Jerash. They went through Gilead, through a beautiful disorder of voluptuous hills and deep valleys. He saw Bedouin and their black tents. In Jerash there were honey-golden ruins. As he and the driver were walking in the Street of Columns, the muezzin sounded. They stopped to light cigarettes, then walked on in silence.

The American Colony hotel was in a pleasant quarter of Jerusalem. It was light and airy with potted plants here and there. There was much paving and uncluttered space around the building. Whidbourne felt something of the atmosphere of a house party. The guests got to know each other's names and shared new-found knowledge and experience. Among those staying there was a group of mature English ladies whom he regarded with some affection, tough old birds doing the Holy Land with Blue Guides and hefty walking sticks. Rural Anglicans almost certainly. At home they would have been in tweeds, shouting at dogs. Their faces had a weather-beaten look which, Whidbourne surmised, might have come from riding to hounds. There was also a rather highly painted middle-aged American woman who introduced herself to everyone as Mrs Prytz, without mentioning her first name. She described herself as an investigative writer, a category that was new to Whidbourne. She said she worked for a magazine, although the magazine was never specified; inquiries on that subject were skilfully deflected. She carried a notepad and pencil everywhere, and was frequently seen to make notes on what was said. She moved with confidence from group to group. She had much to say and her voice carried well.

On the day of his arrival Whidbourne spent the afternoon among the archives of the *Jerusalem Post*, for which Babington used to write. In the evening he strolled into the old city and along the Via Dolorosa. After a light dinner he asked about McKelvie at reception and was told that the professor was indeed staying but had gone out for the evening. Whidbourne went to bed early and slept soundly.

The following morning when he was sitting under a potted palm in the spacious front lobby he saw a rather unusual figure approaching the entrance from outside. From mugshots he had seen in newspapers and on television he recognised McKelvie at once. He was very tall and thin and Whidbourne had the impression that his limbs were not properly connected to his body. As he walked he had a pronounced limp to the right, although he did not seem to be disabled. He was heavily encumbered with a number of objects: a tripod with a camera fixed to it, a briefcase full to bursting, and what appeared to be a short flagpole or slender stick which he carried awkwardly under his arm. These items caused him severe difficulty when he tried to operate the revolving door. He became stationary, imprisoned within a glass segment. He started to shout in great agitation. Members of the hotel staff came to help and for a few minutes it looked as if the entire door might have to be dismantled in order to free him. Eventually he was released and it seemed to Whidbourne that a very large, uncoordinated insect had entered the hotel. He went straight to the lift where he needed further help with the narrow sliding door.

Whidbourne had the morning free and decided to go for a stroll in the Garden of Gethsemane, a place that was familiar to him.

He was walking with his eyes on the ground when he heard a shout.

'Mr Whidbourne!'

It was one of the English ladies. She was by herself. They had introduced each other at the hotel.

'Good morning, Mrs Wibberley.'

'I think it was here, just here.'

'What?'

'Where he prayed, you know. It was awful for the poor soul. He was so alone.'

'Yes indeed.'

She was perched on a shooting stick. Whidbourne imagined pheasants flying overhead.

'The others had had too much to drink, you know.'

'The others?'

'The disciples who were with him, of course. It was the Passover. You were obliged to drink a certain amount of wine at the Passover and they weren't used to it. That's why they couldn't stay awake for him.'

'I suppose that's possible. I hadn't thought of that.'

'My husband's the same, you know. If he has a whiskey and soda after a day's beagling he goes out like a light.'

'It's difficult to know what really happened here that night.'

'Is it? Yours is a timid generation, Mr Whidbourne. You're a lot of shrivelled up cynics, terrified of commitment, with no stomach for the risks of love or faith. I've lived in a more robust time. What fun we had! We were not afraid of being thought soft-headed because we had a faith. As for your art – yuk! I went to an exhibition in London and would you believe it, one of the items on display was an unmade bed. I was nearly sick in the loo afterwards. You're a sad lot, all of you. You think too much. You should trust your gut.'

Whidbourne was not offended. She had softened it a bit with a hint of a smile at the corners of her mouth. He recalled that Babington, though not entirely without faith, had a habit of sceptical inquiry which some found disconcerting. They had been talking about that night in Gethsemane and Babington had asked, if Jesus was some distance away praying by himself, and the disciples were asleep, how did anyone know what he had said in his prayers? Prayers are private and he would hardly have told them.

With some trepidation he put this question to Mrs Wibberley.

She thought in silence for a few moments.

'We shall never know, Mr Whidbourne.'

She stood up, wrenched her shooting stick from the ground and stumped off. After twenty yards she turned and shouted, 'We shall never know.'

She held her stick high in the air and shook it.

'Trust your gut!'

When Whidbourne got back to the hotel, he saw Mrs Prytz fawning on McKelvie in a corner of the lounge. He didn't seem to be enjoying it.

'Mr Whidbourne, c'm here a minute. I want you to meet a famous gentleman.'

McKelvie winced. Whidbourne approached them warily.

'Professor McKelvie, I'd like to introduce a recently arrived writer, the novelist Mr Tony Whidbourne. Mr Whidbourne, please meet the distinguished anthropologist Professor Alister McKelvie.'

They shook hands, embarrassed. Mrs Prytz's fulsome introductions had made it difficult to behave naturally.

'So you've arrived, Mr Whidbourne?'

'If Mrs Prytz says so.'

There was a frosty feeling. Whidbourne said he was expecting a phone call and asked to be excused.

In his bedroom, after rummaging through his papers, he found Babington's review of one of McKelvie's books. It was written when McKelvie's career was well advanced but before he had been awarded the chair of anthropology. Babington did not accuse him of outright plagiarism, but alleged that he had leaned on Fraser's *The Golden Bough* so heavily as virtually to have paraphrased several passages without identifying his source. Babington had written in his rather stilted prose that 'those who are rich in learning should not find it necessary to borrow, but if they do it would be courteous to acknowledge the debt'.

That evening Whidbourne found McKelvie surrounded by the English ladies. Mrs Prytz was among them, notepad and pencil at the ready. McKelvie was being informative about cannibalism.

Whidbourne joined them.

'Eating is close to loving,' McKelvie was saying, at which Mrs Wibberley snorted.

Whidbourne saw the revolving door turn. Kaufman, the Episcopalian minister he had met on the plane emerged and, recognising Whidbourne, came over and sat down. He acknowledged Whidbourne with wan friendliness and nodded to McKelvie as if they knew each other. Whidbourne wondered if he always looked so pale. He said he wanted to make up a party for an excursion to Petra and asked if anyone would care to join him. Apologetically, he added that they would be expected to pay their share of expenses, including hired car and driver. The English ladies declined. Mrs Prytz was willingly recruited and Whidbourne had already agreed to the outing on the plane. McKelvie thought for a while, then said yes, he would like to follow up an interest in the area. It was decided that, provided Kaufman could arrange a car, they would leave for Petra the next morning at nine o'clock. They would stay there for five days.

Kaufman was late and it was eleven o'clock when they left Jerusalem. The car was a six-seater but, although there were only four of them, it seemed to be full of Mrs Prytz. On the journey, she regurgitated well-digested facts about Arabs and their traditions, about the crusades, about how deserts were formed. She advised the company on how to order food, how not to be ripped off in the bazaars. Hardly a problem was left unsolved by Mrs Prytz. Whidbourne now had time to observe McKelvie closely. He was struck by how ornamented the professor was, how many attachments there were about his person. On the little finger of his left hand there was a diamond ring, and on the forefinger of the same hand there was a heavy ring in the form of a coiled snake with a large stone, possibly an emerald. Most eccentric of all a very fine gold chain travelled in a sagging loop from the lapel of his linen jacket to the breast pocket, from which he often took a gold hunter watch. He was a little overdressed for a working visit to Jordan. Whidbourne wondered what this focus on self-adornment signified. He felt that McKelvie was not a vain man; he seemed too uncaring, too indifferent to others to be vain. In appearance he no longer gave the impression of a large insect, much more that of a slightly dilapidated hawk. Because of his height he was still an impressive figure who created space around himself, a no-go area into which even Mrs Prytz didn't dare venture very far.

At Kaufman's insistence they went by way of Amman and followed the old road to Petra. They were driven first through fertile country where dark stains of grass oozed down between the hills. As they passed Madaba, McKelvie who had been silent until then, said that they were travelling through Moab. They went on through mountainous desert to the Wadi Mawjib. There was a deep fissure, barren slopes rising on each side of it. McKelvie offered further information: 'This, I think, though I am not certain, is where the Israelites crossed over when they were coming from Egypt.'

They stopped and got out to stretch their limbs. There was heat, stillness, a huge silence. Then for a few seconds, the tiny buzzing of a fly.

It was dark when they reached the entrance to Petra. Here they were obliged to mount small, wiry ponies, each led by an Arab boy with a torch. Then they entered the Siq, the narrow cleft that led into the ancient city. Although in places it was only two or three metres wide, the sides rose to an awesome height. In the strip of sky at the top they could see brilliant stars. Whidbourne was on a young mare called Lila and the boy leading her was called Mohemedi. 'She is mine,' he said, 'she is beautiful.' Every few seconds he flashed his torch ahead of them. The ground was rough and stony but Lila was surefooted and in the intervals between the flashes she never stumbled. In the darkness Mrs Prytz's voice could be heard, complaining loudly and profanely about the discomfort of her saddle. The goddam thing was pinching her somewhere and she'd have a thing or two to say about it to the tourist office in the morning.

They went to bed wearily in the rest house, a long, low bungalow of moderate comfort.

In the morning they went about in a group, transfixed by the marvels around them. At midday they stopped for a rest, sitting on some boulders. There were other tourists and Mrs Prytz moved among them, gathering morsels of personal information. After lunch, McKelvie detached himself from the party. He was going to the High Place, he said. It was a long walk and he would not be back until the evening.

Whidbourne had feelings of awe and melancholy as he wandered through Petra. The great chambers at ground level were caverns of deception, leading nowhere. Not a separate brick or stone had been placed on another, all had been hewn from glowing sandstone. It was a city of facades, as if a giant film set had been abandoned.

He was having tea with Kaufman and Mrs Prytz when McKelvie joined them after his walk to the High Place. He was asked if he had had an interesting time.

'Yes. Petra, as you may know, was founded by a rather mysterious people called Nabateans and the High Place was where they performed their ritual sacrifices. The whole region round here was, I'm convinced, a sacrificial area. I wish to study it more closely. Human sacrifice is what I've specialised in over the past few years.'

Mrs Prytz was listening rapturously, her pencil moving in her notebook while she kept her eyes fixed on McKelvie's face. Bubbles of saliva were forming and bursting at the corners of her mouth. Whidbourne thought McKelvie looked dejected. Mrs Prytz had noticed this too. She put one elbow on the table, cupped her chin in her hand and leaned towards him, all sympathy and understanding. She asked him if he had had an unhappy childhood and received such a withering look that only she could have survived it. She was undaunted and said she wanted to do a profile of him. Would he begin by telling her about his childhood?

McKelvie told her that as a newborn infant he had been snatched from his mother by an eagle which carried him away and nurtured him. Mother eagle favoured him above all his feathered siblings. He was about to describe life in the eyrie when it got through to Mrs Prytz that she was being made a fool of. She slammed down her pencil and went off in a huff.

McKelvie said he had some notes to write up and went inside.

Not far from the rest house there were a number of caves occupied by Bedouin. Opposite the entrance to one of them there was always a white pony tethered to a stone pillar. One morning, Whidbourne had seen McKelvie standing there for a long time, staring at the cave's entrance. At the rest house there was a young, dark-skinned waiter called Ahmed who was very attentive to McKelvie. They talked often and at length together on the terrace which ran along the front of the building. Ahmed was handsome in a girlish way and Whidbourne began to wonder a little, then dismissed the thought, recalling what he had read in a gossip column, that McKelvie was a serial marrier with an undisclosed number of children by three wives.

The following morning, as Whidbourne was sitting late over his coffee after breakfast, he saw Ahmed and McKelvie leave the rest house together. When they had gone some distance, he watched them through his binoculars and saw them stop outside the cave where the pony was tethered. Ahmed entered the cave and came out with the occupant who shook hands with McKelvie. Ahmed had evidently introduced them. After some conversation, Ahmed left and Whidbourne saw McKelvie disappear into the cave with the Bedouin.

Later that morning, Whidbourne and Kaufman made an expedition with a guide to the monastery of El Deir which they reached after a long walk up a steep valley with nightmarish rock formations. They sat down to rest. Behind Kaufman's voice there was a continuous drone of melancholy, as though he were haunted by some irreversible disappointment. Whidbourne asked him if he had known McKelvie previously.

'Yes, he came to give a talk at one of the schools in my parish, at my invitation. That was some years ago. It was a good talk, about pre-conquest South America, though as a Christian minister I had to make it clear to the kids that I didn't go along with some of his ideas. He holds that the Christian faith didn't arise from a unique event, but that the miraculous element was added so that it could compete with Mithraism, the religion of the Roman empire. He also thinks the visions of the great mystics, including that of St Paul, were caused by temporal lobe epilepsy. He's a sad case, really.'

'Sad?'

'He's done some first class work, really distinguished stuff, but he's slowly going mad.'

'Eccentric, perhaps.'

'No, mad. He thinks the greatest love you can show people is to eat them.'

'Does he like them well done?'

'OK, I know it's funny, but it's sad too, a waste.'

Whidbourne apologised for being frivolous.

Kaufman went on. 'His mind is getting like that zoom function you have on those binoculars. If you operate the zoom at maximum you cut out most of the light so that you can only focus on one small object. In his case it's human sacrifice.'

They walked on a little further and stood looking across a plain which stretched to the horizon. A muffled crump came from the direction of Israel.

'Testing,' Kaufman said, 'everyone's testing these days. What will it all come to?'

That evening, while the others were reading in the lounge, McKelvie and Whidbourne sat down together at a rickety table outside the rest house. Petra was beginning to glow in the mellowing light.

'Well, Tony,' McKelvie said, but left it at that. Whidbourne had noticed the first use of his Christian name and felt like a pupil promoted to intimacy with his teacher. He asked McKelvie if he was enjoying the visit.

'Oh sure, I've been sitting too long at a desk, running a department. That way you lose touch with what's going on, the important things. I'm glad to be doing what you might call a bit of field work again.'

'Field work. I suppose you could say that's what I'm doing too.'

'What's your line anyway?'

'I'm doing a book about Arthur Babington, the Arabist scholar.'

'Huh.'

'Did you know him by any chance?'

'Yeah, I knew the guy. I'd like to have settled accounts with him.'

'Accounts? Was all not well between you?'

For a moment Whidbourne thought McKelvie looked hunched and vulnerable.

'He questioned my professional integrity. Then he died. Dying has always been the easy way out of an argument. Do you know Fraser's *The Golden Bough?*'

'I've glanced through the abridged edition, that's all.'

'At the end of the book, in a bit of ornate writing that's out of fashion now, Fraser likens the history of human thought to a piece of cloth made up of three threads – magic, religion and science. I hold very much the same view of it, but with important variations which I've made clear, and that shit Babington said I took the idea from Fraser.'

McKelvie suddenly leaned forward in his chair.

'Tony, can you keep something to yourself?'

'Of course.'

'I'd like you to do that, this is most private, and most important to my work. There are caves here occupied by Bedouin. One of them always has a white pony tethered outside it.'

'I know the one, I've seen it.'

'The occupant's name is Haareth, with his wife and two sons. Ahmed whispered something to me in private. They're not really Bedouin at all. He says they're direct descendants, in unbroken line, of the original Nabateans who founded the city of Petra. The name Haareth is probably a corruption of Aretas, the name of early Nabatean kings. Stored away in their heads they have all the traditions and rituals of that ancient people. They guard this inheritance most carefully. With Ahmed's help I've gained their confidence. I've talked to them in their cave, they gave me coffee. As an anthropologist I have an interest in magic, from an academic viewpoint, of course. Magic, human sacrifice and, to a lesser extent, the cannibalism that sometimes went with them, those are my concerns. Most of the ancient religions, and one or two of the present ones, are preoccupied with these things. Think of Abraham and his son. Jesus himself was a sacrifice. And we eat our gods to gain their strength and virtue. What else is the Eucharist but eating a god?'

Whidbourne thought this a rather overworked theme, but said nothing.

'Now this is where it gets interesting, Tony. Haareth confirms what I have always suspected: that human sacrifice was practised here. Not only that, but he has also agreed to perform a sacrifice for me, with all the authentic ritual, the chanting and so forth. I'll be able to record the entire ceremony. No one knows exactly what happened on these occasions. People theorise of course, but they don't know. I'll be the first to tell them and I'll add it as an appendix to the next edition of *The Small Divide*.'

'You don't mean to tell me they're going to burn someone alive?'

McKelvie didn't smile. 'They won't commit themselves to that, a goat will be used as a replacement. Mind you, I'll have to buy the goat, but hell, it's only a few dollars for a priceless bit of research.'

'When will this take place?'

'That's not quite decided. We've only two more days here. It may have to be at night.'

On their last night in Petra, Kaufman and his party were all in bed by nine o'clock. Whidbourne lay awake for a while, wondering whether McKelvie was deranged. He was feeling low in spirits. This was his first assignment of a biographical nature and it would be his last. He had undertaken it for Amelia's sake and he wasn't enjoying it. As a writer of fiction he felt he had some measure of control, within parameters of his own choice. What was called 'real life' seemed uncontainable to him. He had the feeling that his feet were close to an unseen abyss. Recently he had read in a London paper that eight children, all under twelve, had been charged with the attempted murder of a five-year-old boy. The boy had been found, horrifically injured, but alive. Gloomy questions haunted Whidbourne: was mankind undergoing some dire mutation that affected us beyond remedy? He didn't know what was troubling him. It had to do with essential things being shifted dangerously, of there being no shelter, no final refuge. He wondered what Mrs Wibberley was doing at that moment, with her shooting stick and her gruff man's voice, unassailable in her leather-bound, prayer-book faith.

A short sharp sound came from somewhere outside. It was a cry of terminal distress, uttered by some bird or animal at the moment of death. From his country childhood, Whidbourne knew the sound signified murder. He wondered if there were stoats in the area.

All were asleep in the rest house when McKelvie crept from his bed. He dressed very quietly without turning on the light. Gropingly, he gathered some things: his tripod with the camera fixed to it, a movie camera, and a separate sound-recording machine of high quality. He slung them onto his back with various straps. Although it was dark he carefully combed his hair, then stealthily left the building. It was about a quarter of a mile to the cave occupied by Haareth and his family. After he had gone a short distance he cursed himself for forgetting his torch. He did not go back; once a patch of cloud had passed there would be bright moonlight. When he reached the cave he saw the white pony standing there, still as a monument. He called out softly. A few moments later Abu, one of the sons, came out cautiously and approached him. He took McKelvie's hand.

'Most honoured, sir!'

There was excitement in his whisper, a message of delighted welcome. Then the other son, Scherzad, came out, followed by Haareth himself. In the moonlight McKelvie saw white teeth under black moustaches, all smiling a welcome. The wife, Oudsia, stood in the cave entrance, a dark figure. She too was smiling. There was a feeling of conspiracy. 'Honoured sir!' The salutation was given by all of them. There was no reason to speak after that. Two very large panniers were brought out and slung onto the little white mare. Several cans of petrol were added, and bundles of dry wood. Finally Oudsia led out a nanny goat. The animal stood looking about her with quick little movements of her head, blinking and bewildered.

They set out on their way to the High Place. The walk would take an hour and a half.

Petra became monstrous at night. Monstrous because there was no human context, as if the facades had grown spontaneously from the rock. The path became rougher and steeper and McKelvie stumbled. Abu held him up. His hold on McKelvie's arm was firm, yet gentle, almost reverential.

'Honoured sir, rest your hand on my shoulder, it will be easier for you.'

McKelvie did so. He enjoyed this comradeship, enjoyed also the feeling of strength in the young man's shoulder under his hand. They were now well above the old city.

There were loose stones under their feet and McKelvie stumbled again, this time rather badly. For a moment he was on all fours. I'm getting old, he thought. Abu straightened him up, took him by the hand and they walked on. This did not embarrass McKelvie, he had often seen young Arab men walking hand-in-hand in towns and villages.

At last the ground levelled out before them and they were in a flattened area. They were at the High Place. At the edge of what could best be called the platform there was emptiness. Down there, the plain stretched away to – where was it? McKelvie tried to get his bearings. Syria? Israel? The men took wood from the panniers to prepare it for the fire.

Then the boys went searching for more. They came and went until they had stacked a great pile. McKelvie set up his equipment. He put his tripod at a good vantage point and primed the remote control on the movie camera. He placed his sound-recording machine on a boulder some distance away. The white mare and the goat stood still. The moon was very bright. Then Haareth put a match to the wood, with some dry vegetation under it. It began to crackle.

Abu was standing beside McKelvie now.

'Who will kill the sacrifice?' McKelvie asked.

'I will.'

'How?'

'With this.'

Abu drew out a long, slender knife from under his clothes. He felt the blade with his thumb and smiled at McKelvie. Petrol was thrown on the fire. The flames rose proudly. The scene was beautiful.

The heat was becoming intense and McKelvie moved away towards the edge of the platform and stood with his back to the fire, looking out into the darkness. His recording equipment was switched on, all was ready. The chanting began, a slightly discordant sound which pleased his ear.

All of a sudden it stopped, and it was then that McKelvie's field work reached fulfilment. His wrists were gripped and held tightly behind his back by someone strong.

'Honoured sir.'

It was Abu's voice.

It didn't hurt very much, it was so sudden and swift, as if a very hot wire had been whipped across his throat, more of a stinging sensation than deep pain. Blood was flowing down his chest, warm and copious. His head was pulled back by the hair to open the wound. He had just enough time to realise that he was being murdered. A surprisingly vivid image of his long dead mother flashed through his mind for less than a second, when she had rescued him from a gang of street bullies. 'It's all right,' she had said as she held him sobbing, 'it's all right now, you're safe.' The image was there for an instant, and was gone. The next slash was made with strength and it killed McKelvie. As if from far away he could hear his windpipe being severed, like the chopping of a cabbage stalk, his heart still pumping out blood.

A long time later, when the fire had burnt out, they cleared up all the incriminating remains and put them in the panniers. Then they began to walk back to the cave in the old city, richer by a little over $3,000 in cash, two rings, a gold watch and chain, and all McKelvie's recording equipment. Silently Haareth reckoned they had made almost seven thousand dollars.

First light had not yet arrived when they set out from Petra, Haareth riding the white mare, his two sons walking on each side of him, Oudsia following them, leading the goat. None of them felt it necessary to say anything. They walked to the town of Wadi Musa where they arrived shortly after dawn. Within twenty minutes they had sold the goat and the white mare but not the recording equipment for which they knew they would get a better price elsewhere. They walked to where their old van had been parked near the wadi, and into the wadi they emptied the panniers. Then this family, who were not Nabateans but nomads on the make, set off in the van, their brief stay in Petra already a fading memory. At crossroads just outside the town, Ahmed stood waiting. Without getting out of the van, Haareth handed him $500 and waved goodbye, saying nothing.

They were heading for Aqaba where there would be plenty of rich tourists. Haareth and his sons sat on the bench seat in front, Haareth driving. Oudsia sat in the back with their precious gains. She tried on the two rings, opening and clenching her hand, eyebrows raised, head on one side, smiling. They were a little too big, but that could be fixed. Then she took out the gold hunter watch, clicked it open, held it to her ear, looked at the time, closed it again and caressed it with a kneading movement of her thumb. She glanced appreciatively at the back of her husband's head. They had married when they were both eighteen and they had years ahead of them.

She allowed the gold chain to trickle between her fingers over and over again. Lovely! It was almost a sensual feeling. Clever Haareth.

After a while, Abu and Scherzad began to sing; a high-pitched song, wavering, losing and finding itself again, seeming to come from a great distance.

Heading for the Rocks

'When will it erupt?'
'Soon. Perhaps tonight, perhaps tomorrow.'
Frau Hopf spoke as it placating a child. She was a little disturbed by the affection she was beginning to feel for Mrs Vardon. During twenty years of widowhood she had run the Pension Désirée with friendly but efficient neutrality towards her guests. Her establishment was cool and clean and Swiss. She abruptly left the terrace and went inside. On spotless tiles she walked briskly to the kitchen where her voice rose to chastise a timid maid.

The terrace floated serenely above the jumbled houses of Taormina. Sarah Vardon was at peace. It was good to be sitting by oneself in the sun. Everything was exactly right. The heat had crushed those small pods of worry that she found difficult to identify. In the pink radiance inside her closed eyelids the irritants of conscience had dissolved. Even the taut, blank canvas in the penthouse studio in Chelsea no longer reproached her. She opened her eyes narrowly for another look at Mount Etna, a vague presence rising hazily in the distance. A few dark dribbles of old lava could be seen near the summit.

Although the weather had been clear for weeks a small cloud now sat rakishly on the volcano and she wondered if it might be smoke. The mountain would be difficult to paint; there were no colours, nothing to touch with the brush, only a sullen monster brooding in the sun. Last night, and on several previous nights, a slender red tongue had darted vertically from the crater. It would erect itself for a few seconds, then subside and, after perhaps twenty minutes, there it would be again.

Richard Vardon came onto the terrace and quickly walked to where his wife was sitting. In his right hand he held a small radio encased in expensive pigskin. He thrust it dramatically towards her and held it within a few inches of her face.

'I'm getting London,' he said. 'It's definitely picking up the BBC. Absolutely no doubt about it this time. I heard a chap talking about sport. I'll be able to get the stock market report tonight. That's a BBC chap talking now, isn't it?'

Patiently she took the radio from him and held it to her ear, listening to the tiny person.

'He could be a Hottentot for all I can tell,' she said, 'let's bring it down to the beach.'

Although it was now October the days were still hot. Along the Spisone beach the male Sicilian whores walked like fawns, eyes alert for unaccompanied women tourists. Sarah Vardon reclined in a collapsible aluminium chair. Beside her, in the shade of a large hired parasol, her husband lay stretched on his back. She glanced down at him, and for a moment had the illusion that he was not her husband but just another man lying on a red lilo. It wasn't that he was repellent in his bathers, he had almost the figure of a young man, but she never cared to look at him for too long when his eyes were closed. If she did so a cold draught of detachment saddened and alarmed her.

They came to the same part of the beach every day and Sarah noticed that others did the same. This time they had new neighbours, a German couple. The wife was young and dark, and although she sat placidly while her husband bathed she had a lively face. He was older. Thick-set and cheerful, he kept on plunging his head into the water, snorting, shouting, threshing with his legs, returning to his wife, arm outstretched for a towel which she handed to him smiling. He had only one arm. The other was a stump which ended just above the elbow.

War.

A sudden gale of communication blew up between the married couple and another group of Germans. They were shouting cheerfully to each other.

'Krauts,' Vardon said, without opening his eyes.

'They're not all the same, you know. I think these Germans are from the south. You can tell from their voices. They're very different from the ones in the north, much more open and warm-hearted, more artistic, like the Austrians or the Italians.'

'All Krauts to me.'

'I know, darling, but one really must try not to think like that.'

Sarah spoke calmly but a little pulse hammered in her neck.

As the German husband dried himself briskly with his good arm, the stump of the other swung loosely. Sarah couldn't help watching it. Somewhere in her body she felt the pain of mutilation. Amputation shocked and intrigued her. That swinging appendage gave her a feeling of outrage. The wife was so young that they must have married after the war. She had just put on a red straw hat which perched coquettishly on her dark hair and she looked very pretty when she smiled up at her husband with her bright red lips and white teeth. Sarah jabbed at the hat with an imaginary paintbrush. One thick, courageous blob would have got it nicely.

This was the scarred decade of the '50s, a decade of wounds, as Sarah realised when she looked about her.

'It's really extraordinary,' she said.

'What is?'

'These beaches around the Mediterranean, they're like battlefields. All these people with arms and legs missing. There's that German with one arm. Have you noticed the Frenchman at the other end of the beach? He has an aluminium leg. It squeaks. I suppose they need oiling. Goodness knows how many people in Taormina are sightseeing with glass eyes.'

'Pretty natural after a world war. What else can you expect?'

'I don't see what's natural about it, and even if it is natural I still don't understand it. There you all were a few years ago blowing each other to bits and now here you all are bathing together and staying at the same hotels and having fun. In a few years you'll probably all be at it again.'

'If you've got a war on your hands you've got to fight it.'

'When you come to think of it, there must be hundreds of thousands of people all over the world with a limb chopped off.'

Vardon sat up. He drew his hand down over his face. He looked annoyed.

'You're being morbid,' he said.

'Millions if you count the Japanese.'

'It doesn't do to think too much about these things,' Vardon said. He started to get dressed.

'It's just that I don't like being baffled by anything.'

'Questioning things doesn't get you anywhere, sweetheart.'

Sarah said calmly that she just liked to understand things, and again the little pulse throbbed under the skin of her neck.

She leant back in her chair and watched the German husband who was having another bathe. He was now waist-deep, standing quite still. Truncated by the water he looked like a damaged Roman bust, noble, though a little heavy.

'It's a pity you're not interested in archaeology,' Sarah said, 'you'd have enjoyed the mosaics at Casale with me when I went there in the bus last week. They've discovered some wonderful things. You must have heard of the Bikini Girls, mosaics of pretty girls in bras and pants, made for an imperial Roman family.'

'They sound nice, but archaeology isn't my line.'

Sarah closed her eyes. At Casale there were snarling beasts and hunters in pursuit. Blood dripped from the boar's mouth and from the leg of the wounded hunter. In those mosaics, beauty and cruelty had been printed into the earth.

'Penny for them, old thing,' said Vardon. He now looked cheerful, ready to go.

'Please don't call me old thing. I was thinking how nice it would be if something marvellous were to happen – just now.'

'What sort of thing?'

'Something exciting. If that volcano were to blow the whole mountain into the sky.'

'Can't say I'd like that, we'd be pickled in ashes like they were—'

'In Pompeii,' Sarah said with a sigh.

Although Vardon's towel was neatly folded he shook it out and folded it again.

'Well, I'll be off, old thing. I'm meeting Roddy and June Topham for drinks at the San Domenico. In fact I may have lunch with them. Roddy and I do business together off and on. See you later at the pension.'

'Topham?'

'Roddy and June, you remember them! He was at Winchester with me. Chairman of *Dalby and Sumner*. Got his fingers in all sorts of pies. We ran into them at Santa Margherita on the way down last year.'

She remembered two martini-sippers, two people who were skilled at performing anecdotes, fluent and accurate in the description of food and wine, frequent jokers, critical of hotel service.

'Give them my love,' she said, with queenly remoteness.

'Shall I leave you the car?'

'No darling, I'll take the bus, it's more fun.'

She watched him pick his way among the prone bodies towards the steps which led up to the road. He was not a man who gazed at mountains. He didn't like pensions and picnics and sandwiches in paper bags. Greying, tall, athletically built, he had a glitter which didn't go with the Pension Désirée.'

Sarah's hair was undyed brown with only a little grey and her rather full figure was still attractive. One of the young Sicilians approached and stood before her, staring at her with such absurd bravado that she laughed full in his face. His features crumpled. She had broken the rules, spoilt the game, the fragile ritual of seduction had been shattered and he moved on.

A cool breeze roughened her skin and drove her from the beach. As she walked away she could hear the mournful cries of the boatman trying to get customers; he and his battered old rowing boat would soon be débris on this postwar tide. When she reached the road she stood waiting for a bus. She looked up at the scattered houses clinging to the stony hills. Above them, the lurching summit of the Castel del Mola seemed about to topple and crush the tourist town. The hills were scrubby with scant vegetation; their anatomy was hysterical and taut, rocky spines burst from their wasted bodies. Down one of those slopes Dionysius the Syracusan tyrant must have fled wounded on a winter's night, his warriors stumbling and cursing in the dark.

Beyond the brightly coloured houses and the bougainvillea there were barren, rocky places where she had walked one day, alone and free. She remembered a dark snake trickling into a crevice between white stones.

They came each year to Taormina in the Bentley. At the end of their holiday they would drive back through Italy in a leisurely fashion, stopping where they pleased. But always, whichever route they took, they made a point of stopping at Salerno to enact a small ritual of sadness. At Taormina they would stay at the five-star San Domenico. In this luxurious and beautiful hotel there was one grotesque thing: a brown and white plaster figure of the saint which stood at a corner of the landing on the first floor, its left arm outstretched to point the way. It was a little less than life-size. Haloed and inanely smiling, it had directed the Vardons every year since the war to their bedroom with balcony and bath. It was always the same room, reserved long in advance by Vardon, and it was the one in which they had spent their honeymoon. He thought it was a nice touch to bring his wife back every year to this place where there was no more love. Sarah was appalled but had never said so. Always when they arrived they were led to their room by the same porter, now growing elderly, and as they walked along the landing that smelt of beeswax her husband's fingers would press the inner side of her upper arm. This inept little action, a fumble towards communication which she knew to be without feeling, showed how hopelessly off course he was, how little he understood her.

This year she decided the charade would have to stop. One morning before breakfast she stood on the balcony of their bedroom and through binoculars saw the white face of the Pension Désirée in a corner of the bay. She watched the sun bring colour to the urns and statues on the edge of the terrace. That afternoon she took a walk through the town to inspect it. It was near the top of a steep, narrow street leading up to the ancient Greek theatre, its front facing across the bay towards the volcano. When she asked her husband, almost diffidently, if they might move to the pension for the rest of their stay in Taormina he agreed without protest.

The other guests at the pension included a retired, very deaf colonel convalescing after an operation, a pregnant wife and her writer husband who were hardly ever to be seen, and a bony young woman from the Foreign Office who stumped over the hills with a rucksack collecting wild flowers, and who had unexpectedly confided to Sarah that she was still a virgin. There were also two very circumspect Swiss ladies on holiday together. Vardon didn't want to leave the San Domenico and go to a place where the people and the food were, well, a little odd, where there was no room service, no bar, and where the guests brought their revolting packed lunches to the beach.

The dining room at the Désirée was resonant. The deaf colonel shared a table with the virgin from the Foreign office to whom he gave an account of his operation every evening, careful to leave out no detail. A five-inch section of his colon had been removed. He spoke in a loud monotone.

'There's yards and yards of it inside you, my dear. They inserted a piece of tubing, plastic I suppose, and everything now passes freely.'

Behind the colonel's voice, the knives and forks of the Swiss ladies sounded like the pecking of discreet hens. Under his breath, Vardon made an impolite comment to the effect that he would throttle the old sod if he heard any more about his guts.

Thunder could be heard. The lights fused. Frau Hopf and the waitress brought in candles.

After dinner, the guests drifted towards the row of chairs that were arranged – as if in preparation for a performance – along the edge of the terrace. The pension was nearly a thousand feet above sea level and they could see the coast sweeping in wide curves to Catania. At these times Frau Hopf managed to create a ceremonial atmosphere, pacing slowly to and fro behind her guests, murmuring to them occasionally, a priestess of leisure.

The volcano was before them, a giant lying on his back, or so it seemed to Sarah, his long torso pimpled with secondary cones, his toes touching the sea. There was no sound of thunder now, but in the distance, over Catania and beyond, spasms of pale light would flare in the sky every few minutes, flooding space with eerie luminosity. Although silent, they gave an impression of violence.

'Look,' Sarah said to her husband, 'the gods at war. Exciting, isn't it?'

'Summer lightning,' Vardon said, and yawned.

Sarah stared into the darkness where the volcano lay in monstrous sleep. There was no fiery tongue tonight. Frau Hopf was standing close to her.

'Well, Frau Hopf, when will the beast come to life? You did promise us an eruption.'

'Oh, he will not be long. I think he is preparing for an eruption now.'

'How can you tell?'

'I have been here for twenty years. You do not live with someone for twenty years without getting to know him.'

'I wonder, Frau Hopf.'

'Will the ground shake?' This came from the Foreign Office virgin.

'Perhaps a little.'

'Will we all collapse into the sea?'

'Oh no, we are on rock here; 5,000 metres of good, solid rock. We may get cinders and ash though for a few days. It makes my terrace very dirty.'

Vardon stood up. 'I think I'll just toddle down to the San Domenico for a nightcap with Roddy and June. See you later.'

That night as they lay in their twin beds, Sarah was almost certain that she felt a tremor. Vardon was snoring gently. She got up and looked out of the window. Yes, the red tongue was there again, darting into the sky. Below it, she could see the beautiful jewellery of fresh lava, a necklace of glow-worms around the summit. She returned to her bed and lay on her back, hoping for another tremor. She fancied that she heard a rumble which was not thunder. She smiled into the darkness. 'Go on,' she whispered, 'let's see what you can do. Do your worst. Have a real go!'

The next morning she wrote a postcard to her sister.

> Having a lovely time is what one's supposed to say, isn't it? More breath-taking discoveries at Casale. Etna threatens. Am worried about Richard. He cannot touch life. I feel there are horrors inside him. We have a virgin here who collects wild flowers. Isn't that perfect!
>
> Love,
>
> Sarah

After posting the card, she walked past the pension up to the Greek theatre where she sat among the ruins for a while. At the pension, her husband and Roddy Topham were talking what Vardon called 'private business'. She had thought that Topham, usually much too bouncy for her liking, seemed agitated when he arrived. She had noticed that after they had huddled together for these discussions they came out looking serious, but that as soon as they joined their wives they put on rictal smiles.

Although the day was warm she felt a shiver. A fleeting premonition had told her that something awful was going to happen soon. Vardon had been talking in his sleep lately. From his restless muttering she had been able to pick out a few garbled sentences, one of which had ended with the words 'fraud squad'.

Some days later she was sitting on the terrace listening to the sounds that came from far below. The lorries, and the little buses galloping about Taormina, crammed with companionable passengers, were trumpeting like elephants; the horns of the lambretta scooters sounded like bees trapped in a flower. Somewhere in the mountains a giant was opening a huge parcel wrapped in crackly brown paper. These growls of thunder – more frequent now – warned that the weather was breaking. Energy was running down. Even the tourists moved more slowly. The cries of the boatman on the Spisone beach were more forlorn; for him the last *lire* of summer were falling.

Sarah was having a bad day. Something like nausea of the spirit was what she had felt soon after getting up. By mid-afternoon she knew what was wrong: her talent was rotting. For the past eight months she had found it almost impossible to put paint on canvas. She knew her talent was a valuable gift. So was she a coward? She didn't think so. Whatever it was that controlled the points had switched her onto the wrong track a long time ago: she had married Richard Vardon.

On their honeymoon in Taormina they had stood holding hands on one of the small terraces at the San Domenico, looking down into a valley. The air had carried up to them a hot scent, a mix of orange blossom, wisteria and cow dung. She was setting out as a painter and this did not at first matter to Vardon who thought of it as a 'ladylike' occupation. He had started his career in the City. Early in their marriage his good looks and entrepreneurial flair had masked other qualities. Sarah's parents were what he called arty. Her father, whom she loved, was a shambling botanist, her mother painted and wore colourful clothes; writers and artists felt drawn to her even in her extreme old age.

It was when she began to have some success and was selling her pictures in art galleries that Vardon's attitude to her talent changed. He somehow managed to make her parents and their friends seem absurd, referring to them with feigned affection as 'the weirdie brigade'. Apart from the demands made by squash and polo, his energy was focused on gathering money. Gradually the Vardons' cars grew more luxurious, the hotels where they stayed more expensive. Large dinner parties were given, usually for business cronies and their wives, at which any arty or intellectual conversation was out of bounds. Sarah's duties as a hostess reduced her painting to an almost clandestine activity and, although stubbornly pursued, it began to seize up. It had left a fire in her which had been smouldering for a long time.

On the evening of her bad day in Taormina they had been invited to dinner with the Tophams at the San Domenico. Sarah declined, pleading a headache, and Vardon went alone. She usually drank very little but after he had left she had three camparis and asked for a gin to be mixed into the third, enjoying the distant crackle of thunder as she drank it. During her dinner alone at the pension, under the disapproving stare of the Swiss ladies, she drank three quarters of a bottle of strong local wine which made the insides of her cheeks sting pleasantly. It also induced a confused feeling of misery and defiance. She felt ready for a fight.

It was nine thirty when she had finished. The dinner party at the San Domenico would have ended, and they would be sitting out somewhere over liqueurs. June Topham's conversation was so fashionably weary that Sarah sometimes wondered if she would be able to make it to the end of a sentence. She needed sharpening up a little. Sarah decided to walk through the town and join them.

The evening was warm and she went out in her light dress and sandals, walking down the steep Via Teatro Greco. As she reached the bottom of the street there was a detonation immediately above her so loud and close that it seemed like a blow aimed at her person. The giant who had been opening a parcel had found and struck her. Involuntarily, she crouched for a moment like a beast, then straightened up and walked on.

The downpour followed almost at once and drenched her. She turned left into the main street, walking slowly with her face upturned as if having a hot shower. The storm grew in strength, the deep gutters became hurtling streams. Old women sewing in doorways glanced curiously at the mad foreign lady in the rain, her dress clinging to her so that she appeared naked.

When she was half way through the town she stopped at the Piazza Nove Aprile. Just off the piazza was the little church of San Giuseppe. On an impulse, she stepped inside and sat in one of the pews at the back. A young priest in his soutane walked slowly down the aisle from the vestry and as he passed Sarah he looked sidelong at this woman and sensed immediately that she was a tourist. He felt distress coming from her. At the door of the church he turned and walked slowly back, made some trifling adjustment of objects near the altar and walked down the aisle again. Sarah was unaware of him, staring straight ahead. He stopped a few feet from her.

'*Signora*,' he said softly. He spoke no English but his hands, held with their palms towards her, said, 'Can I help?'

'I want a word with the one who calls the shots,' she said, without looking at him.

The priest did not understand; with a smile and a little shrug he walked back to the vestry.

Sarah did not know how to pray but had a shivery feeling that something like a prayer was trying to escape from her.

'Hallo, whatever you are,' she whispered into her cupped hands, 'it's me again. I'm not praying, I'm yelling for help. Have you lost my address or something? Do you run a rescue service? If so would you please, please, please attend to Sarah Vardon.'

She left the church and a few minutes later arrived at the San Domenico. She walked clammily through the entrance hall and found Vardon and the Tophams sitting in the main lounge. They looked at her in astonished silence.

It was Topham who recovered first. 'Good God,' he said, 'if it isn't that sexy mermaid, Sarah Vardon!'

Although she didn't like Topham, his bonhomous manner always ignited a response and she couldn't suppress a smile. She turned to his wife.

'Good evening, June. You look a little tired. Is it all getting too too terribly much for you?'

'You just look damp, darling.'

A pool of water was spreading on the parquet under Sarah. Thinking that this could be misconstrued Topham suggested that they move to the small terrace off the main lounge where the lights were dim and Sarah could drip less conspicuously. Vardon felt apprehensive as they sat down. He thought his wife's face looked a bit wild. Topham was a highly valued customer and the head waiter was seldom far from him. Topham called him over. Sarah remembered him as a nice, balding man with the kindest eyes she had ever seen. He had always been especially kind to her.

'Good evening, Giulio,' she said.

He bowed. His face beamed with real pleasure. 'Good evening, Signora Vardon, it is so nice to see you here.' She knew that he meant it, he would always be pleased to see her, wet or dry.

'Sarah,' Topham said, 'I insist that you have a drink with us. What'll it be?'

Sarah turned to her husband. 'Richard, didn't you tell me once that whatever you wanted in this hotel would appear immediately?'

'That's right, sweetheart, you scarcely have to ask.'

She turned to the head waiter. 'Giulio, can I have whatever I want?'

'But of course, Signora, I am here to serve you. I will bring whatever you desire, *naturalmente*.'

'Then bring me Anthony! Bring me my son!'

Sarah's voice was harsh, and could be heard all over the terrace. Its tone had a primitive quality. It brought silence. Then there was sudden movement, the scraping of chairs, the solicitous but firm voices of English people closing ranks against embarrassment. Within seconds Vardon was escorting her from the hotel.

'Poor dear,' June Topham murmured after they had gone, 'was she a little drunk?'

'Perhaps. Did you know she's a painter?'

'No, I did not know that!'

It was almost as if he had mentioned a venereal infection.

'Artists are unstable people,' he said.

His wife nodded sagely.

'Anthony was their only child,' Topham said, 'he was with a commando unit. She's never come to terms with what happened.'

The next morning Vardon got up early and wrote a letter to a business colleague in Geneva.

Dear Louis

Many thanks for your letter which came to the San Domenico. I think the arrangements we have made will be to the benefit of all concerned. Topham is with us all the way. You are right in saying we should deal through nominees. Since the funds involved are now Directors' private capital they need not concern the Annual Report. The little problem you mentioned will not arise as I shall become Chairman in February.

In confidence I sometimes feel that Sarah and I may be heading for the rocks. Her behaviour has been rather strange lately. This could affect important matters. I don't have much faith in those bloody head-shrinkers but I wonder if they might be able to straighten her out. Worth a try perhaps. Will tell you all later. We begin the trek home tomorrow. I'll be in the office on Monday. Be discreet.

As ever,

Richard

The veins of Italy were dry. From the mountains, only the ghosts of rivers sprang and under the bridges as the Vardons drove north there flowed little more than torrents of grey stone. In Calabria they had passed through groves of olive trees, pallid under a film of dust, gnarled and ashen like old men. The tension between them was rising, as it always did when they were approaching Salerno.

'It's not far now,' Sarah said, 'it's about a mile further on the right.'

'No of course it isn't, we've nearly twenty miles to do yet.'

At last they saw the signpost, *Cimitero della guerra*. Vardon parked the Bentley and then they walked up the path that led to the host of white rectangles rising from the level field. To Sarah it was horrible, this abundant pale crop grown from battle. For a few years after the war these annual visits to the cemetery had brought them closer to each other but later they brought tension. They knew exactly where to go and now stood in silence before the headstone:

LIEUT A VARDON 6TH GRENADIER GUARDS
9TH SEPTEMBER 1943
AGED 20 YEARS

They returned to the small lodge at the entrance to the cemetery where there was a visitors' book which Vardon always signed. Sarah watched him write, 'A fine tribute to a job well done.' Those were the words he always wrote, year after year. Their blandness, their triteness, made her wince. How could he pour such banal anodyne over the memory of her son's stomach being filled with shrapnel, the choking on blood. Better to write nothing at all. As they walked back to the car, she felt Vardon's hand squeezing her upper arm. Did he think she could be comforted by this artless gesture? She wrenched herself away from him.

'Let go of me!' It was a cry of anger. 'Men are savages, bloody murderers, all of you!'

She seldom swore. Vardon said nothing.

She turned to him, white-faced. There was a trickle of saliva on her chin. 'I don't believe there's an ounce of real feeling inside you.'

In this she was mistaken. Vardon's heart ached for his son. It was an ache beyond his comprehension which he had never tried to express.

They stayed in Amalfi that night, at the Cappuccino-Convento Hotel where they had booked a room. They had been given a double bed which was not what they preferred. At dinner Sarah was calm again.

'That place *is* nicely kept,' she said, smiling, 'I'm sorry.' She stroked the back of his hand with her finger.

'It's nothing, sweetheart. Shall we have a nightcap?'

'No, let's go to bed. We've an early start tomorrow.'

Shortly before midnight Sarah had a nightmare. She was travelling at very high speed in the Bentley but the driver's seat was empty. It was a mountain road and she was terrified. She awoke sweating. Vardon was asleep. She felt restless and decided on a walk to calm herself. She put on her dress over her nightgown and entered the external lift which ran vertiginously down the face of a cliff. She strolled along the edge of the harbour. The air was cool and gentle. After she had turned to go back to the hotel she heard soft, sloppy footsteps. Someone was half walking, half running behind her.

'*Signora!*' The man's voice was husky. She did not turn round. '*Signora*, you like nice fucko?'

She pretended not to have heard.

'I give you very nice fucko, *signora. Io sono Greco. I Greci sono dei bravi amanti.*'

The man stayed a little behind her and she couldn't see him. She didn't turn her head, nor did she quicken her pace, but walked on until she reached the hotel. The lift was still at the bottom of the cliff. The man had followed her.

From inside the lift she took a good look through the glass doors. He was shabby and unshaven with greyish hair. He was smiling, and in the moonlight she caught the gleam of gold teeth. She pressed a button and shot heavenwards like a saint delivered from the flesh.

Vardon was now awake, lying on his back. When she came in he sat up so suddenly that he might have been worked by a mechanical device.

'Where've you been?'

'Had a bad dream. Went for a walk along the front. There was a horrible man.'

'A man?'

'Yes. He had gold teeth. He was Greek. He said Greeks are great lovers. He offered me sex. A "fucko", to be precise. That's new to me. It sounds rather cheerful, like those things you have in your polo. Don't you have chuckos?'

'The game is divided into *chukkas*. A *chukka* is seven minutes of continuous play. Filthy little wog! I wish to God I'd been there.'

'If you had been I wouldn't have had the offer of a—'

'Did you accept it?'

'Oh don't be silly.'

When she got into bed she was trembling. To her surprise Vardon grasped her hand. A little later, to her greater surprise, they were making love.

They used to make love with lively enjoyment and it wasn't all that bad now, except that Sarah's habit of detachment was a hindrance. Here we are, she thought, two English middle-agers hard at it in Amalfi. She did some arithmetic. She reckoned it was a little over two years since this had happened. She nibbled his ear. 'Hurrah for England!' she whispered, and almost laughed him out of herself.

After a visit to the bathroom she got back into bed. Vardon's climax had been powerful. She wondered what buried need had suddenly brought him on top of her.

Prolonged absence from a girlfriend? She wouldn't have minded if he had one. Well, not really.

'Richard, why is it called the missionary position?'

But Vardon was asleep.

The next morning, before continuing their long drive north, Vardon said he needed to buy stamps. Sarah said that while he was doing this she would have a coffee. He parked outside a small café facing the sea and went in search of his stamps. Sarah went inside and sat at a table near the back. Some men were standing by the bar near the door and among them she was dismayed to see the Greek.

He had seen her too and – oh horror! – he was approaching the table. He would be under the impression that she was travelling alone which would make her an even more enticing prey.

He sat down facing her.

'*Buon giorno, signora.* You are a lonely English lady? I will show you Amalfi. It is a paradise of romance, a place for love.'

It was then that Vardon appeared and stood glaring down at the Greek. He sat down and for a moment they made an incongruous trio. Then the Greek left with a leer which seemed to question the significance of this Englishman. He returned to the bar from where he stared pruriently at the Vardons.

'Is that the creature who propositioned you last night?'

'Yes, but Richard, please, please... oh no!'

Vardon had stood up. After nearly thirty years of marriage it still came as a surprise to her how tall he was when he stood up, and how elegant. He threaded his way fastidiously among the tables and sauntered casually towards the Greek. When he was close to him he smashed his fist into the gold teeth. The Greek was evidently a despised person and it was he, not Vardon, who was efficiently ejected by two waiters. When Sarah opened her eyes her husband's blow seemed to have erased the man's existence; he had vanished, leaving only a disembodied unpleasantness. The bar stools stood in perfect order and the patron was drying glasses. Vardon returned to his wife and they decided to leave. Sarah, crimson-faced, walked with her eyes on the floor. Word of the incident had spread fast. Marital jealousy was understood and respected here: a small crowd had gathered on the pavement and Vardon was cheered as the brave English signore who had defended his wife's honour.

At Modena Sarah spent an hour in the museum. She left Vardon sitting with his airmail copy of the *Financial Times* outside a café in a small piazza close to the Duomo. The houses were shabby and honey-coloured. It was the hour of siesta and the place was deserted, except for an old woman in black who stood motionless, watching him from a dark doorway, her face a waxen mask. Soon, bored and hot, he decided to have a look inside the Duomo. Not far from the altar there was a stone sarcophagus. Lying in it Vardon saw what he took to be a cardinal, caparisoned in scarlet, bejewelled, gloved and grinning. His illuminated coffin looked remote but vivid beneath a glass lid. Under the gaudy apparel the skeleton was padded like a dummy in a shop window. Vardon stared down at the skull. It wore a biretta and looked as if it had been polished. The fleshless smile was suave and jocular, it had an urbanity which was faintly insulting. Vardon looked more closely at the frightful amiability. Two front teeth were missing. Intelligence lurked in the eye sockets. It seemed that the skull had begun to mock him. 'You fool,' it seemed to say. He felt a subtle crumbling of his confidence.

'You fool, you have the certainties of someone who doesn't think. Think a little more. Things may not be as they seem.'

'No,' Vardon said aloud, 'things *are* as they seem.'

He stepped back from the coffin. With hands in pockets and head down he slouched past *The Washing of the Feet*, *The Last Supper*, *The Kiss of Judas*, *Christ Before Pilate*, *The Via Dolorosa* and *The Crucifixion*. Then he returned and, to the surprise of two American tourists standing nearby, he bent down and put his head close to the lid of the coffin.

'Two and two make four,' he informed the cardinal.

He left the Duomo. Once more he found himself in blinding light. The old woman was still standing in the doorway.

When they arrived in Santa Margherita, Sarah found that by careful pre-arrangement the Tophams were there too, staying at the same expensive hotel. Santa Margherita was one of Vardon's playgrounds. Here there would be old friends, fashionable people with a taste for excess, and good night life.

They were sitting at a table under a parasol on a section of the beach owned by the hotel. Waiters hovered in maroon jackets and bow ties. An ice bucket stood on the table and there were many bottles. Vardon had recovered from his hallucination in Modena. He told a story about a man whose genitals had been scorched when he dropped his cigarette in the loo after it had been cleaned with some flammable chemical. Topham made a brilliant joke about genitals which had them all choking on their drinks.

Sarah looked at them with detachment. Artists were the strongest people in the end, she thought, because they could handle chaos. If these people lifted the stone and saw what was under it they would panic.

She felt very relaxed. Life was there to be touched, its grainy surfaces should be explored. It should be devoured like sublime food.

'I wonder if I could have another drink,' she said.

'Of course you can, sweetheart!' Vardon jumped to his feet and got busy with the ice bucket. He was delighted.

They were all delighted. Good old Sarah! She was having a good time, joining the fun gang. Perhaps she might even give up that painting nonsense?

But that wasn't how it would be at all. As she listened to the laughter and the gags she remembered Vardon's sleep-talking and guessed that a net had been flung from an unfriendly place. There would be nasty headlines in the tabloids about a shamed financier. He would fight like a tiger until the net tightened and he was dragged away. Excitement was rising in her throat, an instinct told her that she was about to take charge of her life. More than anything now she wanted her brushes and her palette and her paints. When she got home she would put a brazen splodge of red on the canvas. The German wife's hat, it would all start again from there.

Between half-closed eyelids she watched a young water-skier in the bay. He had the careless freedom that came from long practise and skill. She liked the geometry of the taut rope and the wide arc he was scything in the water. She rejoiced in the brown body, the stretched arms and thighs. She watched until they seemed to dissolve in light and spray.

Ice Thoughts

It was lucky for him that he noticed the taxi parked with its snoozing driver at the airport; lucky also because a card was propped against the windscreen giving the name of the place he wanted to go to written in capitals. He got in. His clothes looked expensive and he was quite tall. His hair was grizzled. His name was Grout.

Leaning forward he tapped the burly driver on the shoulder and told him where he wanted to go.

'That's quite a long drive. You have money? I don't take cheques.'

'I have money. Please start.'

There wasn't much conversation, which suited Grout, but he learnt that the driver's one-man one-car firm was based in the town close to where he would be staying. Its income came mostly from ferrying people to and from the airport. He leant back comfortably and watched the landscape unfold. Years ago, he had taught history at a boys' school. Then a business opportunity came his way through a relation. He grasped it and prospered to an extent that surprised him. Now, at the latter end of middle age, he employed a large staff, his dealings were international and he travelled constantly.

Because of the difficult and beautiful way the country was made, the journey took a long time. He knew it would be cold when he arrived, but when he got out of the car the cold was beyond his expectation.

'Ten o'clock tomorrow then,' he said as he was paying. It had been snowing and he saw the back wheels spin for a moment as the driver left. A short path led from the road to the place that presumptuously advertised itself as a hotel. Grout chose such places out of curiosity, and a slightly mischievous desire to witness the unachieved. Inside, there was not a trace of mortar, stone or brick, as if the house had been knocked together with a hammer and nails. There was a smell of scrubbed wood which he remembered from schooldays. The reception area seemed to be unoccupied, until he leant over the desk and saw an elderly man sitting at a lower level crouched over a book on his lap. Grout cleared his throat loudly and announced his arrival. Without looking up from his book, the man indicated with a finger where Grout was to write his name and address. Then, still without speaking, he reached for a key hanging on a board and shoved it across the desk. His outstretched hand requested a passport.

Grout went in search of his room. The floor levels heaved like a disturbed sea, the landings were narrow and serpentine. Number eleven was a small room. The floor was so steeply tilted that when he entered he had to take a few quick steps forward to avoid hurtling out of the window at the far end. He unpacked his suitcase: clean shirt and underwear, socks, bathroom implements, and notebooks. He put his clothes in a cupboard which tilted drunkenly to one side. He looked round for a basin. There wasn't one (the guidebook had specified 'modest amenities') so he put the bathroom implements in with the clothes. He placed a tattered book, selections from the writings of Martin Luther in the original German, on the bedside table. The book was a relic from his boyhood in Vienna where his father had been a diplomat.

When he had done these things, he opened the creaky window and looked out. There was still enough light to see the surrounding country. He drew a short breath of surprise. In all his travels he had never seen a glacier, and now there was one below him, a great pale slug wedged in the bottom of a narrow valley, hidden from the road by a hedge. It was like something forgotten, left behind in the onward rush of the world. There was no traffic on the road, no sounds came from the direction of the town, nor from a small collection of houses that formed a village nearby. He stared at the glacier for a long time, until he felt the silence becoming hostile.

As he was closing the window he was aware of someone in the room behind him. He turned and saw a woman, probably in her thirties. She was substantially but not too heavily built, and she was standing very still.

Grout smiled, she did not.

'I am the manageress here, my name is Margaret. My friends used to call me Gretchen.'

She didn't smile or change her expression in any way as she spoke. She was imparting information.

'My name is Grout,' Grout said. Then, getting carried away a little, he added, 'Theodore Grout.'

'I know.'

'You know?'

'From the register in reception.'

'Ah, of course. So you're German are you? Or Austrian? I have a lot of Austrian friends.'

'My mother was German.'

Grout went to the window. 'How long do you think that glacier has been there?'

'Always, for ever. Thousands of years. It's going downhill, a little bit each year. It will get us all in the end.'

He didn't bother to tell her that she was mistaken, that because of the warming of the planet we would easily outlast the glacier. As there was no further material for conversation she inclined her head slightly and left the room.

At supper that evening he was served by a very young girl whose blonde hair was in plaits. She was silent, and so shy that it was a kind of wildness. Grout didn't speak in case it might frighten her away.

After supper, he sat reading in an area just off the narrow landing. Although he was often alone he didn't hunger for company. He was heterosexual and was not a virgin, yet he had never married, regarding marriage as an avoidable risk. He shunned nearly all committed relationships in case they might interfere with work. He had a lady friend of east European origin called Veronika. He would visit her in her tiny, beautifully furnished flat. Occasionally they would dine out together in a small, expensive restaurant. Sometimes when this happened she would talk nostalgically about the fate of her relations. Grout would listen attentively, nodding in sympathy. He would cover her hand with his while she wiped away a tear. There was a sexual dimension, diminishing now because they were getting on a bit. Their lovemaking was conducted slowly, seriously, with much thoughtfulness for each other. Neither of them desired marriage. It was a secure friendship.

He went to bed that night thinking about the strangeness of the manageress. Why had she said her friends *used* to call her Gretchen? Were they all in the past?

Next morning the taxi arrived punctually at ten o'clock. Grout asked to be put down by a monument he saw near the centre of the town and told the driver to pick him up at the same point after two hours. He began to explore, walking slowly with an erect gait; too erect perhaps, children tended to giggle as he passed. He sometimes stopped in front of buildings which looked unkempt or unoccupied. He would jot some details in a notebook. Sometimes he would take a photograph with a very small camera. Everything he did he was precise. The driver picked him up after two hours and brought him back to the hotel.

In his room he went straight to the window and looked down at the glacier. His gaze became intent and he imagined for a moment that it was swelling. He wasn't sure if there was a greenish tint around the edges.

As he looked he became aware of a growing sadness. He couldn't place it.

There were sounds behind him. When he looked round he saw the manageress. This time there was someone with her, the shy girl who had served him at supper the previous evening. The girl began to make his bed. The manageress spoke.

'Why do you look so much at the glacier, Mr Grout?'

'Because of curiosity. Think of the chemicals it must contain, the bubbles of history going back thousands of years.'

'Yes, yes.' She was bored. She did some dusting. The girl finished making the bed. As they were leaving the manageress said, 'Try not to think too much about the glacier, Mr Grout, those ice thoughts will bring you nothing good.'

Grout found her manner rather abrupt for a hotel employee, but thought no more of it. In the afternoon he put the notes he had made in town into an orderly sequence, and wrote them down in an exercise book. Then he went out and found a path leading down to the glacier. He stopped at the edge and got an impression of its size, far bigger than he had realised. The centre was higher than the rest, so that the whole shape was slightly convex. Its presence would account for the extra cold he had felt when he arrived from the airport. He sensed the power of its inertia. He stood for a few moments in the chill and silence. The light was going. He went back to the hotel and tried to read a local paper he found lying about.

On the way to his room he met the manageress on the landing. In that narrow space she looked very large.

'Mr Grout, you have been looking at the glacier again.'

'How can you tell?'

'From your eyes.'

Back in his room he wondered if she was mad. He slept fitfully that night. Each time he awoke he imagined the white monster in the valley outside and wondered why it induced such melancholy in him. It surprised him because few things worried him.

The next morning he went for a long walk. He made notes again and took more photographs. He looked for a pub or café where he could have a sandwich but without success. When he got back to the hotel he found the manageress sitting in an armchair in the reception area. Her posture was so relaxed that it looked proprietary and he wondered if she might be the daughter of the elderly silent man he had seen crouched over a book when he first arrived. Were they perhaps the owners of the hotel? The bluntness of her questions suggested self-confidence too strong for a member of hotel staff. The impression was reinforced when she spoke.

'Where have you been, Mr Grout?'

'I went for a walk, took some photographs.'

Grout thought her face was not quite the same as usual. The eyes were more concentrated, almost piercing.

'What do you do, Mr Grout? What is your profession?'

'I start up small companies and make them big ones. I like to see them grow and flourish. In short, I'm an entrepreneur.'

'Where?'

'Anywhere, everywhere. I'm an internationalist. I may be in touch with your government soon.'

Grout went to his room and put his notes and camera on a small table. He went downstairs and ordered a sandwich. The shy girl with plaits brought it to him. After that he went out again, down to the glacier. He put a foot on it gingerly, then withdrew it. He walked along the edge of the glacier for a few minutes.

In the evening the shy girl brought him supper.

The following morning the taxi driver had to take a family to the airport but called for Grout in the early afternoon. He asked to be dropped at the Town Hall and to be collected after a couple of hours. He tried to do some research on property law, and whether there were restrictions on foreigners buying land and houses. The language was a problem and his progress was slow and tiresome. The girl at the desk was helpful and spoke very good English, but Grout felt he was not spending time usefully.

The driver returned punctually and brought him back to the hotel. On the way to his room he met the manageress on the landing. She was blocking his path.

'Mr Grout, I have a question to ask you. I hope you will not mind.'

Grout was disappointed by his visit to the Town Hall and was not in the mood for enigmatic conversation.

'What is it?'

'Would you like to come for a walk on the glacier with me?'

'I'm not sure I'll have the time. It's most kind of you to ask me.'

'Are you so busy, Mr Grout?'

'I'm busy most of the time.'

'I have special shoes I can lend you. It will be interesting.'

'Most kind.'

'Perhaps you should ask the government's permission to come for a walk with me when you get in touch?'

Grout was intrigued by the little sneer. It seemed some kind of anger was growing in her.

'May I pass, please?' He went to his room.

The next day was the last of his visit. He had booked the taxi from early in the morning until late afternoon. He asked the driver to take him about the area with no special purpose in view. The landscape was strange to him, dramatic, with steepness everywhere. Sometimes he got a glimpse of the jagged coastline. The stillness of that day was unusual. On the way back, he decided to put a question to the driver.

'Do you know Margaret, the manageress at my hotel?'

'Margaret Gustiansson? A little, yes.'

'Only a little?'

'She is a strange lady.'

'Strange?'

'She was for twelve years in prison. She came out last year.'

'What was she in prison for?'

'Murder.'

'Who was her victim?'

'An English tourist staying at the hotel. They took a walk on the glacier. She shot him with a pistol. She was found guilty. She went to prison. She came out.'

The driver told a story well. No frills.

'Does anyone know why she shot him?'

'She would never say. She wrote a poem for the judge but he did not like it. Perhaps they had a – how you say? – a little tiff. Perhaps she wanted his shoes.'

'The judge's shoes?'

'No, no. The tourist had no shoes when they found him. It would have been very cold without shoes, you know. The police looked for shoes everywhere. They were never found. She may have buried them. She is a strange lady, you know.'

The day had almost gone. Grout felt far from home.

That evening, the shy girl brought him his supper for the last time. He gave her a generous tip. He felt a bond with her. Something not to be explained.

He went to his room early and packed his suitcase. He got into bed and picked up his book of Martin Luther. Soon there was a gentle knock on the door and the manageress came in. He was mildly relieved that she seemed to be unarmed, unless she had a holster with a gun in it strapped to her thigh. She shut the door very quietly and stood looking at him for a moment. Then she moved quickly to his bedside, dropped to her knees and rested her folded arms on the duvet. She was wearing a low-cut dress. Grout felt only slight arousal when he saw the cleft between her breasts, great white dugs they were, swelling aggressively towards him. Gusts of cheap scent were coming from her.

'Mr Grout, you are not married.' It was a statement.

'That's true.'

'You need a wife, I can tell.'

'I don't think I do. I've always managed for myself and I have a good friend.'

'Mr Grout, Theodore, the people here do not like me. I have no friends.'

'That's sad. I'm sorry.'

'Bring me to your country. I will be a good wife for you, my dearest.'

Grout thought it would only bring more trouble if he said he needed time to think.

'Miss Gustiansson, I'm not really a marrying sort of man.'

'Ah, you like boys. Why did you not tell me...'

'I do not like boys...'

'I am an understanding woman...'

'Not in that way...'

'Why did you not say...'

'I like educated, mature women who don't want to marry me.'

'Theodore.'

'No. For your sake, so that you may avoid further unhappiness, no.'

She suddenly got to her feet, strode to the door and turned to glare at him. She was in a fury.

'I despise you. You are a frightened man. You are afraid of life. I can sense fear in you. You are full of fear. You *shtink* of it.'

She left him, slamming the door. The little building shook.

Grout finished the paragraph he had been reading when she came in. He closed the book and settled himself for sleep. He was thinking how much better a word 'shtink' was than stink.

'I shtink,' he said softly into the pillow and turned out the light.

The next day he paid the bill to the elderly non-speaker at reception and was grudgingly given a receipt. By late afternoon the manageress had not reappeared.

The flight home was in darkness. Grout was travelling in Executive Class. Unusually for him he felt unsettled. He had a stiff drink. Briefly, as the plane started to descend for landing, he felt it would be nice to have arms around him that night. It was only for a moment.

Back in his flat he forced himself to go through his mail very quickly. There were not many telephone messages. He was ex-directory, accessible only to a very few friends and business acquaintances.

He rang a number.
'Veronika?'
'Ah, so you are back.'
'A few minutes ago.'
'How was it?'
'I think there may be opportunities there, but it needs careful thinking about. My visit was strange, really very strange. Shall I come round?'
'All right, but be quick. I am sleepy.'
'So am I. I'll ring tomorrow. Sleep well.'
'Goodnight, my dear.'

Grout got something out of the fridge and poured a glass of red wine. After a bath he went to bed and turned out the light.

As soon as he closed his eyes the glacier appeared, as if it had been lying in ambush. The icy scalp shone in brilliant, improbable light. He knew now where the sadness had come from; what had been worrying him was that the glacier was a wasted asset. He wondered if he could buy the whole valley from the government. How many people could be persuaded to move for cash? He could afford to make a good offer.

Lying in the dark he thought of all the things he would like to do with the glacier. With heavy industrial equipment he would drill holes into it and make corridors that would form a maze. Baroque music would come from hidden sources, constantly changing lights would glow from within the ice. At its core there would be its memorable glory, a hall of magic.

It was in the hall of magic that he fell asleep.

The next day he called on Veronika and told her of his plans for the glacier.

'It sounds exciting, Theo, but don't you think it's just a little bit, well, banal? It's Disneyland really, isn't it, dear? The baroque music would sound lovely, though.'

Grout laughed and invited her out for supper. She accepted. They had a good evening. They always did. After supper they went back to Veronika's flat. She fell over onto the carpet with her feet in the air while trying to take off her tights. There was much laughter.

Time was going by so fast. In the distance, Grout could see a shrouded figure. It was loneliness, life's creepy end.

He had known Veronika for a long time. No woman had pleased him as she did. He knew she had courage, she faked nothing. In the days that followed he began to imagine the advantages of a shared life. He no longer needed to protect his work so obsessively, certain objectives had been achieved.

A week of indecision passed. Grout lived in a block of flats. One evening when he was coming back from the office, the senior doorman, an Irishman called Paul, told him that a lady with a foreign accent had called to see him. He knew at once who the caller was. She was the killer on the glacier, the bringer of sorrow, the bitch-queen of ice and snow.

'She said she would call again, sir.'

'Thank you, Paul. Yes, she will call again. I will make preparations.'

The next morning he took a taxi to Veronika's flat. She answered his ring wearing an apron. She had been washing up. They went to the kitchen where she continued washing up, chatting with her back turned to him. She didn't show surprise when he asked her to marry him.

Speaking into the sink she said, 'Do you really think your feeling for me is strong enough to go through all that?'

'I wouldn't have asked you if I didn't.'

'I thought we were quite happy as we were.'

'Please, Veronika.'

'Oh all right, dear.'

She turned round to face him, smiling.

'I shall need a new dress.'

Grout spent quite a lot of money on a ring. He put notices in two broadsheets. In his acquired status as an engaged man he wondered calmly when the manageress would strike, and whether someone might get hurt.

Sometimes though, when he drew back and looked with a colder eye, he wondered whether such problems mattered at all when seen against the larger scale of things. It might have been the weather that made him feel like this. For several days now the air had been still, the sky low and sullen, packed with clouds of unknowing.

THE DARK TOY

The sunlight glinted on the handlebars of the bicycle that had been for so long desired, promised, at last given. The summer was good, blazing over the inherited lakes and the small, pedalling boy. In the heat-shimmer, the stringbag dragonflies hovered and swerved and coupled. From rafters and in cool grey ruins folded bats hung waiting for the night.

I am Dermot, I am a boy. I am quite strong. I have a cut on my left knee. My eyes are blue. I have freckles. I was born eight years ago in the civil war, on the day Rory O'Connor blew up the Dublin Four Courts. I live in the big house with my father. An old woman, Miss Williams, looks after me. She used to be my nanny. She's kind, but she's very old, nearly fifty I think, and she can't run very well.

The avenue stretched before him, pale and dusty, a gut connecting the big house with the public road. Along this road his father was thundering to Ennis in a Model T Ford, hell-bent on Miss O'Riordan, the new barmaid at the MacNamara Hotel.

I'm alone most of the time, but I'm not always lonely as there is Calnaan who looks after the car. He used to be the coachman. He's the nicest man in the world. I wish he was my father. My only friends around here are the Tierney girls. They live quite close, only a mile away if you go across the fields. There are five of them. I'm not supposed to play with them because they're Catholics, but we meet and play in the old castle down by the lake where no one can see us. I don't see any difference. Grown-ups are stupid about those things. There's Arthur Medlicott too. He's all right but he lives far away on a mountain and he doesn't often come here. Visitors, grown-ups I mean, don't come here much now. When they do I watch and listen. I notice everything about them while they talk, every little vein and pimple, the hairs in their ears and noses. I've forgotten no face that's been here, I remember every voice, all that's said.

Dermot's family was of the Dal Cais, neither settled nor planted, but sown by some early tide of migration. Six hundred years ago, they had hurled themselves down a green and rocky hill with Felim O'Connor's men at Dysert O'Dea and hacked de Clare's force to pieces in the watery fields below. But the Penal Laws had enhanced for them the attractions of the reformed church and of the English landlords' daughters. Through intermarriage with these, and through judicious purchases of land, they had taken on the varnish of Ascendency. Sometimes the Gaelic grain cracked the varnish.

Cahermacrea was a big square house. It looked to the west. When Dermot stood in the porch there were bright tiles under his feet. A grey church spire rose from the village across the fields. In the distance beyond the village a long hill, darkened by trees, lay across the view like a great fat sow. Beyond the hill there was the ocean. Some of the window panes of the porch were coloured, others were plain. He could choose a red world, or a blue or a plain one. The blue world was heraldic, serenely magical; in the red world dragons thrashed and roared in the ocean beyond the hill. The plain world was the alien truth. It was the way things were.

A few minutes ago, when I was standing with Calnaan in the yard, we watched Daddy driving away. I could see his head through the back window of the car. When Mummy died he wore a black hat for a while, and a black band on his left arm. Now he wears a grey hat on the side of his head and he wears brighter clothes. He thinks I've forgotten.

Dermot didn't yet know the boundaries of his father's land. Beyond the big wood there was a lake, beyond the lake there was another wood and another lake. There were wildernesses of crag and thorn, and paths he had never followed to their end. Through this land the Fergus ran to the Shannon and the sea, a stealthy river, secret and smooth.

Sometimes he takes a little suitcase with him. I don't know where he goes. I'm glad he's gone.

Calnaan had been at Cahermacrea since he was a boy, first a stable hand, then groom, then chauffeur. Middle-aged now he was tall and lean, a powerful man. He looked dour but excitable blood, fierce affections and dislikes, ran beneath his skin. He smoked Clarke's Perfect Plug which he flaked into the palm of his hand with a penknife before filling his pipe. He could spit tobacco juice a yard from his mouth. At departures, at funerals and weddings, at all times that touched his heart, tears pricked in his eyes. When this happened, his lips worked furiously, no words came. To fight off the tears he would stamp his feet and wave his arms and shout furiously at everyone around him. His way of greeting Dermot was to extend a brown forefinger, tipped with a grimy nail, for the boy to hold.

When the car turned the corner out of the yard, Calnaan took the pipe out of his mouth and did a super spit. He said, 'Yerrah God, aren't we as well off without him.' His thought just suddenly came out of him before he could stop it. It was my thought too.

This was the country of Thomond, where swords had been raised in battle in the stony hills at Corcomroe and Dysert O'Dea. The lichen-covered ruins of Dromore castle stared across the lake, not feeling picnics or the feet of children. A stone slab over the door proclaimed:

THIS CASTLE WAS BUILT BY TEIGE, SECOND SON TO O'CONNOR THIRD EARL OF THOMOND AND BY HIS WIFE, SLANEY.

At the top of the castle the peregrine falcons nest. They're hungry and wild, beautiful. Their cries are cold.

Behind the castle, under the moss, the ants were busy with doomed purpose, hurrying, hurrying. In Ruan post office, elderly Miss Casey yawned as she steamed open an envelope addressed to the big house. She read the letter inside. Oh my, money was owing. Where would it all end?

Sometimes Daddy's eyes are funny. There's something there that you can't make friends with. There's a portrait of my great-grandmother in the hall. Local people were frightened of her, they called her The Holy Terror. Sometimes when I look into her face I see Daddy's eyes staring at me. Suddenly the old woman starts to come out of the picture and she and Daddy are the same person. When this happens I go and find Calnaan who is always somewhere about and when I talk to him I feel everything is all right. Sometimes though, even Calnaan isn't enough. When things are really bad I need the other thing. I think of it as a kind of dark toy. When I need it I have to go to it. Although I hold it close I've never seen it. Sometimes it has almost come to me.

The avenue ran for an Irish mile through bracken and primroses, tall trees and bluebells, through the Cragatheen wood, then through a meadow to white iron gates and the public road.

We have only candles and lamps at Cahermacrea. It's dark when I go to bed in winter. I go up the stairs alone and later Miss Williams comes to say goodnight. I light a candle in the pantry and bring it up with me. It's thirty-seven paces from the pantry to the foot of the back stairs, forty-nine to the hall stairs. If I go up the hall stairs, there are twenty-nine steps to the first landing, then seventy-three paces to my bedroom at the end of the landing. I hold the candle well out in front of me. This is the first floor. The top floor of the house is empty and I only go there when I need to, only when it is light, though I go to a very dark place. From the back door of the house to the foot of the back stairs it's forty-three paces for me and twenty-five for Daddy if he's in a good mood. If he's in a bad mood he does it in twenty-one. There are flagstones on the passage floor and he has iron tips on his heels. You can hear them all over the house. I try to be in bed when he comes back from Ennis, but if I've left it too late and I hear the car coming I run to the back stairs which is a place he never goes to. He never goes to my bedroom either. Mummy used to sleep there before she died. I wait half way up the back stairs and count Daddy's footsteps from the back door. If he meets me before I get to the stairs I smile and say 'Hello Daddy.' It's always safer to smile because I never know what he's going to be like. He's a wizard shot though, and he can hit a hurley ball right over the house. His hands are so strong I'd like to have him with me if there were wild beasts around. When he's angry his skin doesn't go red, it seems to go dark.

Dermot was approaching the Cragatheen where, even on hot days, there was always a slight chill.

Look at that hawk! She's a kestrel. I know where she lives. I've heard her screaming from her nest in the Cragatheen. She's hovering over the rabbit warren looking for young grazers, her tail spread to keep herself steady, her wings fluttering. Will she swoop?

In the Cragatheen the limestone had a skin of moss; cosy, treacherous in its welcome. There were deep clefts into which sure-footed animals, sheep and goats, sometimes fell and died, trapped, staring upwards. Trees that brandished demented thorns had somehow taken root. It was a mysterious little wood; its strangeness came on you with a sudden fall in temperature. It was half way to the front gates.

In winter I have my bath at night before the turf fire in my bedroom. There are rough towels and shiny copper jugs. When Miss Williams is drying me, she puts the towel over my head and we have to pretend I'm a train going through a tunnel and I have to say 'chuff-chuff'. It's a bit stupid. A few years ago, after I'd been in bed awhile, my grandmother, Grannie McEnchroe, would come creeping into my room. She walked with two sticks and I could hear her coming all the way along the landing because the sticks tapped the boards on each side of the carpet. I'd hear her stays creaking when she came in, and all she'd say until she reached my bed was, 'Sssh'. She'd get hold of my head and pull it to her so that my ear was right up against her mouth. Then she'd whisper Catholic prayers so close I could feel her lips moving inside my ear. She never said goodnight when she left the room, only 'Sssh'. Daddy would have nearly killed her if he'd known because he and I are Protestants. Grannie McEnchroe is dead and now when I'm in bed Miss Williams sings Protestant hymns into my mouth. Sometimes before I go to sleep I wish I'd been with the dark toy, just for a little while, but I try not to go to it too often, only at very special bad times. I don't know what it is. I know it's always there waiting for me. Miss Williams talks to me about a heavenly father who is always kind. That'd be great, it'd make a change. You need someone who's on your side – always.

He got off his bicycle and left it on its side with the back wheel spinning. He ran quickly into the Cragatheen, glancing neither to right nor left, as if following a line drawn on the ground. He stopped and looked down into a cleft.

My bedroom is above the kitchen, and when I wake up in the morning I can hear Annie Kelly stoking the range. She has a stiff leg and I can hear her footsteps, clop-scrape, clop-scrape, clop-scrape. She's the cook. She looks very stern but I can make her shriek by lifting her skirt from behind. I love the rumble of the range because it means that people are about and everything is all right. When the range is hot you can look down into it through a round hole and see the fire inside it. One morning I got up very early and stole downstairs and peeped into the kitchen at Annie. It was still dark, but the glow from the hole was lighting up her face. She didn't know I was there and I felt awful because she looked so sad staring down into hell.

'Is that what hell is like, Annie?'

'Jesus, Mary, and Joseph – the guards! What are you doing, creeping up on me like that!'

'Is that what hell is like?'

'Hell is hotter.'

'What did Jesus do when he went down into hell?'

'Ah how would I know, Master Dermot?'

'He descended into hell.'

'Go on now, I have the breakfast to cook.'

I think the last time I went to the dark toy was after I'd had the bad dream. I dreamt I had walked into the shrubbery early in the morning and it was the most wonderful morning I'd ever known and I knew I'd always be alive and happy for ever. I couldn't look up at the sun, it felt so bright. The grass and all the leaves were shining with little buds of dew, and everything was so still I felt I shouldn't move for fear of breaking my happiness and Oh God I didn't want to be separate any more, I wanted to be the same as the grass and the leaves so we'd all be the one thing and nothing could hurt us any more. And then I saw the Devil. I was so excited I was afraid he'd hear my heart beating. I'd always felt sorry for him, with nobody on his side and maybe needing a friend. He was quite a long way off, standing under my favourite tree, the friendliest tree of all, the laurel that had grown into a kind of house, a safe place with its branches bending over. His back was turned to me. He wasn't how I thought he'd be at all, he was sort of grey-coloured, like clay. Suddenly, he turned round and he was smiling at me as if he knew I was there all the time. He had such a friendly face! And then I saw that the laurel tree had withered and I was frightened. I ran into the house. Mummy was dead and I knew I'd have to go to Daddy with his strong hands. I ran into his bedroom. He was there in bed, but something was wrong. It was Daddy and it wasn't Daddy. I said 'Daddy, I've seen the Devil,' and I ran to him. Then it was horrible because I saw that he was made of sand. When I got right up to the bed I found that his face and his whole body were crumbling like a heap of sand, just like the sand at the sea.

'You'll have another one with me, Miss O'Riordan.'

'Oh no, thank you, Mr McEnchroe, I couldn't.'

'You will, you will!'

'No really, I cannot. I dare not. I have a light head. I only take a tiny drop sometimes. You had me tipsy last time, Mr McEnchroe.'

'A bird never flew on one wing, Miss O'Riordan, that's one sure five!'

'Well, that's true for you. All right so, I'll have something small to keep you company, Mr McEnchroe.'

Miss O'Riordan was creamy, although at twenty-one she had already been well skimmed. She turned her back and poured herself a Crème de Menthe. She was longing to slosh a good drop of the hard into a tumbler but felt that the liqueur would make a better impression. They were alone in the bar. As she poured the drink she felt a disturbing presence behind her. It was formidable, unrestful, imperious. It seemed to fill the air with crackles and sparks. There was too much energy in the room and she would have liked to open a window and let some of it out. She felt extreme but excited wariness and wondered why her arms were goose-pimpled.

Miss Williams brings me to the Protestant church in Corofin every Sunday. I hate it, the smell of the prayer books and cushions, the cold grey stone. Miss Williams smells of mothballs in her Sunday clothes. I try to think of God, but it's very difficult and I can only think of someone wearing a garda cap. When I try to think very hard of what God looks like I can only see Sergeant Considine of Corofin. All the same there's a thought somewhere in my head and I feel that if I could get it out I could understand everything. I wish I could think with the whole of my mind. But I don't want to understand everything. I don't really want to understand the dark toy. And I'd rather not see it, I'd rather just feel it. No one will ever find out where it is.

A familiar face, a wide brilliant smile, greeted him from the bottom of the cleft in the Cragatheen. The goat's skeleton had been there for as long as he could remember. One day, perhaps when pursued, or with the come-hither scent in its nostrils, it had hopscotched itself into this neat natural grave. Dermot had often imagined the day. He had watched the last running and skipping over the crags until the trusted foot slipped. He had felt the cramp, hunger and cold spreading through the wedged body, until the eyes glazed and surrendered. Even now, he thought, the bones were trying to flee. He peered down at them without compassion. This exercise, many times repeated, was detached. He was not interested in death but in dead things. He desired detail. He said aloud, 'You're dead and I'm alive.' A bird sang. When Dermot looked up, his eyes caught the shine of a birch tree. He ran whistling back to his bicycle. He felt exultation, perhaps because death is the stiffener that makes a good strong drink of life.

'All right, so,' she said, raising her little glass. He raised his.
　'Let us be lively even if we only live a minute, Miss O'Riordan!'

'Well, that's a good thing to drink to all right.'
'I'd say you're from Cork?'
'I am so. My people are in business there, you know. My father has a good position. I'm only doing this job for a cod.'
'I'd rather face wild horses in the street than handle a Corkwoman.'
A trill of reproachful laughter from Miss O'Riordan.
She rested her elbows on the counter. 'My relief should be here soon. She's overdue already.'
'You live in the hotel, I suppose?'
'Oh I do, yes.'
'It's a good hotel so long as you have the right room. I hope they've given you a good room.'
'Oh a very nice room, yes. Number twenty-eight.'

I'm glad he's gone. I'm free. I'm riding to the white gates. This is the first time I'll have been on the public road by myself. I've always had to have Calnaan with me, or Miss Williams trotting and fussing and fretting behind me. Nobody knows where I am. I'll have gone and come back before they even miss me. I'll leave the bike in the yard and just walk in all innocent. If I meet Daddy coming home it'll be the finish, I'll never see the bike again. But he won't be back this evening, surely? Nor tomorrow evening. There's no one for him to talk to here, only me. The only trouble right now is Mrs Doyle at the gate lodge, but she sleeps in the afternoon. She's nearly dead anyway. I'll just open the gates and ride out without looking to see if she's there. I'll turn right at the bottom of the village. Then I'll turn right again at the next crossroads by Clancy's house. Then I'll be on the road from where you can just see the Burren mountains heaped in the sky, the road to where I've never been.

Miss O'Riordan was pondering. What do these Protestant widowers do for it? If they did it with the maids, the talk would be sure to get out one day. Off to Dublin or London maybe. Or do they manage without it? Not this one surely?

An attractive man all right. He could talk me into anything. If it doesn't happen today, it'll be tomorrow. Soon, anyway. He'll take me shopping in Limerick. I'll get that outfit in Roche's Stores if it isn't gone. Maybe he'll take me to Dublin. If it isn't today it'll be tomorrow, or the next day. Or next week. Such an attractive man! But my God, the eyes! What sort of a beast is it inside him? Anyway, it'll be soon. His sort can't wait. They're hell-raisers, real hell-raisers.

Dermot opened the white gates, mounted his bicycle for the first time alone on the forbidden public road, and pedalled towards the village. He rode down the village street. An old woman straightened her back to look at him, a hand shading her eyes. Johnsie Frawley the blacksmith, just back from Ennis, gave a tipsy roar. From others there were cries of astonished recognition. He reached the end of the village and turned right. Then he was on the strange road that led to a wilderness of rock. Cahermacrea land was still on his right, but soon he would be passing its boundary. Along the skyline the hazy Burren slept.

When he turned a corner he saw a jaunting car ahead and quickened his pace to get a closer look. It carried two men, one of them lolling, his head moving loosely with the swaying of the car, the other upright and stiff, holding the reins. Both wore tattered hats with the brims turned down. These men had a quality of strangerhood; there was something in them that unsettled Dermot. Even from behind them he could sense something quite different from the village people. A message that they were alien to him seemed to come from their backs. 'Take care,' it said, 'we are not for each other, we will never mix.' The driver's back was very thick with rolls of fat, as if he was wearing tyres around his body, the hair on his creased nape was dark and greasy-looking. Dermot decided to overtake. He pedalled faster until he was close behind the men and his nostrils caught the smell of the horse. He hesitated, then made a spurt. He drew level with the offside wheel of the car and felt that he was doing an awful thing: he was alone where he should not be, alone on the public road and the road seemed to belong to the man holding the reins. He pedalled faster until he could see the driver's face. The man flicked the trotting horse with a whip held lightly in his right hand. He was swarthy and heavy-jowled, staring into the distance. Dermot got a glance from the corner of a dark eye. Then, the head turned and the face took a full but expressionless look at the boy. Dermot smiled. There was no response. Neither smile nor frown. When he made the final effort to overtake Dermot was humiliated by seeing the lash of the whip glide across his left wrist. It was little more than a venomous caress as if a snake had licked him and he hardly felt it, but the deft, lazy action carried a command. He looked up at the man, hoping for a smile or a wink to redeem the moment; but the heavy jowls didn't move and the face looked straight ahead. Dermot freewheeled and dropped back. He stopped and got off his bicycle to watch the two men driving into fields of rock, into old battle-grounds and places of hearsay. Although the sun throbbed with the full strength of summer, he felt an eeriness as the men seemed to melt into the hazy light. He crooked his arms as if to hold something close to him.

At that moment, his father and Miss O'Riordan were lying in a bedroom in the MacNamara Hotel. Protestant seed nourished trouble and complexity in a Catholic womb. Shrill voices came through the window overlooking the Pro-Cathedral, voices of children in the bare-footed thirties, playing in the dust.

With his head down, Dermot rode back through the village. He passed through the white gates again. From her small window Mrs Doyle, a pale, silent woman, watched him, motionless. He rode fast through the Cragatheen. Then, in the haggard at Cahermacrea, he found – oh, thank goodness! – Calnaan; safe, strong Calnaan.

'...rough bad men, Calnaan, really rough. The driver had a terrible face. I felt there was murder right down in his soul.'

'Oh Jay!'

'He never smiled. His arms were as thick as your thighs.'

'Were they, faith?'

'If you'd been there and he'd gone for me, what'd you have done, Calnaan?'

'I'd have hit him a blow in the lug o' the ear.'

'Would it have knocked him out? Would he have been knocked out?'

'What knocked out! He'd have been knocked into the middle of next week!'

'We'd have beaten them both?'

'Me and you could beat the world.'

'Show me your muscle, Calnaan.'

Calnaan rolled up his right sleeve, stretched out his arm and slowly brought his clenched fist to his shoulder. Under the skin a ball gathered and swelled to the size of a turnip.

'Calnaan!'

There was silence between them. There was a little flurry of air. Dermot's thought was drawn away, he was strangely lost.

'Look at me a minute.'

Dermot looked and found Calnaan's eyes searching his face. He had never seen Calnaan's eyes like this, narrowed to slits.

'Sometimes I wonder if you're growin' up or growin' down.'

'What do you mean, Calnaan?'

'There are times like you've lost a bit of yourself, d'you know?'

'I think I know, Calnaan.'

'D'you ever go messin' about in some bad old place?'

'Why?'

'Cahermacrea's a funny old house. The old people tell a lot of stories about it.'

'It's a lovely house.'

'Same thing happened to your father.'

'What?'

'He changed, like. When he was a boy like yourself. There's be times he'd go someplace in the house and no one could find him. There's something wrong in Cahermacrea. I'd like to scour the house like a dirty pan.'

'Changed?'

'It's like he changed into some kind of a...' Calnaan scratched his head.

'A demon? Calnaan, I had a dream—' Calnaan put his hand on the back of Dermot's head.

'Mind yourself, asthore.'

Suddenly, with such force that it was painful, he pulled the boy's head hard against his ribs.

'God blessoo!'

★

Redfern wore a cardigan with leather buttons and carried his small change in a purse. He was powerful in Rotarian circles. The man was grossly facetious, although like many facetious people he was also watchful and shrewd. His conversation had the hypnotic quality of being almost totally predictable. Dermot didn't hold this against him; there was a certain pleasure in steering the ship of boredom. In a few moments he would say either, 'Mind the little people don't carry you off,' or, 'Take care the leprechauns don't get you.' Today Dermot felt it would be the leprechauns.

'Take care the leprechauns don't get you.'

Pale Miss Gemmell was pounding away at her Imperial, tinted glasses framed in tortoiseshell, large upper teeth bared in concentration.

'How long would it be since your last visit, Dermot?' Redfern asked.

'I went over ten years ago when my father died.'

'A long illness?'

'No, he did everything quickly. He just died and got straight into his coffin. I was only there for a week.'

Miss Gemmell cleared her throat. She disapproved of the reference to the coffin.

'I expect you'll find a lot of changes there,' Redfern said, 'a lot of property's being developed in the republic. Prices going up all the time.'

'There's been a lot of arising and going.'

'A lot of what? Sometimes I don't know what you're talking about. No, property's the thing all right. Opportunities. Our firm's strong in the Limerick area. And in Clare too, thanks to your contact with McKeever. We operate through nominees of course, as you know.' Redfern was an estate agent, but his dealings extended beyond buying and selling for clients. Dermot suspected that he was involved in development projects and he seemed to make more money than the accounts of the firm implied. He was a great man for nominees.

Dermot took an electric razor from his briefcase and brought it to the washroom. He started to shave, wrenching his face into smoothness. Not a bad face at all really, considering everything. A little puffy round the eyes just now, but that would go after a few walks in the Burren. Since the divorce he had noticed the faint beginnings of crow's feet. With thumbs at temples he hoisted them away and tried a face-lifted smile. A full head of dark brown hair added an inch or so to his slim six feet. A solitary grey hair had been thatched in above his left ear. He had welcomed its arrival with wary satisfaction. Except for the prominent nose with its jutting bridge his mother's genes, or someone else's, seemed to have rubbed his father out. Or had they? The trouble with genes was that nobody had a free run. Dermot felt that the man was hiding somewhere inside him, that he might suddenly talk out of his face, taking possession.

After clearing his desk he moved swiftly across the room with coat and briefcase. At the door he raised a hand.

'Well, I'm off.'

'Bye-bye, Mr McEnchroe,' Miss Gemmell said, without looking up.

'Have a nice time, Dermot,' Redfern said, 'push the firm, mind the leprechauns don't… oh, by the way, I almost forgot. You'll be seeing McKeever. I'd be glad if you'd give him this letter. You'll be quicker than the post.'

He gave Dermot a sealed envelope. He knew it would be delivered safely, and unopened.

Dermot shut the door behind him. Freedom! At the sound of the lift gates closing Redfern said, 'Funny fellow'.

'H'm.' Miss Gemmell pounded at the Imperial for nearly a minute, a clattering enigma of tortoiseshell and teeth.

She stopped typing. 'You know, I've always felt I've never quite made contact with him. I don't mean he isn't nice, he's awfully nice. Please don't get me wrong, Mr Redfern, no one could be friendlier, but there's something…'

'Yes.'

'Something that keeps you at a distance.'

'Damaged goods, Miss Gemmell, damaged goods.'

Redfern felt he had been definitive. He tilted back his chair and folded pudgy hands.

'You mean…'

'Somewhere, sometime, life has hit him below the belt

when he wasn't ready for it. I can tell that sort of thing a mile away. Those people are all the same. They can mix in a crowd as well as anyone when they want to. They can even be the life and soul. But they remain separate. Dermot's a good mixer or I wouldn't have brought him into the firm, but there's a label stuck on his chest.'

'Do you know, I never noticed it.'

Redfern shut his eyes and counted to three.

'An imaginary label, Miss Gemmell. It says, 'Don't come too close.'

'I've always been interested in psychology.'

'Mind you, he has some very useful qualities. He has loyalty too, I'll give him that. And he can talk people into anything. Sometimes his memory of conversations surprises me; he can recall every detail. Did you know he was in Intelligence during the war? Something to do with interrogation. He can remember what people have said for years. I sometimes wonder whether he's still mixed up in it.'

'I wouldn't be surprised.'

Redfern added darkly, 'He writes stories. I read one of them in a magazine.'

'I knew there was something.'

Miss Gemmell was a woman in a hormonal hurry, she could see forty coming. Redfern's desk was at the other end of the room but, although each faced the same wall, his desk was slightly to the front of hers and she could take sidelong glances. She took one now. A bit heavy in the jowl. Overweight. Scurf on the collar of the brown suite. All the same, he was single.

'I think you handle him awfully well,' she said.

'Oh, the Irish are all right if you know how to take them.'

'I could almost think you were Irish yourself, the way you handle him.'

Redfern simpered. 'My great-grandmother was Irish as a matter of fact.'

Miss Gemmell lifted her pencil high and brought the end of it down hard on the desk, the emphasis of her gesture spoilt by the rubber on the end.

'I knew it,' she said quietly, 'I knew it, I could have sworn it, only I never liked to ask.'

At half past five Redfern asked her if she would care for a drink at the Rose and Crown before he drove home.

Dermot flew to Shannon where he hired a small car. Instead of going straight to the MacNamara Hotel in Ennis where he had booked a room, he made for the coast.

Although a strong wind was blowing the sky was clear, and between Spanish Point and Lahinch the dark rocks had a dazzle where the tongue of the tide had licked them and withdrawn. Far out a submerged reef caused a periodic distortion in the water above it. Every few seconds a great wave was generated. This green disturbance swelled and curved but did not always break. At Lahinch, a village so beaten by storms that it seemed to have hunched its back against the sea, Dermot turned right and drove inland towards Ennis. Clare offered a bleak face to corners from the west. In fact, it was not her face that you saw but her feet. She hid her hills and watery depressions in the east. The Burren mountains were her great toenails, and for twenty miles eastward her bones were thinly covered by a garment of earth, as if she had drawn it up to cover her soft allurements beyond Tulla and Scariff, laying bare the Burren. Dermot felt a prickling in his eyes. There was an integrity about this stony place; in his childhood it had been the edge of the world.

The MacNamara Hotel in Ennis had once been an unpretentious place of the sort that might be found in any provincial town. Then it began to be patronised by American and German businessmen and tourists arriving from Shannon airport. Grievous change had now been inflicted on it by the proprietor. As the guest of a brewery he had toured the southern counties of England in search of ideas for renovation, returning, not with the new, but with a vulgar misconception of the old. By a ludicrous transference of culture he had renamed the hotel, calling it Ye Olde Macnamara Hostelrie. The main bar had become Ye Barde's Taverne and at its entrance a fake beam bore the injunction *Prithee Lower Thy Head*.

There was also a smaller bar and it was into this that Dermot walked after unpacking in his room. He found himself alone with a ginger-haired barmaid, amply, though not obesely, built.

'Good evening,' Dermot said.

'Hello.'

'May I have a whiskey, please?'

'You can of course. What'll it be, Scotch or Irish?'

'Scotch, please.'

'Scotch it is then.'

Dermot sipped. 'Would you care for a drink?'

'All right, so.'

'What'd you like?'

'I don't like to ask you but could I have the same?'

'Certainly you can.'

She poured herself a Scotch, to the brim of the measure and a little beyond. Her dress was low-backed. Skin not bad, though there was the odd pimple. Dermot could detect accreted accents, piled like geological strata above the foundation of her Irish voice, acquired through frequent and sometimes profitable contact with male visitors arriving from Shannon.

They raised their glasses. 'You must be a mind-reader,' she said. 'I was gasping for one.'

'We seem to have the same taste, anyway!' *For God's sake stop it, she's too old for you.*

'I used to drink liqueurs a lot,' she said, 'but I find them a bit too sweet for me now.'

Dermot walked about the room, looking at the awful pictures. Sometimes he found that the really bad had a more compelling quality than the good. The barmaid watched him with sharp appraisal. A nice cut to the Donegal tweed jacket. Protestant trousers.

'You're restless,' she said, 'it's the travelling, I suppose. I seen you booking in a while ago.'

'It's just that I keep looking for something I might remember. I used to come from these parts. I spent my childhood here.'

'Are you telling me?'

'About seven miles from Ennis. I used to come to this hotel with my father sometimes, though not into the bar, of course. I just thought some of the pictures I remember from home might have found their way in here after the auction. You know how it is, you can't help looking for... for what belonged.'

'And is it long since you were over?'

'Quite a few years, when my father died. I didn't come in here though, I stayed with a friend.'

'I've been here quite a few years myself.'

She was no spring chicken certainly, and yet... Dermot thought of lush petals about to fall.

He put down his empty glass. 'Well, I must be off. Lots to do. I'm only here for a few days.'

'See you, so,' she said, her eyes following him to the door.

That evening Dermot called on McKeever to deliver Redfern's letter. Jack McKeever's father had been the McEnchroes' family doctor. Jack himself was a solicitor who specialised in property. He lived in a large bungalow in the outskirts of Ennis. He prospered. The door was opened by a maid and Dermot entered a long hall, sumptuously decorated in what he would have described as informed bad taste. A moment later McKeever was walking towards him with hand outstretched. He was a tall man with scant hair parted far down on the side of his head. Although in middle life and good health, his gait was curious: a conspicuous swaying of waist and hips which was intended to convey world-weary distinction but gave the impression of premature ageing.

'Well, Dermot, long time no see. Come in, sit down. I see you are burdened with a missive.' Something in the jocose formality of the last phrase, accompanied by a little sigh, sent a message of unhappiness. Two very strong drinks were poured.

'Sorry I can't entertain you properly Dermot, I mean dinner and all that, but I've had a marital upset.'

'I'm very sorry to hear that.'

McKeever said nothing more on this subject. He took Redfern's letter and read it slowly and in silence. Then he folded it carefully and put it in his pocket. He was non-committal. 'Property's going like hell around these parts. Did you know the FitzJames estate is offered at around a quarter of a million? I hope to do a deal for them not a thousand miles from here. What brings you over, Dermot?'

'An impulse. They come every so often.'

'Is there a woman in your life?'

'Not just now.'

'Women don't seem to have any real class these days. Not the way your mother had. You were very young when she died, you probably don't remember her.'

'I do.'

'She was a wonderfully calm person. Always dressed in grey. So elegant! I used to think of her almost as a kind of goddess, the way kids do. I remember one day when I was in a boat with my father fishing on Cahermacrea lake I saw her standing very still at the edge of the water, a beautiful woman. I thought she looked unhappy.'

'Did you know my father?'

'I met him once. A disturbing man, like a volcano. Extinct now of course.'

'No, he's still a factor in my life, a dreadful presence.'

McKeever told Dermot of how he and his brother, whenever his father attended the McEnchroes as a doctor, were dropped half way up the avenue and left to play in the Cragatheen until they were picked up on the way home.

'Because they were professional visits you see, Dermot, not social ones. We never paid social visits to Cahermacrea. It was a bit too grand for the likes of us.'

'You'll be writing to Redfern, I suppose?'

'I have that in hand, Dermot.' As Dermot drove away McKeever waved briefly from the door, solitary, sad. Blessed with financial increase.

Back at the hotel Dermot had a snack and some coffee in the lounge. After this he decided on a walk before bed. The streets were almost deserted. He strolled the half mile to the O'Connel monument. The sky had cleared and the air was dry. He looked up at the darkness, the velvet between the stars. It was all whirling, flaming, as if some giant was juggling for his life.

In his bedroom he sat at a small table and, following an old habit, jotted down the landmarks of the day: his talk with McKeever, the great green wave, the lush barmaid with ginger hair above cool eyes. His notes were clinical, his feelings absent.

In bed he lay awake thinking of his small, carrot-haired son, wondering whether his trusting spirit would survive and flourish, or become cynical and dry. There was hope. He remembered reading somewhere that the child never dies. With this thought he went to sleep.

'A scotch, please, plenty of soda.'

'Right.'

'How're you keeping?'

'Oh great. And yourself?'

As she got the drink the creamy, slightly pimpled back was turned to him again.

'And what's the programme today?' she said, pouring.

'I'm going to Shannon. I've lost a book. I think I must have left it at the airport when I was collecting the car.'

'Much chance you'll have of finding that.'

'You wouldn't remember my father coming in here, I suppose?'

'Always on about the old times! Are you looking for your childhood?'

Dermot stiffened a little. He didn't like barriers being crossed without invitation. 'In a way – perhaps.'

'One more push on the cradle and you'd have been all right.'

She said this putting the drink into his hand instead of on the counter. Her smile was full of teeth that were still strong but bore dark fillings that showed through from the back. It was too much of a smile, too understanding. Dermot drew back from the counter with his drink. He disliked percipient women; they were a threat. This intimacy was quite unexpected, almost as if an underwater swimmer had emerged suddenly to embrace him, although she was wearing, not a skin suit and flippers, but the trashy traditional green costume in which it was the practice of the management to dress the female members of the hotel staff on certain days. Dermot had noticed these sullen colleens slinking about the landings and the lounge.

You couldn't call this one sullen, though.

'Why wouldn't I remember your father? Sure I don't even know your name, anyway.'

'McEnchroe, Dermot McEnchroe.'

'Good God!' The words were little more than a soft outward breath. 'Maybe I do. I think so. I'm not sure.'

'Well, I must be off.'

When she said, 'You'll be back?' it wasn't really a question.

It was dark when Dermot got to Shannon. Throughout the day a rising wind had been stirring damp air and was now growing into a storm. The sky was burdened with arriving rain. He could hear no sound of aircraft, there was no bustle. The terminal where he had hired the car had no sense of welcome, with large areas of glass and aluminium. Automatic doors opened for him with sinister deference. There were cold, rectangular pillars, and from the ceiling a dim light was shed grudgingly from long neon tubes through plastic slats designed in the pattern of a fish's skeleton. A few officials sat behind desks like morose dwarfs, shrunken in this void of transience. Dermot had a feeling of such impermanence and drift that he longed for a fireside.

A sign directed him to lost property.

'I think I left a book here a few days ago when I was collecting a car from *Ryanair*. I see their office is closed.'

'What sort of a book was it?'

'It's a big book. It's called *The Denial of Death*, by an American author. It has nothing to do with immortality, it's about human behaviour—'

'Just a minute.' The bored man ran his finger down a list, then rummaged in a shelf under the counter.

'This it?'

'Yes, oh thank God – thank you.'

Dermot signed for the book and left. His hired car was parked a hundred yards from the building. When he was half way across the tarmac the rain started, so suddenly and heavily that he thought one of those malign dwarfs must have turned on a cosmic tap. When he reached the car he was drenched. Back now to Ennis. Back to… back to…

Where the hell was he? The geometry of the airport had dislocated the landscape he remembered from his childhood. New concrete roads and dual carriageways had been scored across the grain of the land. He thought he had taken the road for Ennis, but was now uncertain. He had misgivings that he was driving in the opposite direction towards Limerick. He took a left turn onto a minor road, hoping it would bring him back to Ennis. The road grew less reassuring as he drove, as if doubting itself. It narrowed, dipped and rose, turned this way and that. Some of the signposts were askew, one was broken. The rain was so heavy that the windscreen wipers couldn't sweep a clear arc and he had to open a window to read a signpost. God Almighty, how could he be heading for Scariff? Clare was drowned and he was lost.

At last, in a place which he took to be Feakle, he saw the longed-for sign. Inis. Before taking this road, he stopped to light a cigarette. The wind tugged at the little car and he could feel it rocking. In his damp clothes he had a moment of lucid self-assessment. He was solitary. Who was close and loved? His small, carrot-haired son, now at his prep school? Calnaan? Who else was there? Two or three others, perhaps, people he seldom saw. Among his many acquaintances, few were intimate. The adroit social exercises, the laddishness, the occasional abrasiveness of tongue; these were the bits of armour you had to buckle on for the joust of life, to protect whatever the thing was that lived inside you like a glow-worm.

As he drove on, sure of Ennis now, he felt an appetite growing. It was vague at first, then revealed itself with alarming definition as a depraved longing for the ruined green colleen at the MacNamara Hotel. He would go into the companionable bar and have a large golden Scotch, then another. He would buy her one and they would have a long, cosy chat.

At the hotel he changed his clothes, had a bath and went down to the bar. It was getting on for closing time and the crowd was thinning out. Tonight there was also an assistant barmaid, a thin girl in spectacles. She too was wearing Eireann's green; perhaps this had something to do with Sunday. In the corner, where the counter joined the wall, the ginger-haired one was sitting very still with her elbows on the counter, resting her cheeks on her hands. Between her elbows there was a large Scotch recently poured, the soda still rising. When Dermot entered her eyes turned to him, then to a group leaving the bar, back to Dermot again, then down at the Scotch. He noticed that the balls moved slowly; evidently she had put away a few during the evening.

'A large Scotch, please. I'm glad you haven't closed. I got soaked.'

She made no move to get the drink but glanced down at the Scotch, then up at Dermot.

'Would you be very kind and get me a large Scotch, please,' he said in the voice he used for children and very old ladies.

She pushed the drink slowly towards him.

'You mean that's for me?'

She nodded.

'But how did you know I wanted a Scotch – and how did you know I'd be coming in?'

'It's not difficult to know what you want and I guessed the storm would drive you in about this time. I thought I'd have it ready for you.'

Dermot paid for the drink. She went slowly to the till, gave him his change and settled again on her stool, head down and elbows on the counter. She was crying into her mascara. There were no sobs, no heavy breathing, just an effortless downpour.

'Something wrong?'

No answer. She shed a black tear. Dermot had usually found that if you made fun of a crying woman she would either laugh or scream. He put his glass directly under her face.

'Look, would you oblige me by crying into that? I need some water, not too much, mind.'

Her body began to shake. She was laughing. She straightened up, damply beaming.

'You remind me of someone,' she said.

'You'll have a drink with me?'

She said neither yes nor no, just got herself a Scotch and returned to her stool. She didn't thank him, but raised her glass a little. The casualness was not rude. It excited Dermot. It suggested intimacy. He was beginning to feel curiously unlike himself. A false friskiness was coming into his manner, something he deplored in others. What was he doing? Her skin, he felt sure, was younger than her years. How had she contrived it, what black arts, he wondered, what secret oils and unguents had she used to keep this bloom?

'What's your name?' he asked.

'Vera.'

'Vera who?'

'Vera.'

The last customers were leaving, saying goodnight to the thin girl who was listlessly wiping the counter. She began to clear away the glasses.

'You can leave them,' Vera said, 'I'll see to it. You'll be down early in the morning anyway. Let you be off now.'

Dermot was alone with the ginger hair.

'It's a terrible night,' he said.

'What harm? We don't have to be out in it. We're in for the night with a good roof over us.'

'You'll have another one with me.'

'Ah no.'

'Go on, go on.' There was something stronger than persuasion in his voice; the jerk of his head towards the bottles was almost peremptory.

'All right so, one more.'

She filled their glasses and came back, elbows on the counter again. She was leaning well forward. The alien disturbance moved again in Dermot. Normally the gentlest of men, he now felt himself to be the puppet of a brash, aggressive spirit which would make him talk, would manage the whole evening for him. He leant forward and folded his arms in front of the woman. The white valley of her cleavage was close to him. He was assailed by expensive scent, brought, probably, by some smitten drinker from Shannon.

'You smell nice,' he said.

'That's the idea.'

He looked closely at the green dress and was surprised that the roughness of the material attracted him so strongly. She didn't move when he felt the texture of the short sleeve on her upper arm, kneading it between his forefinger and thumb. It had the quality of sacking, like the dresses he had seen on dolls. It stirred a need in him. He could hear the wind outside. He wanted to be shut up with this woman in a small dark place. The inner turbulence he had been feeling seemed to be taking possession of him. Erotic words poured from this stranger's mouth.

She listened impassively. 'I'm in number twenty-eight, top floor,' she said, 'I'll be up there shortly.'

Dermot took her hand. It was very warm. He rotated his thumb on the palm.

'Couldn't we go now – together?'

'All right. I'll tidy up in the morning. Let you follow well behind me through the lounge. There's a new girl at reception. I don't want her getting ideas.'

Dermot caught up with her on the first landing and put

his arm around her waist. He wondered how a body could generate such warmth without extreme athletic exertion.

He abruptly stopped walking and withdrew his arm.

'What number did you say?'

'Twenty-eight. Why?'

'My room's just along there. I've got to go there first. I'll be up with you in twenty minutes.'

'Twenty minutes? You're in no hurry.'

'I'm sorry. I forgot something. I've just got to do my notes.'

'Notes?'

'Yes. They go cold if I leave them till next day.

'I see.' She bridled. 'Take care I don't go cold.'

'I'm sorry, I have to do them. I won't be long.'

He walked quickly along the landing. She stared after him, wondering if she had made a sensible decision. Was he mad? Notes? For God's sake.

In his room Dermot sat at a table and made his notes with unimpaired concentration: Shannon, the storm, the drunken reeling signposts, the blackness of the night around him in the little car. When he had finished and put down his pen, the licentious itch returned.

'You were great,' she said.

The sheets were rumpled. Dermot lay curled low down, regretful, feigning sleep. He raised his eyes cautiously and found that he was looking into an armpit, a nest of grey wire. She was lying with her arms up, her hands under her head. The blank light was not kind to her. How could he have done this? He had taken her lustily as soon as they were in bed, and again in the small hours. Now he couldn't bring himself to touch her.

'What about a little kiss?'

Oh God, I couldn't, I couldn't.

'Isn't it funny,' she said, 'the way fate brings people together? You and me lying here.'

Dermot groaned, just audibly. He was wary of post-coital wisdom. The subjects he dreaded were Art, Philosophy and Life. And he had experienced worse: a woman he had got to know after the divorce used to lie back blathering about reincarnation and whether animals had souls.

'Everything is chance,' were the next words from this one. 'Do you know, I might almost have been your mother.'

Dermot was out of bed and struggling into his shirt before she spoke again.

'Where are you going?'

'Back to sanity.'

'Where's that?'

'Look, I'm awfully sorry to be like this. It's just that I've forgotten something. I've got to get to the post office quickly.'

She lay still as he dragged a comb through his hair. He stopped to kiss her on the forehead, a remorseful kiss of goodbye. He turned to smile at her from the door. 'This has been wonderful. See you soon. Bye now.'

'So you're going to the post office?' She seemed about to say something more, but left it unsaid. Dermot was unable to fathom the look on her face.

He shaved and had a bath, obtaining only partial redemption from the soap and hot water. After breakfast, as he was on his way out through the lounge, the girl at reception called out to him.

'A letter for you, Mr McEnchroe.' It was a small envelope with very large, careful handwriting.

Dearest Dad

I hope you are very well. I came first in histry last week. Yesterday I rode the bisicle with both feet off the ground.

It will soon be hols. Lets go to the west of Ireland. I want to see the wild waves again. Last night I dreamed about a huge bird with wings so big they shut out the sun and made the world go dark.

Best love,

Bobby

Dermot walked, wet-eyed, to the post office in Bindon Street. 'I want to send this letter to England. May I have a stamp, please?'

'You can to be sure.'

He was alerted by the voice of the young man, hardly more than a youth he seemed, behind the grill. It stirred something in him, a yeasty, undesirable excitement. And something like apprehension. 'Grand day,' came from behind the grill.

'Yes.'

Above the vertical bars of the grill there was a horizontal gap. Through this Dermot saw his father's eyes, his great-grandmother's eyes, above a long nose with a jutting bridge. They had the glare that he remembered.

'There you are, now.' From under the grill his father's strong, blunt-fingered hand emerged, pushing the stamp towards him.

Dermot posted the letter and tried to draw a curtain in his mind against what had happened: the features, the energy in the voice, the emphatic manner, the hand. He recalled the strange look on the barmaid's face and had to quell a feeling of nausea.

One summer twenty years earlier at Cahermacrea, Calnaan was lying in his bedroom off the back passage. It was a hot afternoon. He had lived alone in the house for a long time now, the master settled in with whoever she might be, in Dublin. The place had been the subject of a compulsory purchase by the Land Commission. He recalled the day the bailiffs came, and how he had managed to save the boy's most precious thing, his toy aeroplane. Now the house was being demolished by a firm of builders from Dublin. There was the sound of hammering, the fall of mortar and stone. They had started at the front and were working their way towards the back where Calnaan was lying on his bed. He could hear his memories being smashed. He had come to Cahermacrea as a stable boy and could just remember the old master, Dermot's grandfather, in whose presence he had felt awe and admiration. He could knock you down with the look in his eye. What a seat on a horse the old man had! Ex-cavalry, 17th Lancers he was. Two big wolfhounds behind his chair in the dining room and he'd throw them bones over his shoulder. No one was ever in want when he was here. A great heart. There was never his like in Clare again.

Chip, bang, crash, wallop. They were getting closer and they were laughing as they worked. Calnaan felt the room shaking and he could hear the voices of the young men.

Calnaan rose from his bed, went out and shouted to the men.

'Let yee stop a minute. Let yee leave my room till the last.'

'We can't do that, it'll fall in on you.'

'Leave that room till the last, no two ways about it.'

They were gathered round him, a very tall, elderly man. He had a presence which made them silent.

'No two ways about it.'

So they chopped the house away around Calnaan. Two days later the noise stopped and the young men waited. Calnaan got up, rolled his blanket and a few belongings in his mattress which he tied with a cord and hoisted it onto his back. He carried it across the fields to his sister's house in Ruan. He did not once look back.

The day was clean and clear, the sky cast down a wide, cold glare of scrutiny. This was strange weather, dark and stormy one day, bright the next, like the blinking of a huge eyelid.

Dermot found that the white gates had gone; so had Mrs Doyle and her tiny house; each in that order had been erased. The avenue was now a minor public road, muddy and unremarkable. The once resplendent trees had been felled, the parkland tilled. He stopped at the Cragatheen. It was no longer a wood, here too the trees had been felled for timber, leaving exposed the giant molars of limestone with, here and there, a few bushes of thorn.

There was thick moss, posh as a carpet. Dermot walked carefully over it and looked down into the familiar cleft. The faint signature of the goat's skeleton was still there. The place depressed him and he didn't like following the ghost of the old avenue. He decided to drive back to the village, leave the car there and take the path across the fields to Cahermacrea.

He stopped outside the Moroneys' cottage. Bridy Moroney had been in service at Cahermacrea. She had had seven children, not all of them sired by her diminutive husband Micky. Dermot talked in through the open door. Bridy, her great hips askew, waddled towards him. Micky, now eighty-eight, sat on a chair in a dark corner.

'The Lord save us!' Bridy said.

'Well, Bridy, how are you?'

'In the name O' God, Master Dermot, is it yourself or your father? You're the dead image of him in his young days.'

'You remember him of course?'

'What remember! Let me tell you, he was a man of great spirit. There was a bit of the devil in him, but musha, he filled the house with life when he came in to see you.'

'He changed.'

'Ah, sure he fell into bad company. Never mind that. He

was a wiry young man. I remember him ridin' in the point-to-point at nine stone seven. He hunted every inch of the county with the Clare Harriers, God bless him. He was afeard of nothing on a horse. Some of the jumps he'd take would bring your heart up into your mouth.'

'A great man with the gun,' came in a squeaky voice from Micky, who had not moved from his chair in the shadows.

'Wasn't he the single-rise champion of all Ireland at the clay pigeon shooting,' Bridy shouted, 'didn't he lead th'Irish team over t'England for the international!'

'He did to be sure.' Dermot remembered rows of silver cups in the dining room.

'Listen here to me,' said Bridy, 'when the team were on their way home didn't he dance a beautiful jig on the platform at Euston station! The station master came along to stop him because he was drawing a crowd. Would he stop? Come here to me.' She drew Dermot's ear to her mouth. 'He said, "You can kiss my Irish arse".' A shriek came from her. 'Aah God!' She spun a full circle on her feet.

Micky's reedy voice came again. 'There was a great bit of Irish in him. God be with the times when he'd shoot a snipe with one foot on a crag and th'other in the air.'

A river of confused feelings was running through Dermot as he walked across the fields. To hear his father spoken of with admiration and affection, described almost as a folk hero, had come as a shock to him. The man had been fierce all through, a concentration of instinctive life. Yet on his deathbed he had almost aroused Dermot's pity. His mind had wandered.

'We'll go shooting, Dermot.'

'Yes, Daddy.'

'Bring me my gun.'

'All right, Daddy.'

'The beautiful one with the Damascus barrels, the one that's never missed a bird.'

'I will, Daddy.'

He began to speak like a bewildered child.

'My rod and my guns, where are they?'

Life drained out of him until he slid down into what Dermot had always imagined as a long, dark tube.

'I felt no grief.' He spoke the words aloud as he walked to Cahermacrea.

He could make out the contours of the house from the jagged gums of the walls which were two to three feet high. He went straight to where the porch had been and scraped his heel on the scanty grass, back and forth, until he saw the tiles of the floor, bright and new, an embalmed remnant of his boyhood. Nostalgia, he thought, was too much despised. It was partly a search for renewal, a desire to begin again.

The fat beech hedge that had once enclosed the shrubbery was now emaciated, a line of skinny overgrown trees. The friendly laurel bush, under which he had seen the Devil, remained vainly protective in its shape, naked as if brutally undressed, blasted by neglect and wind. The whole place lay under the curse of time and weather.

At the door of a small slated cottage built on the site of the dining room gaunt Calnaan stood. Although he stooped a little, he still gave an impression of height. Rather than a stoop, it looked more like a finally chosen posture; his body had settled for this. There was a frost of stubble on his face but his eyes were bright. Dermot walked towards him. The brown forefinger was extended.

'How arroo? Arroo good?' was all Calnaan could say before his lips began to work in the battle against tears.

'Not too bad, Calnaan. Yourself?'

Calnaan spat. 'And the son, God bless him?'

'At school.' Dermot suddenly realised that no holds were barred with Calnaan, you could express love without feeling a fool.

'He's wonderful, Calnaan! Eyes full of trust. You wouldn't believe the fun we have together.'

'The crayther.'

'Freckles and red hair.'

'He didn't steal that, faith. Your grandfather had a streak of red in him, God rest his soul.'

Calnaan's mouth began to work again. He stamped about flailing his arms, turned away, then swung round on Dermot as if to assault him.

'Come in can't you, I have the tea wet.'

A white cloth had been laid on what Dermot recognised as the old kitchen table. An aluminium teapot, fruit cake, biscuits, soda bread and stormy yellow butter were waiting. Calnaan poured the strong black tea.

Later, they went out and walked over the ground of the old house. Calnaan, flowering from the ruins, carried a pitchfork. With this he prodded the earth, identifying floors: the tiled hall, the drawing room, the library, the storeroom, the pantry and kitchen. Dermot regarded the savagery of change. All the refuges of childhood, the back stairs, the landings, the hiding places, the snug night-nursery, all had dissolved into the cold air. We are of the caves, he thought, it is cosiness that is our real need. Mere masonry is at our roots.

Calnaan jabbed his fork into the ground again and twisted the shaft. There was a grating sound.

'Them's flagstones. This was the back passage.'

'The back passage, yes.' It was here that his father's iron-tipped heels would ring while he hid on the back stairs. All the same it couldn't have been easy for him after his wife died, coming back to a big empty house at night, playing gramophone records in the drawing room until he felt he could sleep: *The Isle of Capri, Old Faithful, Home on the Range, My Blue Heaven, Miss Otis Regrets.* The overdraft, the mounting debts, the devastating losses on the land, only half of it arable. His knuckles used to be raw from punching the wall as he went upstairs to bed. Dermot was startled by a faint stirring of compassion inside him. 'Let you come in again,' Calnaan said. The invitation was imperative, he had not adjusted to the grown Dermot. From a box in a corner he drew bottles of stout and put them on the table. Calnaan didn't eat in this cottage, only slept there, going down to the village for meals cooked by his sister. This hospitality must have been planned with care, the food and stout bought with his small pension, all carried along the rough path from the village. They drank several bottles over reminiscences.

'It's as well you go to the car now,' Calnaan said, 'before the stout takes a hold of you. I'll walk down with you to Ruan.'

As they walked questions poured from Dermot.

'How's old Johnsie Frawley?'

'Dead.'

'And Annie Kelly, Where's she now?'

'Dead.'

'And Father Ryan, who used to hunt?'

'Dead this long time.'

'What about old Jane Brady, the washerwoman?'

'Oh, same as ivver, all blather and piss like a barber's cat.'

Their shoulders touched and a cackle of laughter flew from them. Dermot took a sidelong look at Calnaan. Nearly ninety, surely?

As if he had read Dermot's thought Calnnaan said, 'I wonder will I make it into next year, ha?'

'You will of course.'

A salty wind was blowing into their faces from Lahinch, from the wastes of the ocean beyond.

★

Lakes and ruins were asleep, every leaf was still. The hawk swooped, the baby rabbit felt the talons and the meticulous thrust of the beak. He screamed and was borne away.

> *'Now the day is over,*
> *Night is drawing nigh,*
> *Shadows of the evening*
> *Steal across the sky.'*

Miss Williams' hands formed a funnel between Dermot's mouth and her own. Her lips were very close to his. She sang out of tune and her breath was a little sour, though all her life she had drunk the sweet milk of faith. Dermot could not forget the lick of the whip, it would be there for ever, that little touch of languorous power. The incident had fouled the whole day's happiness.

> *'Now the darkness gathers,*
> *Stars begin to peep,*
> *Birds and beasts and flowers*
> *Soon will be asleep.'*

He would wait for a few minutes after she had gone, then he would get up. He would go to the dark toy.

'I'll tell you one thing for sure: no matter what happens, no matter what you've done, you need someone who's always on your side. Always, always, always and for ever.'

Miss Williams put her lips very close to Dermot's mouth.

> *'Grant to little children*
> *Visions bright of Thee.*
> *Guard the sailors tossing*
> *On the deep blue sea.*
> *Comfort every sufferer*

*Watching late in pain;
Those who plan some evil
From their sin restrain.'*

Miss Williams tucked in the sheet and quietly left the room. Her footsteps grew faint along the landing. One minute more and she would be down in the drawing room. It was time to go to the dark toy. Dermot got out of bed, very slowly opened the door and closed it softly behind him. He crept bare-footed to the stairs that led to the top of the house. As he ascended, the furniture and decoration grew sparser. There were no pictures on the wall of the first flight, no wallpaper on the second. On the third the carpet had withered. The sap of the house was falling. He reached the bare boards on the top landing. There was a feeling, almost a smell, of long absence.

The smell of dead maid.

Dermot crept to the front of the house and into a room where the floor was littered with the junk of past generations. There were boxes and trunks full of once-cherished belongings; old toys, a phonograph and other mechanical objects, heavy, well-made things. They gleamed in their remoteness, seeming on the verge of marvellous function, but were now enigmas which had withdrawn all response to baffled hands.

Dermot gazed at the church spire across the fields. The heart had gone out of the day. He leaned his head against the wall. Those walls were nearly three feet thick. Surely they would stand for ever?

Yes, I am alone, but not lonely. Even if Calnaan wasn't here I could stop loneliness. I can make things up. I can make up people. I can make them talk. I can make up worlds. I can make things happen.

He tiptoed to the back of the house, to the maids' deserted quarters. He entered a room and stood still, excitement rising. He went to a corner and with his fingernails prised open a door which was flush with the wall, and crawled into a small, built-in cupboard, closing the door tightly behind him. Darkness. One side of the cupboard was a bare wall and in this there was a recess, its opening little more than a hole. No light had ever been here. With tender caution, he put his hand into the hole. It may have been because of forlorn wistfulness that he imagined feeling a turbulence there, a flurry of air, that rushed into his hand. He had never seen this thing. It might have had the shape of a doll, or perhaps it was formless. He was sure it had a fibrous quality which he found comforting. He felt a kinship with it so close that it was almost unity. It was his last resort, his own core, this small thing hiding in the dark.

Printed in the United Kingdom
by Lightning Source UK Ltd.
125348UK00001B/46-60/A

9 781847 481788